"She does not seem to have a great fever," Ben said, turning to her mother, but Lady Larkspur had something to say about that.

"I am very warm," she insisted.

"Perhaps you would feel a good deal better if you did not have the weight of ten blankets upon you," he retorted, and threw half of them off the bed.

"I will surely die without them," she insisted, and moved quickly to recover them.

But Ben was even quicker, and caught her around the waist before she could reach them. Her body pressed against his, and when she turned breathlessly to look at him, her sweetly scented hair fluttered across his face. Through her thin nightdress he could feel the beating of her heart, sure and strong, and the soft uncorseted roundness of her breasts.

In the course of his professional life, he had necessarily developed an intimate knowledge of the female anatomy, but he did not recall ever having so unprofessional a response to it. . . .

SIGNET

REGENCY ROMANCE
COMING IN APRIL 2005

Lady Larkspur
Declines

Sharon Sobel

A SIGNET BOOK

SIGNET
Published by New American Library, a division of
Penguin Group (USA) Inc., 375 Hudson Street,
New York, New York 10014, USA
Penguin Group (Canada), 10 Alcorn Avenue, Toronto,
Ontario M4V 3B2, Canada (a division of Pearson Penguin Canada Inc.)
Penguin Books Ltd., 80 Strand, London WC2R 0RL, England
Penguin Ireland, 25 St. Stephen's Green, Dublin 2,
Ireland (a division of Penguin Books Ltd.)
Penguin Group (Australia), 250 Camberwell Road, Camberwell, Victoria 3124,
Australia (a division of Pearson Australia Group Pty. Ltd.)
Penguin Books India Pvt. Ltd., 11 Community Centre, Panchsheel Park,
New Delhi - 110 017, India
Penguin Group (NZ), cnr Airborne and Rosedale Roads, Albany,
Auckland 1310, New Zealand (a division of Pearson New Zealand Ltd.)
Penguin Books (South Africa) (Pty.) Ltd., 24 Sturdee Avenue,
Rosebank, Johannesburg 2196, South Africa

Penguin Books Ltd., Registered Offices:
80 Strand, London WC2R 0RL, England

First published by Signet, an imprint of New American Library,
a division of Penguin Group (USA) Inc.

First Printing, March 2005
10 9 8 7 6 5 4 3 2 1

To Allison, Jason and Elizabeth
For whom I helped to develop the first chapters,
but whose stories are entirely their own to write.
With love.

Chapter One

*O*ver the plump white shoulder of her oldest and dearest friend, Lady Larkspur noted the entrance of yet another single gentleman into their lofty company. Too tall for her taste and tanned beyond what might be called fashionable, the stranger nevertheless looked like the sort of man who would have once intrigued her sufficiently to require an introduction.

But no longer. Happily, Lark was beyond such girlish concerns now, and on this evening required only the presence of her own dear Hindley Moore.

"He is very late, Lark," whispered Miss Janet Tavish into her ear, "but he will not come any sooner by your watching for him."

"You are right, of course," Lady Larkspur answered, even as she remained vigilant. The newcomer passed off his greatcoat to one of the waiting servants and ran long, thin fingers through his dark hair. He turned, and as he scanned the festive crush, Lark imagined his eyes lingered a moment too long upon herself. They were very light, almost certainly blue, and seemed a little out of character with his saturnine features.

She quickly looked away, only to meet the bemused, knowing expression on Janet's own sweet face.

"Who is it, then?" Janet smiled.

"Who might it be but Mr. Moore?" Lark shot back, more irritably than her good friend deserved. "I thought I saw him enter, but it appears I am mistaken."

"Of course," Janet agreed, as always. She reached up to straighten the lace at Lark's breast, an act of intimacy surely forgivable among old friends. "But in all these months, I never saw you look upon your beloved with such an expression on your face."

Lark glanced back at the stranger, silently ordering her lips and eyes to feign perfect indifference. Lord Southard, her brother-in-law and host of this evening's ball, had already engaged him in conversation. They laughed at some private joke, and the stranger clapped John companionably on the shoulder. Really, this was impossible! Who was he?

"I surely do not know what you mean, Janet. Between Hindley and myself there are special—"

"Is he already arrived, Lark?" interrupted a voice at her shoulder. Lady Larkspur did not have to turn to know her oldest sister now joined them, and she did not have to ask who "he" might be. Truly, this began to prove very tiresome.

"He is not yet here, Del," Janet answered for her. "And I fear if he does not come soon to claim his lady, she will likely be seduced into dancing with another."

"How can you say such a thing!" Lark protested. "Hindley and I have an understanding so perfect and delightful, I would never be induced to look upon another. To dance with someone else would be a punishment."

"Your loyalty is admirable, dear sister. I only hope the gentleman deserves it."

Several moments passed in silence, as each of the women managed to look upon anything but the face of one of the others. They all knew of Hindley Moore's long association with a certain Miss Eleanor Davenport of Oxford, and of how that lady had disappointed him when her betrothal to another was announced six months ago. Almost immediately, Mr. Moore turned his attention to Lady Larkspur, the only remaining unattached daughter of Lord and Lady Leicester's five children and one possessed of a very persuasive dowry. Lark, who at twenty-four had already stood as bridesmaid to three younger sisters, welcomed Mr. Moore's advances with a happiness that might have been born from a certain desperation.

"I believe he does," Lark said quietly, finally meeting her sister Delphinium's interested gaze.

"I am happy for you, dear Lark. I wish you happiness ever equal to what I share with John." Del smiled as she looked across the company to her husband and raised her hand in a sign of greeting. "But I fear my guests have become impatient for the music to begin, and we ought not wait any longer. Father intended to announce your betrothal to Mr. Moore before you stepped out for the first dance, but it must be deferred until his arrival. I am sure he will be along soon. Shall we plan to raise a toast when we break for dinner?"

"I am sure the announcement will be as well received then as now," Lark said graciously, though she truly would have preferred to stand up with Hindley for every set. Now, in his absence, she would be obliged to remain against the wall with the matrons and the girls unlucky enough to have no partner.

"I am sure of it," repeated Del with an air of finality. "And now I see John signaling for me to join him. I hope I have the endurance for this long evening."

Lark glanced down at the smooth, flowing lines of Del's pale blue gown, doubting if anyone present, save their immediate family and a few close friends, knew she was increasing. Two little girls already slept upstairs, and John and Del entertained high hopes for the birth of an heir—as surely as Lark's own parents once had before the births of their five daughters.

With a knowing smile, Lark followed Del's gaze in John's direction. He still stood with the dark stranger, their heads bowed together in some serious discussion. The newcomer broke away first, raising his brow in a gesture of surprise and looking over the company. Before his eyes could once again settle upon her, Lark reclaimed her sister's attention.

"But first—name the gentleman who engages John so completely. I am sure I have never seen him before."

Janet started to laugh, but was quickly stopped by Lark's deft little kick to her ankle.

Del stood silently, perhaps asking herself the same question.

"Why, he is very handsome, is he not?" she asked.

"It cannot possibly matter, unless we wish to direct him to our good friend Janet Tavish."

"I am not at all—" Janet began, undoubtedly to remind the sisters of her affection for the local curate.

But Del interrupted. "He must be Mr. Queensman. He and John were in the Americas together during one of the conflicts, but I do not believe they have seen each other in many years."

"He is a soldier, then?" Lark asked a little too readily.

"No, he is not—at least not in the usual sense. He is a physician, and he accompanied the troops on their campaign. When John went down near the fort at Lake Champlain, I believe Mr. Queensman attended him. They became friends at that time."

"How fortuitous for John. Must we thank Mr. Queensman for saving his life?" asked Lark, a little tartly.

Del looked at her in surprise. "I most certainly shall. But it will not be my only reason for greeting the gentleman with warmth. Quite by coincidence, he is also somewhat related to us."

Now it was Lark who was surprised. Surely she had never heard his name before, and she was often admired for her remarkable memory. But soon she nodded her head with a growing sense of recognition.

"Is he yet another beggar?" she asked disdainfully. "Someone who imagines he stands in line to Father's title if none of us manage to produce a son?"

Such hopefuls occasionally presented themselves at Leicester Park, full of mighty expectations and little thread on which to hang them.

Del must have been impatient to go to her husband, but she remained long enough to put her sister in her place.

"I do not believe he needs to beg, dear Lark. If there are no little boys to carry on the name, the title and estates go to Lord Raeborn, as well you know. But he is very elderly and himself has no direct heirs. His closest relative, by a common grandfather, is apparently Mr. Queensman. Father explained it to John, who then passed it on to me, and now I to you. It is very unlikely it should ever come to it," Del said, patting her flat stomach. "But a man possessed of such expectations could hardly be dismissed as a beggar. You will be pleasant to him, I hope, if he dares to speak to you?"

"I doubt he will have the opportunity," Lark said pertly. "I expect to spend all my time with Mr. Moore."

"Once he arrives," Del reminded her, and retreated before Lark could think of a suitable answer.

Mr. Benedict Queensman of Brighton surveyed the large crowd already assembled at Southard's ball, wondering if he would be able to recognize his cousin after the lapse of almost ten years. Then, as a young man of twenty-one, he had been present at Raeborn's marriage to a lady young enough to be his granddaughter, and was happily reminded by the enthusiastic—if elderly—groom of the likelihood that a tiny heir might supplant him in whatever expectations he dared to harbor. Ben wished his relative all the best and comforted his own dear mother, assuring her his expectations were, as always, very slight. In addition, he pointed out that the purpose of his current rigorous studies was to train to do something useful in his life, rather than going to waste in the elevated, idle life of a gentleman.

As he stood with his friend John, on the threshold of a glittering society event, he recalled the youthful idealism of those days long past, and how the trials of war and illness and deprivation might have done much to change his point of view. But, curiously, they had not.

He wished himself away from London, finished with the affairs of business and family that had brought him here two weeks before, and back with his patients and his experiments at the small hospital to which he dedicated all his time and energy. He was needed there.

Here, even in the home of his old friend, he was just another eligible dancing partner for a young lady's pleasure. And such pleasure might turn to aloofness once someone reported to her suddenly curious mama that Mr. Queensman had a shop, of sorts, in Brighton and almost never took residence at his London townhouse.

"You must learn to smile more, Ben." John clapped him cheerfully on the back. "Or else my guests will think you far above them, and Del will begin to worry about the success of her party. And I will not have her fret, for she hopes to deliver another package to the family in six months' time."

Ben looked at his friend's face and marveled at the great happiness etched there. He had a sudden vision of those same features when first he had seen them, on a distant battlefield, and knew it was for such rewards that he would never tire of being a physician.

"My best wishes, John," he said with genuine pleasure. "If you would but introduce me to your lady, I might congratulate her as well."

"Of course you will not, old man. Remember, you are not a medical man in this company, only another eligible gentleman at our party. My wife will not appreciate your indelicate knowledge of the upcoming event, no matter how much joy it presently gives us." John paused and looked out over his sea of guests. "But you must be introduced at once. Delphinium knows your part in my restoration to health and is eager to meet you, as well. If only I might find her . . ."

Ben used the respite to once again seek out his cousin. In the corner, near the buffet, a bald-headed man cornered a lady of perhaps fifteen. She looked terrified. Yes, that could be Raeborn. Recently widowed, and still childless, the old goat would undoubtedly be pursuing the fifth Lady Raeborn. And as Raeborn grew older, each lucky lady seemed to get proportionally younger than the last.

"Ah! I see her! She looks very engaged in what must be the latest gossip, but if you can get her attention, her curiosity might be sufficiently aroused to pull her away from her sister and friend. There! Do you see her just to the right of the matron with the feathers?" John asked as he gave a subtle wave.

Ben saw the feathers and then the matron and, waiting a moment while two red-jacketed officers passed, finally the object of his companion's adoration.

How alike in taste he and John must be, Ben thought, for Lady Southard was the very woman who had attracted his interest when he first entered the ballroom. With something feeling surprisingly like envy, Ben once again noted the brilliant hair, neither red nor blond, the large brown eyes that unblinkingly returned his gaze, and the lovely proportions of a form that managed to look slender but not at all delicate. Her flowered gown, of some lacy stuff, dipped modestly at the breast, revealing smooth pink flesh that seemed to heighten in tone even as he studied her. Unlike the two blond beauties who framed her, she appeared to rely entirely on nature to groom herself, for he could see no artifice in the landscape she presented.

Ben let out a deep breath and turned to his fortunate friend as he recollected himself. It certainly would not do for him to be in any way attracted to the wife of his old friend. He only hoped John would not seek his professional advice about his lady's condition, for he did not think he could behave very professionally once he put his hand upon her.

"Well, what do you think, man?" John asked. "Am I not the luckiest man on earth?"

"I think . . ." Ben began, and then hesitated when one of the two blondes gave them a brilliant smile and waved her fingers. In the line of her cheek and in the manner in which she held her chin, he could see some resemblance to the object of his sudden desire. "Is that Lady Southard, then? In the pale blue gown?"

"Is she not an angel? I knew within five minutes of meeting her, Delphinium was the only woman I could ever love."

Ben almost said something about the young lady who had often visited John in the army hospital in America, but one look at his friend's face silenced him on the subject. Instead, he professed a very gentlemanly kind of interest.

"It is an unusual name."

"Undoubtedly." John smiled. "When you meet her parents, you will understand how Lady Leicester manages to get her way in almost everything."

"Lady Leicester? Is she not the watercolorist of whom my own mother is overly fond? She who produces fields of daisies on canvas and spreads their seeds even as far away as the drawing rooms of Brighton?"

"I did not know you to be an authority on the arts . . ."

"I do not consider the lady's watercolors to be art—"

". . . for you are quite right about the daisies. The family is naturally grateful that Lady Leicester did not produce more than five daughters, for I fear the next would have been graced with a most common name." John laughed at a joke Ben did not see.

"I beg your pardon, John. I fail to understand . . ."

"She would have been 'Daisy.' Knowing nothing about garden varieties, I did not understand it myself at first. The five Leicester sisters are all named for flowers: Delphinium, Larkspur, Columbine, Lily and Rose. Del even tells me there is a bit of redundancy there, for larkspur and columbine are pretty much the same flower."

"How remiss on Lady Leicester's part," Ben said dryly. "And are the sisters all very much alike as well?"

John hesitated, and Ben thought perhaps he had insulted him, for his host had already made clear he thought his lady above all. But it seemed John only considered the question to answer him honestly.

"Four of them are very much alike, and my brothers-in-law and I often congratulate ourselves on our good taste and good fortune. But Larkspur is unique both in appearance and in disposition, possessing little of her sisters' sweetness and delicacy."

"And does the brother-in-law who married her share in the others' self-satisfaction?"

John smiled. "There is the rub. She is the only one who remains unmarried, though not for lack of effort on the part of her anxious sisters. However, she seems to have found someone who is prepared to deal with her high spirits, and the announcement of their engagement is to take place tonight."

"Is the gentleman to be congratulated?"

John laughed. "I suppose so. But I do not believe he is yet arrived, so that pleasure must be deferred."

By the third set, the anxious expression on Lady Leicester's face finally caused her only unmarried daughter to retreat to safer realms. Lily seemed to have nothing better to do than to post herself at the door and periodically send Rose along with the message that no Mr. Moore had yet appeared, and Del apparently felt that the gentleman's absence signaled some deficiency on her part as hostess. Columbine thrice reminded her older sister that there were many other eligible partners available and if Mr. Moore should find himself jealous at the sight of his darling dancing with another, it would serve him right for coming so late.

Larkspur began to feel something of the same thing herself. What had begun as mere frustration evolved into anxiety and then irritation at the neglectful behavior of Hindley Moore, and Lark wondered if it would prove unlucky to announce her betrothal in the midst of an argument—for she fully intended to have one once he arrived.

Unappreciative of all the concerned glances sent her way, Lark escaped her sympathetic audience and sought to find some comfort with a glass of lemon water. The buffet tables, not yet spread with dinner, provided a sort of sanctuary, shared only with a few elderly men and two girls too plain to be popular dance partners. Lark felt herself a suitable companion to them just now.

Knowing they were as curious about her as she was about the whereabouts of Hindley Moore, she raised her glass in a silent toast and smiled politely.

But before she could replace her glass on the table, one of the gentlemen broke away from his companions and approached her. Wheezing, and slightly out of breath, he reminded her of a straining pocket watch in need of a dose of lubrication oil.

"It is Lady Larkspur, is it not? It is many years since I saw you, not since you were a little girl. And you have grown up very nicely, my lady, though in a very different style from your beautiful sisters."

Lark bristled at the words, for she was oft reminded of her sisters' natural assets over her.

"Thank you for reminding me of it, sir. You seem to have the advantage of me, however, for I do not recall our acquaintance."

"Forgive me, my lady. I hope it is not too presumptuous of me to approach you, but you must excuse my impertinence as the reward of old age. Let me give you full advantage of our relationship: I am Lord Raeborn, a cousin to your father."

Lark offered her most disarming smile. "Of course, my lord. I have heard of you. And is the young lady with whom you were just dancing your daughter? Or a cousin whom I ought to take under my wing?"

The watch works sputtered and threatened to come to a halt.

"I have not been blessed with children, my lady. The young woman in question is Miss Alice Herrick, a very fetching girl."

"I see," said Lark, and thought she did—all too clearly. The old man, unable to produce a child, nevertheless could still pursue one. She wished Miss Herrick well and hoped her fleet of foot. "I believe this is her first season."

"As I daresay it is yours, my dear," smiled Raeborn.

Lark smiled back, and wondered how severely the man's vision was affected by old age. No one else would think her a green miss enjoying her first bloom into society. As a lady of twenty-four, she practically sat upon the shelf.

And if Raeborn knew her family as well as his familiarity presumed, he would also know that three younger sisters were already married. Next to sweet little Alice Herrick, Lark felt practically a matron.

"It does not signify, sir, for it is certainly my last."

"I am disappointed to hear it, my lady."

"And yet there is no reason why you should be. It is for the best of reasons. I am to marry Mr. Hindley Moore," Lark announced with a pride belying the irritation she felt with her intended.

"My felicitations, then," said Raeborn, and as he bowed, Lark realized the gentleman did, indeed, own one reason for disappointment. She remembered Del's fleeting words, recalling to her the curious fact that if neither she nor her sisters produced a son in the years ahead, their father's estate would be bestowed upon this man. Lark, anticipating marriage and motherhood, would necessarily decrease the odds of such an event occurring.

"Thank you, my lord."

"Of course. And is this the lucky gentleman who approaches with our host? Why, no, this cannot be Mr. Moore, for he looks somewhat familiar to me." Lord Raeborn squinted towards the candlelight and pursed his gray lips in consternation. "I believe it is . . . of course! Here is a young man of a relationship even closer than we find ourselves, dear little cousin."

Lark bristled at his words until she caught their full implication, and then she felt agitation of another sort. What Raeborn already saw, and she did not, must be the approach of the dark stranger, John's friend and Raeborn's heir. If she were absolutely honest with herself, she would have to admit she had sought refuge to avoid his occasional glances as much as to deflect speculation about Hindley's absence.

"Raeborn!" John's voice, always so cheerful, resonated like a slap across her face. "Behold a gentleman who wishes to renew his acquaintance with you. He is so infrequently in town, and you so infrequently out of it, it appears your paths have not crossed in many years. And yet you must be in each other's thoughts and wishes."

Lark thought John intended to be disarming, though possibly not as much as soon became evident. She saw Raeborn flinch at his words, and guessed the older man often thought of the younger when he faced the fact of his own mortality. She felt a glimmer of sympathy for him, for she knew what it was to be powerless against the future.

"And what luck! I shall accomplish another introduction here," John continued, "for here is a young lady whom I would very much like you to meet, Ben."

Lark knew she owed it to her brother-in-law to put a cheerful face on these proceedings, but turning to greet the newcomers proved a very difficult business. She sought to understand a reason for it, for she quite adored John and ought to feel kindness towards the man responsible for restoring him to Del. But Mr. Queensman's presence frankly disturbed her, making her more aware of herself and her frailties than ever before in her life.

"Lark?" John said quietly, the confusion evident in his tone.

Lark turned around, feigning surprise at the interruption. She saw John first, and fixed her eyes on him, as if he were the only gentleman deserving of her notice.

John frowned. "I hope I am not coming between the two of you."

"Of course not, John. Lord Raeborn and I were just comparing remembrances of the family. We are distantly related, you know."

"Excellent! For I bring you yet another cousin to share in your conversation. Mr. Queensman, may I present my sister-in-law, Lady Larkspur? Lark, Mr. Queensman is also my old friend, having been responsible for saving my life in America."

"We owe you a debt of gratitude, sir," Lark said politely, and finally looked up at him. Mr. Queensman appeared very tall, even taller than John, and his eyes were most decisively blue. They settled upon her with uncommon warmth, and Lark knew what a moth must feel as it drew towards a candle flame. She lowered her lids. "But if, in fact, we are cousins, it is only in such a distant way as to make any relationship nonexistent. It is very, very distant."

"So very bad as that, my lady?" Mr. Queensman said, and Lark heard his voice for the first time. Very deep, it echoed with a resonance that made his words clear even if he spoke quite low. It was the sort of voice capable of taking command of a situation, and it seemed replete with the confidence that once so ordered, its commands would be obeyed.

If Lark were not already disposed to be nervous in his society, such an attribute would have been enough to set her against him.

"Why, it is not so very bad, sir," Lark said, lowering her own voice. "We, who have nothing in common aside from a few twigs on an overgrown family tree, have only few occasions to ever meet. I cannot imagine why we would wish to do so more often."

The air of confidence surrounding Mr. Queensman wavered, but just for an instant. He narrowed his lids and lifted his chin slightly so that he seemed to study something above her head. She hoped he asked himself why an otherwise pleasant young lady would rebuff him, and then she thought perhaps she might begin to explain it to him.

Of course, she really did not understand it herself.

Nor did John. She saw the confusion and annoyance in his dark eyes and noticed when his hand came up protectively to his friend's shoulder.

"Come, Ben. Let us leave Lady Larkspur to her conversation with your cousin, for I fear we have interrupted something of import. And there are so many more people to whom you must be introduced."

"Have I not already met every young lady present? And every dowager who ever knew my dear mother? Come, John, grant me a respite from such delights. The music is playing, and I yearn for exercise. I have a mind to ask your kind sister-in-law if she will stand up with me for the next dance."

"I am sure you will find dancing with Lady Larkspur a delight as well, Ben," John said defensively. Lark felt a certain pity for him, for as the most agreeable of all men, he could not help but be mystified by the unbidden tension between his guests.

Lark put on her most fetching smile, which Lord Makepeace had once compared to the rising sun of a summer's day. "I am sure your friend would find it so, John, but it is a pleasure to be denied him. After all, I am practically engaged to marry Mr. Moore, and I owe all my dances to him."

Mr. Queensman looked around him, as if expecting to

discover a member of their company of whom he had remained hitherto unaware. "And yet your gentleman allows you to provide your own refreshment and does not accompany you to the buffet? Or is my cousin Raeborn his trusted emissary?"

Lark glanced at the old man, who had remained silent all this time. Mr. Queensman's question seemed to send him into spasms of happiness, such that he could barely catch his breath.

"Your cousin is not, nor could he be, since neither Mr. Moore nor I has had the pleasure of his acquaintance before tonight," Lark explained quickly. "And as it turns out, Mr. Moore is not yet arrived."

The barest touch of a smile tickled Mr. Queensman's lips.

"How very loyal you prove yourself, Lady Larkspur, though I daresay you will let your Mr. Moore know of your disapproval concerning his tardiness. I hope he has an excellent excuse."

"It is none of your business, sir."

"You are right to put me in my place. And yet I feel a natural bond with all men who find themselves in some sort of discomfort or trouble. Perhaps it is an affinity nurtured by my years in military service." He glanced at John, and Lark understood at once how the ties between them remained secure. "So would I not be helping poor Mr. Moore by dancing with his lady and deflecting some of her anxiety? He surely could not have prohibited it. And we are cousins, in any case."

Lark opened her mouth to protest, but the words did not come. She felt momentarily powerless to defy him and unwilling to embarrass John by refusing to dance with his friend.

Raeborn stepped into the breach, clapping his hands like an excited child.

"Excellent! Excellent! One must admire your talents of persuasion, my boy! It is no wonder the king likes you at his side . . ." Raeborn continued his praises, but Lark ceased to hear him.

What sort of audience did Mr. Queensman enjoy with the king?

"It is settled, then," Lark heard John say, utterly relieved. "I believe the next dance is a reel."

"No," said Mr. Queensman, and Lark knew her guess about the authoritative nature of his voice was well founded. "It is not settled until the lady agrees."

Three sets of masculine eyes settled upon her, and Lark felt lost in the forest their bodies made around her. She looked up at Mr. Queensman and wondered why he insisted upon granting her even the illusion of independent choice.

"I will tolerate the diversion, Mr. Queensman, if you will but understand that my dancing with you is a most singular event."

"I never thought otherwise, my lady," he said, his eyes not leaving her face.

And so Lark was propelled into the center of the room by the combined forces of John's long sigh of relief, Raeborn's stupid and insistent clapping and the strength of Mr. Queensman's muscled arm. Though she looked straight ahead of her and never said a word, she was fully aware of the interested glances in their direction and her sisters' frank curiosity. Lily and Rose, who seemed to regard Mr. Moore as their maiden sister's Last Great Hope, looked ready to break in between them and therefore save Lark for her intended.

For her part, Lark only prayed Hindley Moore would witness the scene for himself and feel well put out and truly jealous. Mr. Queensman, for all his arrogance, might have known something of what she felt when he offered to deflect her anger.

"I am very eager to meet your Mr. Moore," Mr. Queensman said.

"And why is that, sir?" Lark asked, though she waited to speak until they faced each other along the line of the reel.

Mr. Queensman, in his turn, waited until the first steps of the dance brought them closer before he answered. "Owing to his present negligence, Lord and Lady Southard's guests have not yet seen you during the course of the festivities. And such continued absence would prove a misfortune, for you are quite the most beautiful woman here."

Lark did not trust herself to speak at first, for never did her most ardent suitor offer up such hyperbole, not even in pursuit of her father's fortune. And Hindley Moore, who spoke her praises at every opportunity, never looked as if he entirely meant what he said.

"To what purpose is your compliment, sir?" Lark finally asked, genuinely perplexed and just a little bit flattered.

"Must a compliment have a purpose, my lady? Need it be anything more than observation?"

"I believe so, Mr. Queensman. Otherwise we would all be expending a lot of air with very little direction."

He seemed to consider this as they continued to dance, and Lark wondered—with just a touch of regret—if her practical view made her somehow less beautiful. If not, then they must present a very splendid spectacle as they danced, for she did not think there was a man who measured up to him.

Of course, Hindley had not yet arrived.

"Then your society is very different from my own, my lady. There is little artifice in the small community of Brighton, and one may freely speak one's mind without generating undue suspicion."

"Can such a thing be possible? Has not our king built a great palace there and made the place his home?"

Benedict Queensman laughed and his whole face seemed transformed. He looked approachable, his guard let down.

"What you imply is perhaps treasonous, my lady, but I must admit you are absolutely right. Since the completion of the Pavilion, a continuous caravan of royal followers has entered Brighton, building their own monstrosities along the beach and changing the temperament of the town. The locals have gained much by the sudden influx of wealth and demand for products, but there is growing sentiment that much has also been lost."

"And are you one of the offenders, Mr. Queensman? Do you travel in the circle of the king?"

"I do not travel with him at all, Lady Larkspur. However, I am often invited to the receptions at the Pavilion when the king is in town. I have also . . . ah . . . advised him concerning certain matters of health."

"You are not his personal physician, then? I thought Lord Raeborn implied it."

"I am not. Nor would I wish to be. I am my own man, my lady."

Lark rather thought so.

"Then what brought you to Brighton, sir? Are you a fishing enthusiast?"

"I prefer swimming with sea creatures to killing them. But that is not what brought me to Brighton, in any case. My estate is there, a modest inheritance from my mother's family. But I also operate a small hospital in the town, one I established when I returned from the wars. It keeps me very busy."

"I daresay it must, if we have never seen you before in London."

"I confess, London is among my least favorite places."

Lark took this comment as implied criticism against herself, as if she were the Lord Mayor himself. But the music was nearly at an end, and she wished to have the last word on the matter and their little interlude.

"Then we most certainly will never see each other again, Mr. Queensman, for it is one of my most favorite places."

She smiled as the fiddler played his last, and graced her partner with a curtsy designed to show off the most tantalizing parts of her anatomy.

But as he reached for her hand, Lark felt herself gripped by much smaller fingers than he possessed. Mr. Queensman did not have a chance to protest as she was dragged off the floor.

"Janet! What is the meaning of this? Could you not allow the man to escort me to the tables?" Lark protested as she turned around and then twisted to get out of Janet's firm grasp. "He will think us very poor mannered—"

"It should be the very least of your concerns, sister," admonished Columbine, coming up from behind.

"Why, what is this?" Lark said quietly and let her arms go limp. Janet and Columbine stood before her, and between their shoulders she saw Rose and Del making their way through the crowd. "It is not good news, I fear."

"Nor is it, Lark," said Janet. "We would have interrupted your dance but that it would have called too much attention to yourself. And you will already suffer the consequence of more attention than you could wish."

Delphinium, looking more like the elder sister of their childhood than like the lofty Lady Southard, joined them then and pressed Lark into the corner. Someone else came up behind, and Lark assumed it was Lily, completing the set.

"Does she already know?" Del asked Columbine, as if she spoke in the presence of a child.

"Know what?" Lark asked irritably.

"Brace yourself for the worst, dearest," Del said, reaching out both hands to hold Lark by the elbows. "We have just heard the most dreadful report from Mr. Calvin, who only just arrived at the party. It is about your Mr. Moore."

"Hindley?" Lark gasped. "Is he . . . dead?"

Would she be a widow before ever being a wife?

"It is much, much worse than that," Del said slowly.

"Whatever can be worse?" Lark asked, her voice barely a whisper.

Sound was suspended in the Southard ballroom, and the sisters and their friend seemed quite alone.

"Mr. Moore has eloped with Miss Eleanor Davenport, on the very eve of her wedding to another. They have departed to the north, where a marriage may be performed in haste."

Lark closed her eyes, unable to believe the indictment her sisters brought before her, the perfidy of the man she had trusted. Her life, her direction, seemed full of chaos and disarray, and she felt herself falling backward into some great dark pit. The candles and bright colors of the room swirled above her, and she reached out to grasp hold of something. Little fingers pressed against her arms and shoulders, but, like tendrils of early spring ivy, they were not strong enough to secure her.

And so she fell, into the darkness. In her last conscious moment, she felt a painful shock of surprise. Instead of dropping against a soft, perfumed, sisterly breast, she felt something hard and unyielding beneath her shoulders and was surrounded by the fresh scent of sea pines.

Her last thought was of Margate, of summers spent walking along the beach.

Chapter Two

*B*en Queensman sat across the broad oak table from Lord Raeborn and observed his elderly cousin with a practiced, professional eye. Though he seemed very lively this morning, almost boyish, the unmistakable signs of a life spent in utter disregard of one's physical well-being were plainly evident.

Raeborn's liver-spotted hand, holding his teacup, trembled slightly as he poised it over a platter of chocolates while scooping up several rich selections at once with the other hand. His open mouth, accepting the sweets even as he rambled on about one matter or another, revealed a row of very yellow teeth and gums too far receded beneath his chapped lips. His scanty hair, knowing none of the benefits of soap and warm water, abandoned all hope and fell away from his head to take refuge on his slouched shoulders.

Ben looked down at his plate and pulled a strand of hair from his omelet. Dark and curly, it could not belong to his cousin, but neither did it speak well for the cook in the dark, damp kitchen on the lower level of Raeborn's townhouse. Hungry, but no longer possessed of an appetite, Ben pushed his plate away.

"And so the matter must be resolved soon, I understand, for her father is most desperate to see her settled," Raeborn mused, stuffing another chocolate into his mouth. A line of dark spittle stained his chin.

"Pardon me, sir, but were we not talking of the king?" Ben asked, confused.

Raeborn made a gesture of impatience, entirely justified, and spilled his tea. As no servants stood ready and prepared for such a mishap, the warm liquid began to spread across the table, threatening the silver.

"You will never get far in London society, my boy, unless you can follow a multitude of topics with exactitude. Believe me! I understand it all too well!" Raeborn settled back into his chair and patted his stomach. "The king already left our table, so to speak, replaced by a gentleman of greater interest to me. Lord Leicester."

"Yes, of course. I called at his home yesterday, where Lady Leicester greeted me most graciously in her studio. She is an artist of some talent, you know."

"Yes, yes, we all know it," Raeborn said, still impatient. "More to the point—how is the girl?"

For reasons he did not pause to understand, Ben refused to say the name of the only girl left in the Leicester household, the one who had seemed the most popular subject of gossip in the week since Southard's ball.

Perversely, he answered, "The twins appear in good health, and Lady Southard makes a most gracious hostess when her mother is occupied with her painting."

"That is all well and good, but they none of them hold a candle to the redhead. Do you not think she is extraordinary?"

Ben felt his heart beating so insistently, he wondered if Raeborn could hear it.

"She is very pleasant, certainly. But she is in seclusion. Her loss must be deeply felt."

"Her loss is nothing. Hindley Moore groveled at Miss Davenport's feet since her first season and only turned to Leicester's girl in his disappointment. No one knew what she saw in him, nor why she would desire another lady's leavings. If there is a loss, it is Moore's." Raeborn looked thoughtful as he ran a finger through the spilled tea. "And another man's gain."

"I am not sure I understand you, sir," Ben said calmly.

"Leicester is desperate! She is the last of his daughters still at home, though far from the youngest. She does not have the look of her sisters, nor the disposition, for she is reputed to read all sorts of books and plainly speak her mind. Gentlemen are nervous in her presence, for she will not stick to subjects like the weather and the state of her rosebushes." Raeborn paused to catch his breath, and Ben felt concern to see a bright red flush on his face. "And now she is jilted! It will be a rare gentleman who will want her now!"

"Perhaps she is not wanting a gentleman, either."

"Impossible! And, in any case, it does not signify. The

word is out her father wants her married—and quickly—to
cover up this mess. He will settle a great deal of money
on her."

"It sounds as if Lord Leicester intends to be more generous to her future husband than to her."

Raeborn looked mystified by this declaration. "And why
not? She is only a girl."

Ben sat back in his chair, feeling infinitely more worldly
and superior than his cousin.

"My good man, have you not just tried to convince me
the lady is anything but just a girl?"

"Yes, I suppose you are quite right. But then, you surely
see it my way, as well."

"I am not sure what way it is, sir. In what direction do
you intend to lead me?"

"Down a path of joy, my boy. The lady Larkspur must
be married soon, and she will bring a multitude of advantages into a match. Knowing the condescension of her partner, she will be grateful, and therefore tolerant, helpful and
obedient. She will grace his table and warm his bed. And,
as she will have much to do to catch her more successful
sisters, she will be anxious to produce an heir. Could ever
a man desire more in a wife?" Raeborn looked specula-
tively at Ben. "But I sense he will have to spring quickly
to secure her."

Ben felt again the insistent beating of his heart and wondered when he had regained the disposition of a schoolboy.
He, who always considered himself cool and rational, now
seemed to lose himself whenever he thought about a lady
who had shown him not the slightest bit of preference. She
had not even bothered to be polite to him.

"I . . . I hope you do not mean me, sir?"

Raeborn's eyes opened wide, and he flushed to the thinning roots of his hair. His mouth opened and closed like
that of a fish gasping for breath, and his whole body went
rigid. Suddenly he let out a bellow, so hysterical a sound
that it was several minutes before Ben realized his cousin
had laughed.

"You? Good God, boy! I am sure you are the last one
Lord Leicester would consider for his daughter. You'd best
look in Brighton for some sturdy miss." His finger wagged
until it seemed to turn on himself and thump against his chest.

"I am speaking of myself, of course. Lord Leicester's chit needs a husband, and I believe I am just the one to make her father happy!"

"I will speak to her, and speak to her alone!" Lord Leicester blustered as he banged on the door of Lark's bedchamber.

Janet Tavish cried out as she pressed her fist against her lips, and Columbine looked nervously at Del. Del, just as distressed, could do no more than shrug and turn to Lark, who seemed to sink deeper into the nest of her pillows.

"What would you have us do?" Lily whispered from her corner.

"He will break down the door," Rose added timidly.

"Then let him," Lark said with more courage than she felt. Her father paused in his assault, and she wondered if he had gone for reinforcements. "He will have a broken door, and I have a broken heart. I am ever the poorer, for his injury can be fixed."

"He is very worried about you," Del said. "As are we all. It is a week since he-who-shall-remain-nameless disappointed you, and you have hardly eaten or taken a step out of this room. You shall waste away like this, and lose whatever chance remains of redeeming yourself."

Lark pulled her covers off and sat upright. "Redeem myself? As if I am the one who offended, insulted and ruined the life of another? As if I am responsible for disappointed hopes and shattered dreams? I, for one, have nothing to redeem."

"That is not quite so, Lark," Columbine said, though she did not meet her sister's eyes. "There are those who think you rejected Mr. Moore by not showing him proper degrees of affection and loyalty. Mrs. Winthrop says you drove him into Miss Davenport's arms."

Lark made a sound appropriately dismissive of such nonsense. "A fine statement coming from that old battleship! She who could stand on the cliffs of Dover and rebuff a fleet of French warriors! What does she know of it?"

"Nothing," said Del. "She knows nothing. But, for some reason, she, and others like her, seem to have Father's ear."

"And Mother?"

The sisters looked at each other.

"Your mother seems engaged on a very large canvas of water lilies. She gave Mr. Queensman an audience but almost no one else merited one," Janet said. "Mr. Queensman is the man—"

"I know who Mr. Queensman is," Lark said quickly. She had thought of his deep voice and blue eyes more often this past week than anyone might have imagined. In her dreams he inexplicably took the place once held by Hindley Moore, and she once woke up believing he held her in his arms. "But I do not understand why he presumed to come to our house and speak to Mother."

"Oh, he spoke to all of us," Rose said, with a spirit unbecoming a married woman. "But Mother also welcomed him, whereas she would no other. Perhaps it was to offer her gratitude."

"For what?" Lark's eyes narrowed as a suspicion dawned.

Once again her sisters would not meet her eyes.

"Well, dear," Del began, "we did not wish to embarrass you by reminding you of this, but when you fainted, Mr. Queensman caught you in his arms. And then, acting most discreetly, he carried you upstairs to one of the guest chambers and made sure you were not in any danger."

Lark said nothing for several minutes, now knowing she had not imagined the feel of warm hands on her skin, pressing against her heart and neck. No wonder she did not think herself still with Hindley, for his fingers had never strayed farther than her wrist.

"He is a physician, Lark," Del said, almost apologetically. "And Dr. Wainwright would have taken too long to summon."

Dr. Wainwright was probably thrice Mr. Queensman's age and about as compelling as a block of wood.

"And so you allowed—"

"We allowed nothing, Lark. Mr. Queensman did all that was well and proper and pronounced that you had received a dreadful shock. He instructed us to keep you warm and thought you might be more comfortable in your own bed. He was very . . . doctorly."

He does not look it, Lark thought.

"He is a gentleman, Lark!" Lily added. "If Lord Raeborn does not—"

"I know all about Mr. Queensman's expectations. I do not wish to hear another word about him. I would rather hear about Father, and understand the nature of his anger."

Before the sisters could reply, a different sort of banging was heard at the door, something like the sound of metal on metal.

"I believe he is knocking the hinges from the door," Lark reflected as she sank down again. "How like Father to keep everything neatly in its place. I daresay he wishes the same for me."

The heavy door yawned open, hanging precariously on its splintered frame. Four of Lord Leicester's daughters rushed forward, followed by a nervous Janet Tavish. Lark remained where she was, and stuck out her lower lip.

Leicester stomped into the room like some warrior king. The laces and floral sprays filling the chamber, not to mention the presence of six delicate ladies, belied any sort of challenge. But Leicester looked ready to do battle.

"Girls!" he barked, making the single word both a command and a curse. His daughters, recognizing his rare mood, made haste to gather up their needlework and books and escape. Lily stopped short at the door and returned to pull Janet away before Lark's friend could do anything more than glance helplessly at the bed.

"Yes, Father?" Lark said when she could no longer hear their footsteps in the hall. "You have gone to great lengths to speak to me."

"And you have gone to great lengths to avoid me, girl," he said sternly.

Lark shifted uneasily in her nest of pillows, unwilling to admit the truth of it. "But I have hardly moved from my bed, sir. I have been sadly indisposed."

Leicester grunted and sat down on the chair vacated by Del a few minutes before. His look softened, and Lark felt a little tickle of delight at realizing herself still capable of bringing her father to her own terms. She sighed and leaned back against the pillows, waiting to hear her father's apology for his rude invasion of her sanctuary.

"It is a sad business," he acknowledged. "And a great disappointment for you. You were fond of Moore, I know, though I confess I never thought him completely worthy of you."

"It is sweet of you to say so, Father, but I did love him so." Lark sighed, knowing she was already weary of the refrain she had so often spoken in the past few days. Whomever, whatever, she thought she loved must not have existed anywhere but in her battered heart, for now she realized she did not know Hindley Moore at all. Indeed, repetition of her protestation of love for him did nothing so much as diminish the truth of it in her mind, whereupon it almost as easily left her heart. Perhaps she did not so much love the man as she loved the gallant part he performed in courting her, during which he made her believe she too was someone other than herself. In the quiet of her invalid's room, Lark ruefully came to understand that what she loved was hope, briefly disguised in the person of Hindley Moore.

The closed door, intended to foster her deception, did admit certain truths. But she would never reveal them, not even to her family and closest friends.

Her father nodded thoughtfully. But for recognizing his mannerisms all too well, Lark might have feared he knew her fickle heart. He was not agreeing with her, but was instead rehearsing a speech intended for her benefit. As he had seen fit to destroy the ancient woodwork in an effort to deliver it, she suspected she had more to fear than she had hitherto imagined.

"That is precisely the cause of my concern," Leicester said, still nodding.

"You need not worry so, Father," Lark said comfortingly. "I am sick of heart now, but I will surely mend. I have thought myself in love before, but survived to outgrow such sentiments."

"Precisely," Leicester repeated. "But I do not believe your endurance is due to an affinity for martyrdom on your part, girl. I am convinced you are unable to choose your lovers with any degree of discernment."

"Father!"

"Do not dispute me, girl! I recall, with perfect clarity, Lord Dunlap, who thrilled you for one season and married Lady Mandeville at the end of it. And then Mr. Barrows, who seemed to have greater expectations in Germany than in London. Lord Vanyard? I believe you loved him passionately. And why have I not seen the Duke of Kelsford for these two years past? And now—"

Lark extricated her hand from the blanket and held it up.

"Enough, Father. You are making me quite ill. I admit I have chosen neither wisely nor well, but I am resolved to be more circumspect in the future. I shall endeavor to learn more about the gentlemen I meet and take greater care in deciding to whom I shall deliver my heart for safekeeping."

"You shall not."

Lark looked at her father in surprise, thinking her vows very prettily expressed.

"You shall not choose anyone at all in the future, my girl." Leicester stopped his nodding and rose to his feet. "I will do it for you."

"You cannot," Lark whispered, barely making any sound at all.

"I can and I will."

"My sisters were all free to choose their husbands."

"Your sisters managed to do it efficiently and without scandal. You, on the other hand, have made us the object of derision through all society. Lady Fontaine felt compelled to ask Delphinium if we would like you to accompany her to France this summer to remove you from the public eye."

"France! You cannot be thinking of finding me a husband there!"

"And why not?" Leicester roared. "I have been paying for you to have French lessons for fifteen years!"

"You are so ashamed you would have me lost to you— perhaps forever? An exile in the land of our enemies?"

Leicester's look softened, though not enough to provide his daughter with any degree of security.

"I would not have you so far, not even to salvage the family's reputation. Indeed, the husband I have chosen for you is a good deal closer. He is a gentleman in need of a wife, and presents his suit in very sincere and practical terms. Do you recall meeting our distant relations, Lord Raeborn and Mr. Queensman, at Delphinium and John's gathering?"

Lark felt her body grow warm, remembering Mr. Queensman only too well. He had the severe look of a sincere and practical person, and a physician would surely find a wife an asset in his busy life. Of course, Brighton society was not what one might have wished, but the king's presence in town would be the harbinger of better things to come. And Lark suddenly felt sure she could soften Mr. Queensman's look and make him find reasons to laugh. If the gentleman had already expressed an interest in her, then it must be requited. . . .

"If you desire me to answer Mr. Queensman's suit, Father, I will obey," Lark said with more modesty than she felt.

"Mr. Queensman?" Leicester cried, his voice rising again. "Mr. Queensman? My girl, if I am setting you up for marriage, I assure you it will not be to a mere physician with an estate in Brighton! Nor to one whose expectations are tenuous at best! I do not care who strikes a better pose, or dances a better reel! Your childish admiration is to no avail here. Mr. Queensman!"

"If not Mr. Queensman, then whom?" Lark asked, and then, "Oh, no!"

"Oh, yes," Leicester said softly.

"You cannot tie me to such a man. He is most dreadful. And he must be . . . why, even older than you, Father."

"Thank you very much," Leicester said tersely. "But I think you will find Lord Raeborn quite an amiable husband. And with luck you shall be a mother within a year, effectively blotting out the doctor's expectations. So much for Mr. Queensman! What could you have been thinking, girl?"

What indeed? Why would she imagine her father settled on a man she merely disliked, whose presence made her uncomfortable? Her punishment in being tied to such a one would scarcely be sufficient to redeem her disgrace. Instead, she must be married to a man fully repellent and utterly stupid.

So would she be made to pay for Hindley's treachery.

"I am thinking I shall suffer through every minute I am married to Lord Raeborn."

"It is too bad. You might have considered the consequences when you gave your heart to those who proved inconstant. You will find Raeborn to be a devoted husband, I have no doubt."

"Father." Lark reached out, pleading. "Please do not do this to me. Please reconsider."

Leicester backed away, avoiding her hands and her supplication.

"It is too late, girl. I will not be blamed for the same offense as those others to whom you foolishly gave your heart. I will remain steadfast. And I have already given my promise to Lord Raeborn."

"I will kill myself on the day ere we wed," Lark said dramatically, as she poised a butter knife over her breast. She waited until she had Janet's full, horrified attention and pressed its dull point into her flesh. "My reputation, so sullied by the ultimate act of desecration, will make me the heroine of legend. Disappointed maidens will gather at my grave and throw flowers upon my head."

Janet, looking from the knife to her scone, gave the barest glimmer of a smile. "Not roses, I hope. You know how they make you sneeze."

"In any case, it could not matter, for I shall be rotting in the earth."

"That is revolting, Lark. You sound as if you have been reading Italian novels." Janet glanced over at the small desk in the corner of the Leicester drawing room, where Richardson's *Clarissa* lay open. "Your situation is nothing as bad as novelists would devise."

"Is it not? Do you not think rotting in the ground preferable to rotting in the house of a very ancient and infirm gentleman? Do you not think the feel of the dark earth must be more comforting than his hands upon me? I shall wake up ill every morning and pray for every night to end quickly."

Janet said nothing, and Lark knew her dear friend shared her fear and revulsion.

"My own father is some years older than my mother," Janet said comfortingly.

"Your father is not yet as old as my Lord Raeborn!" Lark cried and felt a renewed sense of despair. "He may die ere he begets a child on me, ere I reach my twenty-fifth birthday."

"Then your troubles will be at an end, will they not?" Janet asked hopefully. "You should then be the Countess

Raeborn and have your own home and finances. You could do what you wished and marry whom you chose. It would not be so very bad."

Lark paused for a moment's reflection. "It is very wicked to imagine one's happiness dependent upon the death of another, is it not? But if, in fact, I do not produce a little Raeborn, then neither will my happiness be complete. I should only be the dowager countess, for the estate would go to another."

"Surely he would not oust you from your home."

"Perhaps it would give him pleasure. It is Mr. Queensman."

"Mr. Queensman? The doctor? But why do you think him ungenerous? He stood up to dance with you at Delphinium's ball. And later, when you fainted, he proved himself most considerate and kind."

"It is his profession, after all. And I am sure he danced with me out of a sense of obligation to John. For I keenly feel some disapproval there, something to set us off as opposites. When he learns I am to marry his cousin, his censure will be ever more intense."

"Then you are to marry him?"

"Mr. Queensman?" Lark gasped.

Janet made a gesture of impatience. "Of course not. Lord Raeborn."

Lark sank onto the chair at the desk and dropped her head wearily onto her elbows. Beneath her, the thick book she had been reading felt warm against her flesh.

"I cannot," she said. "And yet I know not how to avoid it."

"I assume a knife to the heart no longer seems a suitable option?"

Lark smiled. "I believe I love life too much to quit it, even if I am doomed to a dreadful marriage."

"I am much relieved to hear it."

"That I shall have a dreadful marriage?" Lark said.

Janet shot her a withering look. "It may not be as dreadful as you fear, dear Lark. After all, we know no ill of Lord Raeborn, and he may prove very kind and considerate. Even jovial. And if he behaves honorably, you must do the same."

"I have often been admired for my acting abilities, and shall employ them to advantage in my marriage," Lark answered solemnly. She looked down at the reddened palms of her hands and splayed her fingers like a lacy fan. Between them lay *Clarissa,* the tragic story of a young lady brought to ruin by her family's cruelty. Abused by a man in whom she placed her trust, Clarissa never recovered from the mistreatment, and descended into a decline. Lark had not read more than five hundred pages of the book, but she already knew its heroine would die before its conclusion. Brooding about the tale, Lark fingered the pages and ran her hand over the sturdy leather spine. "I am a very good actress," she said.

"So you are," Janet acknowledged absently. "But I hope you are not contemplating an escape to the stage."

Lark stood up, dizzy with the strength of her sudden resolution. With perfect clarity, she knew how she would avoid marriage to the odious Lord Raeborn and garner enough sympathy to redeem her shaky reputation. She would neither obey her father nor appear to defy him. And most important, she would be granted the reprieve she needed to set herself on course.

"I feel faint, Janet. I believe I am going to . . ." Lark crumpled to the ground at Janet's feet.

"Dear God! Lark! Do you hear me?" Janet threw herself down and grasped Lark's shoulders. "Do not move. I will call for your parents."

Lark opened one eye, and felt a pang of guilt for tormenting her very best and truest friend. Janet sat back on her heels, openmouthed and utterly confused.

"I—I thought you were dead," she gasped.

Lark pulled herself to a seated position and straightened her hair.

"Not even nearly so," she said, feeling very satisfied with herself. "I only acted as if I were dead."

Janet stared at her.

"Do you not understand, Janet? I shall escape this hateful marriage to Raeborn as Clarissa Harlowe avoided hers to Lovelace. I shall go into a decline, lie secluded in my chamber and make all sorts of pronouncements about the frailty of love and life."

Janet did not look at all convinced.

"I shall refrain from eating, and take no exercise. I shall avoid all contact with society."

"And you believe this to be a solution to your problem? I say it creates a greater one. I do not wish to spoil your surprise when you reach the conclusion of the book, but Clarissa indeed dies for her efforts," Janet said as she pulled Lark to her feet.

Lark reached for her friend's shoulders and shook her gently.

"But I shall not!" she said almost joyfully. "I shall merely be playacting at illness and pretend great deprivation of health."

"And how long will you manage it? Do you not think Raeborn will merely wait on your recovery?"

Lark frowned. "I do not know. But he is a very old man and cannot be too patient. After all, he may not have much time in front of him. And besides, a sickly girl is not promising if one wishes an heir in a year's time."

"Your sisters will not be very happy to hear your plan."

Lark looked at Janet in surprise, for she had not yet considered such complications. She loved Del, Columbine, Lily and Rose dearly, but could not be confident they would keep her deception a secret from their parents.

"Then they must not know of it, Janet. Only you will know the truth, and you must not tell a single soul."

Janet shook her head, as she had through years of girlish pranks and mischief. Ever more cautious than Lark and not nearly so willful, she nevertheless always remained loyal.

"This is very serious, Lark. This is far beyond throwing your governess's wig into the pond."

"I know it only too well, dear Janet. It shall be the performance of my life." Lark took a deep breath and contemplated the long and lonely months ahead of her. "But if I—we—succeed, my reward shall be the return of that life into my own safekeeping. Is it not worth the risk?"

Janet ran nervous fingers over her brow. "I sincerely hope so," she said and sighed as if all the weight of the universe now lay upon her narrow shoulders.

Ben Queensman entered his cousin's dark townhouse and sniffed the mustiness in the walls. A very unhealthy situation, he thought to himself and decided to mention it to Raeborn. He scarcely knew the old man, but already he felt the bonds of kinship. And if the Leicester chit did not manage to produce an heir for him, those bonds would be even more keenly realized.

He looked around the hall, wondering where the servant had gone and if he ought to follow. After all, Raeborn had sent for him most urgently, and undoubtedly stood ready and waiting in one of the rooms nearby. He would not need to be announced.

Footsteps approached, and Ben could just make out the silhouette of the servant at the opposite end of the hall. The man hesitated but said nothing, and then passed through a door to the right.

Ben waited a polite interval, then followed. He heard the sound of talking, in a man's falsetto voice, and wondered if he was about to interrupt a little scene of lovemaking. Raeborn seemed to be speaking endearments in a hushed voice, making little chirping sounds.

Slowly, Ben approached the door, having no desire to enter into such a scene. His cousin was free to marry whomever he pleased, and Ben wished him all the best, but somehow, inexplicably, the thought of Raeborn with the beautiful red-haired girl troubled him beyond measure. He could not say why.

The door stood ajar, and Ben paused on the threshold to glance within. Raeborn stood over a wicker cage, waving his fingers about and making little kissing noises over the bars. A little blue budgie hopped about excitedly and flapped its clipped wings in appreciation of all the attention it received.

Ben stepped through the door and cleared his throat.

"Did you wish to see me, my lord?"

"Ah, excellent, Queensman! I did indeed, for I did not know where else to turn." Raeborn passed a little sprig of greenery to the bird, who promptly dropped it into a water dish.

"I am honored, sir, for we are only recently acquainted as kinsmen."

Raeborn waved Ben's words away dismissively. "Yes, yes, there is that, though much was lost when your grandfather decided to change the family name to Queensman. So common! The age-old deference due the name of de la Reine suggests a greater sensibility on the part of my branch of the family."

"It is only a name," Ben said firmly. "Blood runs a good deal truer."

"So they say. But I have not brought you here to discuss the elevated branches of our family tree."

"Indeed, my lord?" Ben asked in surprise.

"It is to discuss my marriage to Lady Larkspur. There is a problem."

Ben had thought there might be, for if the lady were as willful and spoiled as reputed, she would not go happily into the arms of such a one as his cousin. Undoubtedly some persuasion would be in order, or supplication from Raeborn's emissaries. Uneasily, Ben imagined he knew for what purpose Raeborn invited him to his home.

"I daresay it is one you can solve with the strength of your own abilities, my lord. Lady Larkspur surely can be made to come around to the idea."

"Yes, of course. There is no question of it, as I already have every assurance from her father. Leicester is honorable and well respected, and his word is as good as done. Plans are already under way for the wedding." Raeborn straightened, as if imagining the scene and his well-rehearsed place within it. "But it must be deferred."

Ben said nothing, but walked over to the birdcage and retrieved the greenery for the tiny bird. He was rewarded with a bite to his finger.

"I see you will not ask me, my boy, and yet it directly concerns you."

"I barely know the lady."

"You know her well enough, and most particularly in a way of great use to me," Raeborn said on a note of urgency. "She is very ill, perhaps dying. And you, sir, are a doctor."

Ben straightened now, bringing himself to a height nearly a foot over his aged cousin. The man appealed to his professional talents, which were considerable, and to his pride, which might be reckoned even greater. But for all that, he had already examined Lady Larkspur more than a week ago and did not think her failing in any way but as a triumphant fiancée at her sister's ball. Indeed, she then seemed a good deal stronger than her disappointing circumstances would have indicated.

"What ails her?" Ben asked, readying himself to embark on a voyage of clinical discovery. "What are the symptoms of her illness?"

Raeborn sighed. "Who can say? She does not eat, nor can she leave her bed. She lies in the darkness, moaning and feverish. Her speech is garbled, though she calls for Mr. Moore and . . . others. You understand, I have not seen her myself but rely on reports from her concerned family. They have applied to their own physician, but the man can find nothing but a general malaise. He can do nothing for her."

"And why do you think it might be otherwise with me?"

Raeborn looked surprised.

"Do you not think I ought to have my own representative in this affair—someone to protect my interests? I have offered for the lady and have been accepted. Her health is an investment for me, as surely as any other piece of property. As such, I believe I deserve to receive my own assessment, and from a professional. It is fortuitous you are now in town, for I know not where else to turn."

"I am not sure I ought to concern myself with this affair, my lord," Ben said, feeling certain of it. "The lady does not seem to enjoy my company."

Raeborn laughed humorlessly. "I am not asking you to escort her to the races, my dear boy! I could not care even less if she thinks you an untutored oaf. I only want you to visit her, consider her condition and advise me of her state. If she is as ill as her family reports, she will not even know you stand in the same room."

Chapter Three

As soon as Ben Queensman entered the sickroom in Lord Leicester's fashionable townhouse, he knew very well the lady was aware of his presence. Neither of them spoke a word, nor was there the slightest movement in the huge bed, but the very air they breathed seemed replete with some fiery energy. Though he could not see her face, he guessed she watched him standing, waiting, daring her to make the first move.

The air itself, while hot and full of strange currents, smelled surprisingly sweet. A large bouquet of purplish flowers—larkspur perhaps?—threatened to topple a delicate table, but they alone could not account for the scent. Indeed, it felt as if something of the outdoors entered the bedchamber with him, for Ben could sooner imagine himself in a field of barley than in the company of a dying girl. And, so imagining, he added conviction to the suspicion he had harbored since Raeborn told him of his beloved's ailment—he believed Lady Larkspur's illness to be nothing but artifice. The chambers of the sick and infirm were filled with all the odors of humanity and earthiness, but they never smelled like spring meadows.

And yet the family appeared utterly convinced of Lady Larkspur's decline. When he had arrived at the house ten minutes ago, all four sisters were standing in attendance, their faces full of worry and care. Behind them, Miss Janet Tavish sat huddled in a chair, barely able to meet his eyes. And Lord and Lady Leicester hurried into the hallway almost at once, too concerned to let a polite interval pass after they heard his knock at the door. These were not the signs of a masquerade, the object of which could only be to release Lady Larkspur from her betrothal to Lord Raeborn; rather, they were signs of genuine grief.

"Do you not wish to see her, sir?" Lady Leicester asked tentatively, presuming to give him a little push into the room. And then, in a soft voice, "It is all right, darling. It is only Mr. Queensman to offer us his opinion."

Ben glanced down at the worried mother and guessed she had been working out her anguish at the easel. A smudge of blue paint stained her cheek, making her look almost as young as her five daughters. During the few times they had met, he felt her aloofness from the rest of her family, but now he guessed her concern for Larkspur was serious enough to warrant her removing herself from her studio. Her place in the sickroom was certainly necessary just now; he could not presume to examine a young woman without her mother present.

"I will not hurt you, my lady," he said as he approached the bed. "Nor will I do anything to add to your present distress."

From the tumble of blankets a small white hand rose up and attempted to brush him away.

"At least she still lives," Lady Leicester murmured, and reached out blindly for the nearest chair. "I fear she may not have long."

Ben did not doubt he might allay such a fear, but he looked first to find the evidence to do so.

Slowly, noiselessly, he came closer to the large bed in the center of the room, dismissing his unbidden memories of fairy tales in which the prince dared awaken a sleeping beauty. A pity his own motives were so mercenary; he came not to rescue a maiden but to expose her. And, in any case, the princess was not his for the asking.

Ben pulled aside the gauzy white fabric arrayed around the canopy and gently pushed away the edge of a blanket obscuring Lady Larkspur's face. With her bright hair spread upon her pillow and a lace nightdress buttoned neatly to the neck, there was nothing of the customary dishabille of the fevered patient, nor any evidence of discomfort. She looked like nothing so much as a porcelain doll.

Suddenly her eyes shot open, very wide and far too clear.

"I do not believe we need your opinion, sir," she said. "The very fact of your presence adds greatly to my pain and distress."

"I am sorry to hear it, for it goes against my oath to aggravate your condition. If it alleviates your concern for my trespass, allow me to reassure you I am here on behalf of my cousin Raeborn, who fears for your well-being."

The bright eyes closed, a little too tightly.

"Please tell dear Lord Raeborn to give up all hope and abandon me. I will not hold him. Advise him to find happiness with another."

Ben felt grateful her eyes were shut, for he could scarcely conceal his grin.

"He will not, my lady. He tells me he loves you dearly."

She looked at him again, her eyes full of distrust and dislike.

"How could he say so? Your cousin does not know me at all!"

"Calm yourself, my lady. Such a display of vehemence could damage your already weakened heart," Ben said soothingly, and chose not to add how it had already damaged her cunning performance. Before she could turn from him, he reached out to touch her forehead and was surprised to find it damp and clammy. He frowned.

Lady Larkspur displayed the wit to flutter her long eyelashes and seal her traitorous lips.

Silently, he ran his fingers down her lovely face, feeling the firm, smooth skin under the layer of moisture, and her admirable bone structure. With his other hand, he pulled away the layers of blankets to examine the rest of her, and she promptly crossed her hands over the bodice of her nightdress. And there, just where her wrists met, he saw several drops of water staining the fine cloth.

Ben bit down on his lip as he looked beyond the bed to a basin of water on a nearby table. A linen cloth hung at its edge, its drippings threatening the fine veneer of the wood.

How excellent her deception! But how much more convincing she would have been if she had bothered to douse her entire body in water just before his arrival.

"She does not seem to have a great fever," he said, turning to her mother, but Lady Larkspur had something to say about that.

"I am very warm," she insisted.

"Perhaps you would feel a good deal better if you did not have the weight of ten blankets upon you," he retorted, and threw half of them off the bed.

"I will surely die without them," she insisted, and moved quickly to recover them.

But Ben was even quicker, and caught her around the waist before she could reach them. Her body pressed against his, and when she turned breathlessly to look at him, her sweetly scented hair fluttered across his face. Through her thin nightdress he could feel the beating of her heart, sure and strong, and the soft uncorseted roundness of her breasts.

In the course of his professional life, he had necessarily developed an intimate knowledge of the female anatomy, but he did not recall ever having so unprofessional a response to it. Surely, if he had believed her truly ill, he would never have had such a reaction. And since she was already promised to his cousin, his unruly desires must be suppressed.

He attempted to mask his confusion before she could even guess at it. Still holding her, he reached with his free hand to his leather bag and withdrew his most useful of instruments. Affixing one end to his ear—an awkward business, since he still held the lady upright—he pressed the other against her back. She wiggled, an act for which she surely was not aware of the consequences on his state of mind. And body.

Her heart, somewhat accelerated in pace, showed no signs of quitting her anytime soon.

"I can hardly breathe," she gasped, and tried to pull away.

Here might have been the one symptom of truth, for his own tight grasp of her put pressure on her diaphragm, and their awkward proximity might very well leave her breathless. Gently, and regretfully, he pressed her back down against the pillows and covered her with the undermost, thinnest, blanket.

"Is that better?" he asked as he put back his instrument.

"No," she insisted. "I do not feel better at all."

He deliberately fussed with the clasp on his case and glanced towards her mother before he spoke. Lady Leicester, apparently unconcerned with the proprieties in the case, dozed in her cushioned chair.

"I am surprised to hear it, my lady. For I cannot find anything at all wrong with you," he said softly.

Lark glowered at him from her nest of pillows and narrowed her eyes.

"Then you must be a very poor physician, if you cannot discover the cause of my malaise!" she cried out.

He raised his brows.

"And you, my lady, must be a very poor patient if you cannot invent symptoms convincing enough to prove me wrong!"

"I invent nothing! I have been ill since the evening of my sister's ball, barely able to leave my bed. My . . . my limbs are quite weak and my thinking in complete disarray . . ."

"And yet you appear very clear and lucid just now."

She paused and glanced towards her mother. Ben admired her tenacity, for he guessed her scheme was entirely of her own working and would have little support if he chose to challenge her in front of the others. It would be easy to defeat her, and thus bless her marriage to Raeborn.

But for reasons he did not care to examine too closely, he preferred not to do so. Not yet.

Lady Larkspur cleared her throat. "It comes and goes, I am told. I doubt I will remember anything of this interview an hour from now," she said with a deep sigh.

"A pity," Ben answered, "for I believe it will remain fixed in my memory for many years to come."

"And why might it be so? What interest do you retain in this affair?"

"Why, none at all, except for a professional one, and a sense of some obligation to a relation."

"We are scarcely related at all, sir."

"So you have told me at least as many times as we have met. I am often admired for my keen intellect, and therefore I assure you your words have been completely understood. But you misunderstand me. I did not refer to our own tenuous connection, but rather to the stronger one I share with Raeborn. He and I have not enjoyed many occasions on which to meet, but my present business in London—and his concerns—have brought us together for a common purpose." Ben's own convictions strengthened as he spoke, and he added, "He is not a bad person, my lady."

Lady Larkspur looked at him with patent distrust.

"I am sure he is a perfect gentleman. I hope he will not be shattered when you tell him I am not the woman for him, for I am incapable of becoming a wife."

"You seemed perfectly competent a week or so ago when you expected to marry Mr. Floor," Ben said and lifted her hand from the blanket. It felt warm and dry.

She tried to pull away. "You have pained me all the more to remind me of his perfidy! Please do not do so again!" Since he would not release her hand, she chose to turn her face away. "And his name is Mr. Moore."

"Forgive my error. Perhaps it is due to the low estimation in which I now hold the man for the damage he has done to you."

A muffled sound came from the pillows, and Ben realized she was trying to stifle a laugh. It was the first time she had exhibited anything other than scorn in his company, and he marveled at his unexpected ability to produce such a response.

"But he is best forgotten, even if forgiveness will not come easily," Ben continued quickly. "Your present state of grief will pass, and your recovery will be complete. Raeborn assures me he will wait."

Ben knew he tested her, purposely inciting her to reveal the true state of affairs. He realized he wanted nothing so much as her admission of playacting her illness, and gambled that his consoling, conciliatory tone would achieve it.

"He must not sacrifice himself for nought," she sighed melodramatically.

"You are too modest, my lady. I would not consider winning your hand in marriage to be of little consequence. The rewards would be very great."

"So is my pain! Please leave me, Mr. Queensman, for I fear there is nothing you can do, for all your reputed skills!"

So rarely had a patient dismissed him, he felt unprepared for the flicker of anger it produced. The lady would not have Raeborn, but she would not have him either. And so it cut at his pride.

"But I did not say I could do nothing, my lady. I could find nothing wrong, but physicians rarely concede their own powerlessness." Still holding her, he unbuttoned her nightdress at the wrist with his free hand, and pushed up her sleeve. "It is an age-old cure I propose, one guaranteed to release the fever. It would be a pity to scar your flesh, but you give me no alternative."

She sat up at once, and pulled her arm away with a strength unusual in a woman, let alone one on her deathbed. Ben had the grace to look surprised, though he had managed to get the very response he desired.

"I will not be bled!" Lady Larkspur hissed at him. "I remember what the butchers who called themselves physicians did to my grandmother, and I will not be so violated! You call yourself a doctor, sir, but if you do what you propose, your services would be better employed at the charnel house!"

"Lark! Dear girl, you are returned to us!" Lady Leicester cried from her chair, and rushed to the bed. "Mr. Queensman, we are forever indebted to you for the restoration of our daughter, for she seems entirely back in spirit. Whatever did you do to enact a cure so quickly?"

I threatened her with real physical pain, Ben thought ruefully, knowing how unworthy it was of him to have done it. Instead, he said nothing, merely watching his artful patient being gathered into her mother's arms. Over Lady Leicester's soft shoulder, Lady Larkspur scowled at him.

"It is an experimental treatment, rarely used, madam. It jolts the patient into an excited state and rids her body of ill humors."

"Dare we hope its effects are permanent? Is my daughter's progress assured? I am eager to give the family the good news, sir. Her father will be forever grateful."

As the lady spoke, her recalcitrant daughter started to slip from her arms like sand through a sieve. Her eyes closed, and she made little gasping noises, as if she were deprived of air to breathe. Lady Leicester set her down gently on the pillows and turned to Ben, her expression distraught.

If the damned girl does not die of her own willfulness, someone ought to hasten her progress, he thought angrily. To subject her caring family to such torture seemed unforgivable.

"What has happened, sir? We cannot lose her, for we love her so." Lady Leicester lifted a paint-stained hand to her forehead. "What shall we tell Lord Raeborn?"

On the other hand, to force a young girl to marry an aged man who cared for her only as an investment for the future was unforgivable in its own way.

"My lady," he began slowly, "we must tell Lord Raeborn and your family that she is not yet recovered."

From the pillow, the bright eyes flickered.

But Lady Leicester demanded his attention. "Is there any hope for it? What must we do? Please understand, Mr. Queensman, our family will spare no expense for her recovery. And your generous cousin made a similar offer, though there is no reason. We are quite able to manage, of course."

"I am sure Raeborn did not doubt your ability but only meant to ensure your willingness. Perhaps he also intended to confirm his own interests in the case, which he tells me are considerable," Ben said diplomatically. Indeed, if Raeborn made such an offer, it appeared his interests were greater than even Ben imagined. The old man had never been known for his open hand.

"Of course. He assures us he has admired Larkspur from afar for many years and is prepared to treat her kindly." The good mother's voice faltered over the last few words.

"I am sure of it. And yet . . ." Ben hesitated, wondering how to phrase his question without sounding like a medieval herbalist. "Is there any talk of love?"

"Love?" Lady Leicester was justifiably amused. "Why, Mr. Queensman, you are more of a romantic than I would credit you! How can there be such a thing, when Lark and Raeborn have scarcely met? And remember, she only recently gave her heart to another."

"That is precisely the problem. My lady, your daughter is lovesick, for she has been dealt a blow to her heart by one who disappointed her most severely. Raeborn's current declaration eases nothing, but may only add to her burden."

"I see," Lady Leicester said, though clearly she did not. "Do you propose we marry them hastily, so she may come to love your cousin? Would that do?"

Ben was not prepared for the lady's decisiveness.

"I believe such matters take some time."

The lady's smile broadened. "Mr. Queensman, if I may be a bit impertinent, have you ever been in love yourself?"

He had nothing to lose by telling her the truth, or at least most of it. For he could hardly reveal that her recalcitrant daughter was the only lady he had ever met who managed to ignite certain unbidden sparks in the solid timber of his sensibility.

"I have had little time in my life to engage in such sport, my lady. I have studied hard and have used my knowledge more energetically than most physicians. As you may know, I operate a small hospital for the poor in Brighton. It requires a good deal of me, and I have yet to meet a woman anxious for such a rival."

Lady Leicester patted his hand with motherly comfort. "I am sure there is such a lady, Mr. Queensman. She will not be the sort of spoiled young chit you are likely to find in fashionable circles, but a woman of developed character. Perhaps someone who has been ill herself, and will think on your patients with compassion."

"I will not give up hope, then."

"But what do you propose to do?"

Ben felt at a loss to defend himself, for unlike Raeborn, he imagined no set path to finding a wife. And, no matter her kindness, he did not intend to explain such things to Lady Leicester.

When he did not answer, she added helpfully, "With my daughter, sir. If it is only love that can cure her, how may we hasten its arrival?"

"Ah, yes," Ben said gratefully. "Love may very well do the trick, but it is not the only solution I propose. Lady Larkspur must be distracted from her extreme distress and would do well with a change of scenery. Remaining here in bed, receiving only family members and doing little to alleviate boredom cannot be beneficial to her health. I prescribe a change of scenery."

He left the bedside to approach the shrouded window and drew the heavy velvet aside. It was a glorious day, the sort that would tempt him to leave his hospital and walk upon the beach if he were in Brighton. The window clasp moved easily between his fingers, making him suspect it had been used often, and recently. He opened the pane, welcoming in the sweet air of the garden below.

"Should we bring her outside? I thought it myself, sir! For I have ever been an advocate of a daily walk and outdoor endeavor. I believe my daughters have been healthier for it . . . until Lark took ill."

Ben turned and smiled encouragingly. "I thought it myself, my lady, for it is unusual to see a family of five natural beauties. And so we shall return Lady Larkspur to her sisters' excellent company. But I think a turn in the park insufficient to produce the sort of cure we desire in this case. I should like to remove your daughter from London and bring her to the seaside."

Lady Leicester frowned. "We once summered in Margate, when the girls were very little. It is no longer fashionable, but I suppose we might rent a cottage near the beach."

"It sounds perfectly delightful, but I rather thought she might do better in a sanatorium."

"Goodness! That seems very severe! Are they not reserved for the very ill or the very old?"

"Indeed they are, my lady. But are we not talking about your daughter's life? She will be in excellent company."

"And are there such things in Margate?"

Ben took a deep breath. "There are not. But I am thinking of a very fine destination farther south, where the king's own physician has established a respite. Mr. Knighton attracts only the finest patients."

"In Dover? Or Eastbourne, perhaps?"

"Not quite. In Brighton, in the very shadow of the king's new Pavilion," Ben explained. "And there is yet another advantage, of course. It is very close to my own home, so I will be available to look in on Lady Larkspur from time to time."

From beneath the cover on the bed, the lady Larkspur aroused herself sufficiently from her stupor to cry out a hearty protest.

"It is the worst of all possible occurrences," Lark complained for the hundredth time, pulling at the flowers on her bonnet.

Miss Janet Tavish braced herself against the leather cushions of their small prison while the carriage took a sharp turn. The ride already exceeded the endurance of her patience, and she thought anything preferable to once again reiterating their awkward circumstances.

"I thought the worst circumstance was to be married to Lord Raeborn," she murmured wearily. "Or that you would die."

Lark loosened a silk flower and sent it flying against the window. "There was never any danger of it, as well you know! But who can say what vapors I shall breathe in this cursed sanatorium! I may well die from exposure to others!"

"If you do, you will at least be rewarded in your last moment by knowing it was all for the evasion of a hateful marriage. I have not anything near your excuse, Lark."

"Whatever do you mean?"

"As your companion, I will be exposed to the same illnesses. If I take ill and die, I will gain nothing."

Lark pursed her lips, in the way she did when she tried to be coaxing. It was a look Janet knew too well. "Is not our friendship worth anything? I shall put up a monument to your memory and cherish you always."

"It is a great consolation," Janet grumbled.

"And does not this journey provide others?" Lark continued. "If not for the fact I am supposed to be dying, it might be a delightful holiday."

"My dear girl, I think you fail to consider the severity of our purpose."

Lark fell back against the cushions and looked unhappily out the window. She could already see the sea and sniff the salt in the cool air. Within an hour they should arrive at Mr. Knighton's sanatorium.

"I do not," she said sadly. "If only fortune had smiled on me and persuaded Lord Raeborn to look elsewhere for a wife. If only my father had relented and allowed me to recover myself in due course. If only that insufferable doctor had minded his own business—"

"Mr. Queensman? I do not think anyone else considers him offensive. In fact—"

"I do not wish to hear it, Janet! Why he is universally adored by my traitorous family is beyond my comprehension. And why they should trust him over anyone else is absurd. He does nothing to warrant it."

"Perhaps not, though his attendance to Lord Southard in America must warrant some respect. And have you not considered his purpose in bringing you to Brighton?"

"His purpose? It can only be to torment me further."

"Unless it is to grant you time during which Raeborn might reconsider his suit or offer his admiration elsewhere."

"You forget he is aligned with that odious gentleman and seeks to further his cause."

"But he has no reason to do so, since the success of Raeborn's marriage might deprive him of an inheritance."

Lark sighed, having worked herself into this corner before. And yet she could think of no other reason for Mr. Queensman's insistence on bringing her to Brighton but to allow her an escape from a marriage to his cousin.

"I might manage to drown in the sea," she mused aloud.

"You are so able a swimmer, no one would believe it," Janet reminded her.

"But the sea is hardly the pond at Leicester Park! There are waves and currents and all sorts of beastly creatures lurking about."

"I am sure there are, but we will have the protection of a bathing machine and a dipper if we venture out to swim. Lily told me Martha Gunn herself is employed at Knighton's, having been recently persuaded to leave her position at Margate. She is reported to be very diligent."

"And dips her customers only in the safest waves? I think I should resent her intrusion."

"Most certainly, if you wish to drown. Mrs. Gunn will surely not allow it."

Lark was preparing a suitable retort when a shaft of bright light broke through the glass of their window. She squinted at the view and promptly forgot her discontent.

"Oh, Janet, just look at it! And here we shall spend the next months? It is heaven compared to the city!"

Indeed, the grandeur of the sea stretched out before them. The day was so clear Lark imagined she could see the cliffs of a distant shore. The blue water, dotted with the occasional fishing boat, looked calm and peaceful, harboring none of the dangers of which Lark professed great concern. Gulls flew gracefully about, several showing the courage to come very close to their moving carriage.

"You look a little too healthy, my dear," Janet reminded her.

"Have no fear, for I have sufficient time to compose

myself properly," Lark said with confidence. After all, in recent weeks, she had become very expert at it.

"Perhaps not. Do you not think those turrets are the towers of the Royal Pavilion? I have read they resemble nothing so much as turnips, and yonder bulbs certainly match the description."

Lark followed Janet's gaze out the opposite window to what likely was the building popularly called the King's Folly, built at great cost, and still not completed. There were many who considered it an architectural nightmare. Lark rather thought it looked a sultan's dream.

"We are very close to our destination," Lark whispered, the great burden of her role restored to her. The last several hours, in no one's company but Janet's, she had allowed herself to imagine them young girls on holiday, with no cares but to keep their faces out of the sun and dress warmly enough for the chill of the evening. But her life was not destined to be so simple and pleasurable, for she now faced a whole new audience who needed to be convinced of her failing health.

And the renewal of one old association, who was not disposed to be generous in his feelings towards her.

"Goodness! Could this be Mr. Queensman himself?" Janet cried. Lark opened her eyes. She knew to expect the beast, but must he insist on showing up at the very gate of hell? "He is very solicitous and kind to greet us. It could not be his official place to do so."

"Perhaps he owns no official place, relying entirely on his association with others. What do we know of him, after all?"

Janet smiled, and Lark bristled to see her so cheerful.

"Nothing, I suppose. And yet I can report he is very handsome and I doubt he relies on any padding in his costume. I believe what we see is genuinely Mr. Queensman. Such honesty speaks well for his demeanor in other things. Which is more than I can say for you, my dear friend."

Lark leaned forward, preparing a riposte. But when the carriage jolted to a stop, she knew she could ill afford the time to put her companion in her place. Instead, she slumped back against the cushions and closed her eyes, just as the coachman opened the latch upon the door.

"Mr. Queensman! What a lovely surprise!" Janet cried, and the carriage shifted to one side.

"Miss Tavish, is it you?" came a deep voice, all too familiar. "Welcome to Brighton! It is most kind of you to accompany your friend on this journey, for the presence of one so close to her can only be beneficial to her health. I trust you had an uneventful journey?"

Janet sighed. "The roads were good, and nothing impeded our progress. But I fear my friend suffered greatly at every bump and turn on the road. She sleeps now, though fitfully."

"I see," Mr. Queensman drawled. He seemed so close that Lark could feel the warmth of his body. Even through closed lids, she sensed he blocked the sun from the doorway of the carriage as he helped Janet down the wooden steps. "I have made certain that her room is prepared for her and a wheeled chair is available. Unfortunately, the one Knighton offered did not meet my qualifications, and so I am having another delivered for her."

"I am sure it is no problem, sir," Janet said agreeably. Lark wished herself closer so she could pinch her. "In town, Lady Larkspur grew quite accustomed to one of the servants carrying her about."

"I am glad of it," Mr. Queensman said briefly, and suddenly Lark felt arms gathering her up and lifting her from the seat. She did not have to open her eyes to know who presumed to carry her in so ignoble and presumptuous a fashion.

In a moment, the sun fell upon her face, and she could hear the voices of the grooms as they set upon her array of trunks and carpetbags. The scent of the sea was strong and invigorating, and, closer, she thought she detected sandalwood and pine. She turned her head, rubbed her nose against worsted cloth and felt something hard beneath it.

"She looks somewhat better since I saw her last, Miss Tavish. Has her diet improved?"

Janet stammered some response, even though Lark had already tutored her with all the answers. Damn the man for having such an effect on them all, she thought angrily. Did he intend to thwart her every move?

She sighed noisily and waited for him to notice her. But

he would not. He continued to talk to Janet and bark out
orders to the servants as he propelled her into a building.
Opening her eyes just a slit, she saw them enter a large,
sunny room and proceed down a long corridor. Lowering
her head, she also glanced upon the smooth, firm skin of
Mr. Queensman's jaw and a white starchy collar.

"Where am I?" she dared to ask.

Janet's face suddenly blotted out all else.

"Why, you must remember, Lady Lark. We are in Brighton, at Mr. Knighton's sanatorium. It is a very elegant
place, by the look of it."

"And is this one of the servants?" Lark asked nastily.

She heard his laughter rumble from deep within his chest.

"I am your servant, my lady," Mr. Queensman said, "and
one already known to you. You will be happy to know
you might avail yourself of my services for all of your stay
in Brighton."

"Why, Mr. . . . oh dear. I cannot recall your name. You
are Raeborn's nephew or cousin or some other relation,
are you not?"

"It does not signify. But as I am your servant, you may
call me Ben. It is my name, and owns the advantage of
being very easy to remember."

He paused just then, and with surprising grace pushed
open a door. Lark blinked and took in the stark but clean
appearance of the room assigned as her prison cell over
the next months.

"It is a very common name, certainly," she said, and
yawned. "If I should ever have the occasion to use it, which
I firmly doubt, I shall endeavor to remember it."

"See that you do, my lady," said Ben Queensman under
his breath, and dropped her unceremoniously onto the bed.

Chapter Four

*F*or a prison cell, the room proved fairly spacious. Mr. Knighton spared no expense in the furnishings and accoutrements and provided enough room for a battalion of visiting guests to be seated and entertained. While such a realization would never have occurred to Lark before her confinement in his sanatorium, she now recognized how several of her fellow inmates scarcely left their rooms, and preferred to welcome their family and friends into their private quarters.

Lark did not expect to receive many visitors, and if one or more of her sisters managed to make the journey to Brighton, she would be pleased to greet them in the large hall provided for such reunions.

But a spacious chamber, for her, held other advantages.

"I shall miss dancing, to be certain," Lark said wistfully to Janet. She curtsied to an imaginary partner and hummed the tune of a Roger de Coverly as she took the first lively steps. Without such exercise, her muscles had already grown weak from inactivity and she was more likely to be restless when confined once again to her seat. "Please join me, Janet."

"I do not know how to dance the part of the man," Janet apologized as she stood.

"I know it very well," Lark said playfully and bowed to her approaching partner. "Do you remember when we were all little girls and practiced our steps in the nursery? I was quite taller than the rest of you and always made to play a masculine role when we danced. On occasion, I still forget myself at an assembly and stand on the wrong side of the line."

Janet laughed and turned the corner on an imaginary gentleman. "Your mistake might not be noticed, for you are still quite tall and must often look over your partner's head."

Lark smiled ruefully and seized the moment to do a little

twisting movement, which felt uncommonly gratifying. She sighed.

"You are right. It is always a pleasure for me to stand up with a gentleman of an uncompromising height." She recalled, a little uncomfortably, how Hindley Moore's small stature had proven prophetic. And how, on the evening of his defection, she reluctantly accepted another's invitation and was momentarily rewarded with an excellent partner. Well, she did not expect to ever dance with Mr. Benedict Queensman again.

Lark stopped suddenly, and an unsuspecting Janet nearly sidestepped right into her.

"Are you tired?" Janet asked breathlessly.

Lark laughed. "You, of all people, know I can scarcely be tired when I have had so little occasion to exert myself. No, I am only concerned we might be overheard by someone walking down the hall, and my deception would be rudely uncovered."

"And yet you must exercise, Lark. Your legs will be in a sorry state if—"

"Of course, Janet," Lark interrupted her impatiently. "I know it only too well. But perhaps we ought to refrain from our improvised musical accompaniment. Or come up with a better scheme."

Janet said nothing, and Lark knew she would not make a suggestion until Lark ventured forth herself. The invalid stretched her arms silently as she studied her friend's bemused face, realizing again how grateful she ought to be for years of devotion and loyalty. She doubted anyone else would remain a party to her deception and agree to seclude herself so far from popular society. When this business concluded, and they could return to all they had abandoned, she ought to reward Janet handsomely for her sacrifice.

But for now, Lark turned her back on her companion and walked to the wide window overlooking the expansive Brighton beach and the azure sea. The day was glorious, another in a string of sunlit days gracing them since their arrival. As a result, they could expect to spend the afternoon on the wide veranda of the sanatorium, reading or playing cards with some of the other guests.

But the others would not awaken for several hours, and the beach and gardens looked nearly deserted.

"You are—you cannot be thinking of a walk upon the beach, dear Lark!" Janet said nervously and stepped up beside her.

"I am sorely tempted, to be sure," Lark admitted. "But we cannot afford such luxuries. In any case, it is possible we will have access to the beach soon enough, for a bright caravan seems to have arrived."

Janet peered over her shoulder. "What is it, Lark? I have never seen such things."

"Nor have I," Lark said thoughtfully. The little wooden sheds, large enough for one or two occupants, were lined up perfectly along the shore and were all adorned with red-and-white ballooned awnings. "But I am quite certain they are bathing machines, designed to take swimmers out into the waves and protect their modesty with those rather large hoods. Do you see the little tracks of wood laid out upon the sand? I believe they are needed to help the horses guide the machines over the sand pebbles. It is a very cunning invention, is it not?"

"Yes," Janet said doubtfully. "But surely there is too much husbandry in their design. How little room we must have in a little box such as that to change into proper garments and store our discarded robes!"

"You are right. It looks very cramped. But then our reward must be our unfettered freedom upon the waves! Will it not be glorious?"

"Indeed," Janet grumbled. "But how much more glorious it would be if you could play the part of the man, as you once did. Gentlemen are not so constrained and can swim wherever they wish."

As if to punctuate her point, two men and a large dog suddenly appeared on the beach just beyond Mr. Knighton's array of bathing machines. One of them glanced towards the building and, apparently satisfied they had no audience, started to pull off his shirt. The dog bounced excitedly into the waves, chasing a gull. In a moment, the two men followed, leaving behind a pile of clothing on the pebbly beach.

Janet squeezed the flesh of Lark's arm, but said nothing. Nor did they turn away from the window, as propriety certainly demanded.

"Yes," Lark breathed, a little unsteadily. "It would be

glorious to be a man, and to be allowed to follow the dictates of one's own heart."

From her wheeled chair on the wide veranda, Lark lazily watched the progress of the workmen as they completed the positioning of the bathing machines upon the beach. Each stood about twenty feet from another, on its own track. An open book lay on Lark's lap, but she had abandoned its trite story at least an hour before in favor of studying all those who joined her in the sun and those who gathered along the waves. Janet, apparently finding her own book equally unsatisfying, asked permission to wander off and explore something of the town.

A cheer went up from the corner table, where several of Mr. Knighton's patients played at whist. Lord Scafell and Herr Schwarzwald, brothers-in-law alike in disposition and ailment, made an uncompromising team, and were accustomed to defeating all opponents. In spite of their deserved reputation, they were nevertheless challenged every afternoon, on this day by Lady Crawford and the bright-eyed Miss Hathawae. Judging by the looks on the gentlemen's faces, the challenge had been met.

Nearby, in a chair facing the building, Mrs. Wertham labored at her needlework. Lark had offered to help her on more than one occasion, for the lady's fingers were twisted with disease and age, but the stubborn worker continued tenaciously, pausing only to change the color of her yarn and to complain about the noisy gulls.

Entertainment of a sort was provided by Colonel Wayland, a blustery gentleman who seemed to have little to do but to recount his exploits in America and remind anyone within earshot that he would not have been confined at Knighton's but for the severe injuries he had sustained in his battles against the Indians. Usually such sentiments were followed by an invitation to examine his scars, though it was likely to be refused. Janet, however, believed Herr Schwarzwald already had a passing familiarity with the colonel's scars, and she said as much to Lark.

Of the great man, Mr. Knighton, they heard nothing. The nurses and servants appeared to have their orders, and the daily lives of the sanatorium inmates moved along in an organized, peaceful manner. No one seemed to have any dire needs, nor did anyone seem to improve in health. The arrival of the bathing machines, however, heralded some great changes in their situations, and everyone appeared to be very excited about testing the waves. For now, the water was reported to be cold enough to induce paralysis, but only days away from being stimulating.

One of the servants approached Colonel Wayland's chair and bobbed very prettily as she handed him a card. Wayland, scarcely pausing in his speech, nodded, and the girl turned to wave in a gentleman from at the doorway.

Lark twisted coyly in her seat, eager for some diversion and nearly certain she would see Mr. Gabriel Siddons, a young man who visited his uncle almost daily. She was not disappointed, but turned back quickly, lest she appear too interested. While he always seemed to have important matters to discuss with the colonel, her vanity insisted he also enjoyed the moments he spent in a mild flirtation with her.

"Good afternoon, Lady Larkspur," the soft voice purred. She thought she heard a hint of a foreign accent, but could not place it. "You look very pretty sitting in the sun, but do have a care for your nose. It is far too elegant to be spoiled by freckles."

Lark smiled to herself, welcoming the flattery and attention. "Thank you for your concern, Mr. Siddons. If I imagined I would ever be well enough to—"

She stopped abruptly, for as she watched the colonel's nephew approach, another gentleman appeared at the door. The little servant held up her hand to stop him, but he brushed her off with a word of which the authority and arrogance could be detected even at a distance. Mr. Siddons, noticing Lark's distraction even as his uncle began some sort of litany of current complaints, followed her gaze and frowned.

Lark looked down at her lap and picked up her book, hoping Mr. Queensman would not notice her. But his advancing footsteps warned her she would not be so lucky.

"Mr. Siddons," he said, "I am surprised to see you here, where our paths might intersect at any time. I understand you are a frequent visitor to Knighton's Sanatorium. Could it be the daily arrival of French goods holds some appeal for you?"

"Queensman, you must know I scarcely miss my homeland at all. It can only remind me of unfortunate events." He paused as he brushed an imaginary tear from his cheek. "I come to Knighton's to visit my uncle Wayland, a dear old gent who would otherwise be quite alone. I do not mind making him happy. But if you must know, the genuine appeal of my recent afternoons here is the company of this excellent but suffering lady. May I introduce Lady Larkspur?"

"Ah, yes, Lady Larkspur," Benedict Queensman murmured as his shadow fell across her page. "But we are already acquainted, better than the lady would prefer. Indeed, it is to check on her progress that I come to Knighton's, for I represent the interests of her concerned admirer. Lord Raeborn will be happy to know you are looking so well, my lady. I attribute your improved condition to the sea air."

Lark slipped lower into her chair as she looked up at him. She thought he looked fairly well himself, though something about his face looked different.

She coughed and put a linen handkerchief to her lips. "Why, Mr. Queensman, could it be you? I am flattered you are able to spare the time to visit me, for you must be very busy with your own little hospital."

"Yes," Mr. Siddons said in a severe tone. "However do you tear yourself away from the ragged refuse who must come to you more in the hopes of filling their stomachs than of any kind of cure? Or do you prefer to avoid them, lest you catch some of their contagion?"

Lark saw anger and indignation momentarily touch Mr. Queensman's face and watched as he—literally—swallowed a retort. She, of course, had never inquired as to the type of hospital he managed and could not help but wonder why a gentleman would be so engaged.

"I have often considered the greater hazards to exist in polite society. What passes for generosity and good cheer are often merely bandages over nasty wounds," Mr. Queensman answered coolly.

Mr. Siddons recoiled, as if from a blow. He opened his mouth to say something, but was reminded of his avowed purpose in coming to Knighton's.

"Boy! Come here! I wish to speak to you!" Colonel Wayland barked.

Gabriel Siddons bowed low to Lark and ignored Mr. Queensman altogether as he turned towards his uncle. As he sat down beside him, Lark overheard the old man demand a full accounting of their conversation. She would have enjoyed hearing Mr. Siddons' version of it, but Mr. Queensman would not allow it.

"I am glad to hear you are flattered by my visits, my lady, but honesty compels me to remind you that I do it for my cousin Raeborn. He has already written thrice, anxious for news of your health." Mr. Queensman drew up a canvas chair and sat down upon it before Lark gave him leave to do so. "And if I had known I would encounter someone as unpleasant as Gabriel Siddons, perhaps I would not have come at all. He abused my hospital most wrongfully, but he is right to think it improvident for me to take time away from my real patients."

His implication, of course, was that "real" patients were genuinely ill. But Lark felt no strong inclination to demonstrate the symptoms of her decline just now, for she felt curious about the work he did and those who came to him for help.

"Are all the people in your hospital very poor? However do you manage? And what if you are needed while you are here vis . . . ah . . . assessing the situation for Lord Raeborn?"

Mr. Queensman looked faintly amused but neatly concealed his smile. "I do not manage alone. To answer your first question, I can tell you I have several generous patrons, including the king himself, who supplement my own investment in the hospital. And, as to the other, I work with many doctors and hire the most helpful nurses. In fact, my purpose in coming to London last month was to interview three young men who were interested in joining me. Lord Southard had a particular recommendation."

"John?"

"Indeed. Why are you so surprised?"

Lark was not sure herself. "I—I suppose it is because Delphinium—Lady Southard—never said a word to me."

Mr. Queensman lifted his chin and squinted into the wind. Lark used the opportunity to study his face, and she soon realized what seemed different about his features. His hair, usually thick and wavy and sometimes falling on his brow, was slicked back and shiny. As the edges lifted and curled into the breeze, she realized they were wet.

"Perhaps it is because she knew her younger sister would have no interest in young physicians," he said after a time.

"Of course." Lark nodded, unable to resist the opportunity he gave her to insult him. "That is precisely the case."

"A pity. I daresay young physicians would be very much interested in you, my lady."

"Sir! Your behavior is insupportable! I will not sit here—"

"Of course you shall, Lady Larkspur, for you insist you are unable to rise from your chair. It is a pity, but my feeble professional talents are unable to decipher why it is so." He turned away from the wind and rested his knowing blue eyes on her guilty face. "But please forgive me if I have worded my phrases badly; I daresay my associates would hardly aim so high as to be interested in you as the object of their amour. Rather, the particularities of your case, an opportunity to understand how one so young and apparently healthy could succumb to such distress and weakness, would present a very educational study."

Lark wondered if he might be trying to scare her into confession. So he would succeed, if she were the sort of spineless girl to whom he was probably accustomed.

But the success of her recent deception confirmed she was stronger than that, and she lifted her face as she returned his challenge. "If you imagine for one minute, sir, that I would allow a strange man to touch me, you are very much mistaken."

He gazed into her eyes, and she wondered if he could read her mind.

"I would never presume to imagine it. It is something I myself tried to resist when called upon to do so in London. But, in any case, physicians necessarily acquire the permission of their patients before they bring in others for consultation." He suddenly looked away, making Lark feel oddly bereft. She watched his hand waver over the tray of pastries between them and then swoop down to capture a quince tart. As if his uninvited presence were not enough to spoil the tranquillity of this lovely afternoon, his impertinence proved additionally grating. "Of course, most patients faced with uncompromising illness welcome the opinions of a team of experts. It is likely to bring them closer to a cure."

Lark said nothing as she looked for an escape from the cunning trap he had set for her. What might prove a plausible reason for rejecting a source of hope? It needed to be strong enough to perpetuate the deception she chose, yet delicate enough to convince Mr. Queensman to play along with her. She did not doubt he knew the truth of the matter; she only wondered when he would expose her.

"Have I not been instructed to trust your own excellent judgment in the matter, Mr. Queensman? Lord Raeborn would hear of no other's opinion, and even my own father preferred your advice over that of our family's doctor. Who am I to dispute their wisdom? I am ever an obedient daughter."

Mr. Queensman laughed, and the tension between them dissipated like morning fog. Lark knew she had won this point, but the realization gave her no joy.

"Indeed, you are young enough to be Raeborn's daughter, though happily you are not. But ought a marriage be so unbalanced as to give all authority to the husband? I thought women rather favored their own ability to rule in certain kingdoms."

Lark bit down on her lip, knowing he sported with her last shred of pride. And how cruelly ironic to understand that Mr. Queensman held the very cure to what truly ailed her, but must be the last man to believe her cured. She could already envision his look of triumph when he handed her over to his aged cousin.

"Lady Larkspur? Have you no retort? I would think you, of all people, would be rather opinionated on the subject."

"I am, sir. I assure you, I am. But as the contemplation of my future holds such little promise, I do not feel my opinion to be of much lasting value. Do tell your cousin how it goes with me, how little hope I have of any happiness."

Before Mr. Queensman could answer, a shadow fell between them, and Lark once again looked up into the cheerful face of Mr. Gabriel Siddons. Behind him, his uncle seemed very much involved in the Battle of Saratoga, a conversation from which Mr. Siddons surely was happy to escape.

"Well, Siddons?" Mr. Queensman asked rudely. "I hope you interrupt us so you can apologize for distressing Lady Larkspur. Your talk of my poor charges has disturbed her greatly."

Mr. Siddons bowed in mock deference. "I am sorry to hear it, sir. And, in fact, I do apologize to both of you. My uncle informs me you are here in an entirely professional capacity."

"Did we not already make it clear enough for you?" Mr. Queensman growled.

Mr. Siddons waved dismissively. "My uncle merely confirmed it. In fact, he is intrigued by it, and asks me if you would be so kind as to also consider his own condition and attend upon him."

Mr. Queensman glanced over to where Colonel Wayland sat, apparently indifferent to their conversation.

"I have no authority here," he said. "That I might come on occasion to see Lady Larkspur is possible only through the generosity of Mr. Knighton. But at a guess, I should think your uncle has little of which to complain but the gout."

Mr. Siddons smiled. "I do not doubt it, but am grateful for your consideration. Would I ask too much if I beg you to tell him your opinion? It would mean much to him. And you need not fear Lady Larkspur will be lonely, for I shall entertain her while you are gone. We are already very good friends."

"Are you indeed, sir? How very congenial for the lady, who eschews all other relationships," Mr. Queensman said nastily.

"Though surely not at Knighton's, where she is loved by all," Mr. Siddons pronounced.

Mr. Queensman seemed to consider this carefully. "I wish I could say it gives me joy, but, alas, the lady's problem is she suffers from too much love. It is a rare affliction, but one affecting Lady Larkspur beyond measure."

Lark wanted nothing more but that the sparring would end, and so she raised a hand of peace between the men.

"Mr. Queensman, you must not take Mr. Siddons so literally! He merely means I am somewhat appreciated by the company here. I display infinite patience with my fellow guests, who often have not lived in the real world for some time but delight in lengthy narratives on the subject. Why, just this morning, the colonel retold the story of his march up the Hudson River to Albany, though I have certainly heard it five times before. If, indeed, he loves me, it is because I do not remind him of that fact."

Lark's honest pronouncement seemed to intrigue Mr. Queensman, who turned towards the colonel with renewed interest.

"Do you reassess your diagnosis, sir?" Lark asked, looking conspiratorially to Mr. Siddons. "Is it possible gout is not the cause of the gentleman's infirmity? Do you fear some foreign ailment, brought on by America's savage environment?"

Mr. Siddons laughed politely, but Mr. Queensman looked quite serious.

"I am unfortunately familiar with them all, not the least of which is the damage by gunshot. I only wonder I do not know Colonel Wayland, for we undoubtedly traveled the same rugged paths."

Mr. Siddons did not respond, and Lark thought he looked very uncomfortable. Knowing his good nature, she thought perhaps he did not wish to remind Mr. Queensman that colonels were not likely to rub shoulders with mere physicians.

"I should like to talk to him," Mr. Queensman said in a curious voice.

"Do, my good man." Mr. Siddons recovered quickly and winked at Lark. "He will be happy for your interest."

"But not at present," Mr. Queensman amended and stubbornly settled back into his seat. Lark wished he would go away.

Several moments passed in an unnatural silence.

"I see Mr. Knighton has ordered the bathing machines installed," Mr. Siddons said conversationally, at last. "They were not yet in place when I was here before. Was it only yesterday, Lady Larkspur?"

Lark appreciated his effort to change the mood of their meeting, and answered quickly. "Indeed. I first saw the workmen early this morning when I looked out my window. The modesty hoods with their bright stripes were already in place, and it appeared as if a band of gypsies had arrived on our poor beach."

"Not poor at all, my lady," Mr. Queensman said quickly. He looked at her carefully as he added, "Mr. Knighton owns the finest stretch of beach in Brighton. Many of us poorer fellows enjoy the waves here in the early morning. If you had but awakened sooner, you might have witnessed our daily expense of energy."

Lark felt her face burning when she realized she had indeed witnessed such a scene. She thought of the dark, lean bodies free of encumbrances and the enviable abandon with which they entered the water. They had looked like Neptune's own minions, powerful and compelling.

"Lady Larkspur? Are you well? You look suddenly feverish. Or perhaps it is the sun casting too bright a light upon you." Mr. Siddon's concern interrupted her unbidden thoughts.

Mr. Queensman's hand came up to brush back her curls and rest upon her forehead, where it surely lingered longer than needed.

"Lady Larkspur does not have a fever," he pronounced, looking into her eyes. Lark would have turned away if his hold had not been so insistent. "But the sun may be too intense. In fact, I believe the lady may be spending too much of her time staring at the sea."

Once again Lark silently cursed his intrusive perception, his spiteful ability to read her mind.

"If I do not entertain myself with watching the waves, I shall go mad," Lark protested.

"What do you suggest, Mr. Queensman?" Mr. Siddons asked eagerly. "Some indoor amusement?"

"It is an excellent suggestion, sir. When first I met Lady Larkspur, she demonstrated an innate talent at indoor activities."

"I know just the thing," Mr. Siddons. "I have recently purchased several dissected maps from Mr. Wallis and his son, who are surprised at the success of their little games. They mount paper maps upon wood, and cut them all awry, so one must endeavor to restore them to order. I intended to bring the maps to my uncle, who is very keen on geography. But I shall reserve several for your pleasure, Lady Larkspur."

"I fear I am not so keen on geography, sir," Lark said meekly.

"Then it is just the thing," Mr. Queensman quickly pronounced. "After all, we do not wish for you to enjoy yourself too much while at Knighton's, my lady, for then you would never wish to return to Raeborn. Mr. Wallis' dissected maps might very well pain you into recovery."

Lark neither answered nor looked at him in response. She only wondered how likely were the early-morning currents to drag someone out to sea.

Benedict Queensman dug his heels into the pebbly beach and glanced up at the windows of the sanatorium. The curtains almost certainly were drawn in each room and nothing stirred on the veranda but a few gulls enjoying the crumbs on the floor.

"Are you not coming, Ben?" Matthew Warren stretched his body and dropped the last of his garments onto the ground. Ben wondered what this otherwise modest young man would think if he knew his movements were observed by curious feminine eyes, eager for forbidden education. Unwilling to satisfy them, Ben stood in his tailed shirt, thinking he already revealed quite enough.

"I may go in as I am, Matthew. It is the way we are accustomed to swimming on my estate."

Matthew Warren looked down at his own nakedness. "I do not doubt it, but were you not the very one to assure me a different sensibility prevailed at the beach? And who will bear us witness? The patients at Knighton's could pose no difficulties. The men may envy us a bit, but I daresay the women have already seen anything we have to offer."

"Perhaps not all," Ben said carefully, but nevertheless he started to pull his shirt over his head. In a moment, he was a fitting companion for his new friend and felt the benevolence of the warm sun on his tanned flesh. He rubbed idle fingers over the hair on his chest.

Matthew looked thoughtful. "Are you speaking of your cousin's fiancée? I daresay it might make for some awkwardness at family gatherings, but you did say you are not all that close. And as he is very elderly, surely the lady is of some experience."

"She is not," Ben said decisively and dropped his shirt onto his trousers. "She is younger than we are ourselves and grew up among five sisters. I am certain she is quite unfamiliar with what we have to offer."

Matthew laughed and started towards the water.

"You never mentioned she was a shy, delicate thing."

Ben followed, but before diving into the waves, he said, "If I never said it, it is because she most definitely is not."

"I think I desire a spyglass, Janet," Lark sighed wistfully as she turned from the window. The early-morning light cast a rosy glow on her white nightgown and put brilliant highlights into her hair.

Janet looked up from the dressing table, where she was affixing a lace collar to her day dress.

"As you have never indicated any interest in sailing, I can only surmise you wish for one so you might gaze upon the men in the water. It is most indecent of you, and very rude to consider me your companion in it."

"Oh, Janet, you need not be such a stick! However else might I prepare myself for marriage if I do not observe the peculiarities of the masculine form? Otherwise I should die of fright on my wedding night."

Janet did not seem very impressed with the argument. "I thought you intended to die before your wedding night. Is it not for that very reason we are here?"

Lark waved her hand impatiently.

"Of course. But Mr. Queensman is trying so very hard to cure me, I fear he shall succeed. I wish he would just stay away and leave me to my misery."

Janet smiled. "Or leave you to Gabriel Siddons? He is not so very handsome as Mr. Queensman, but he is quite agreeable."

Lark closed the draperies, determined to resist all temptation. "He is. He almost makes me recall the happiness of a flirtation and the expectation of calling hours. He is considerate and amusing—everything Mr. Queensman is not. And he has promised to bring me a present."

"Oh, dear. It cannot be proper," Janet reminded her.

"I believe that in normal circumstances it would not be. But as I am quite confined here with little else but your good company to amuse me, Janet, I cannot bear to say no."

"What does he promise? A pretty volume of verse, perhaps?"

Lark frowned. "Nothing of the kind. He will bring me a dissected map."

"A map! And to someone who did not know the direction to Brighton from London? I could cry for the wonder of it!"

"You need not be so dramatic. I simply could not refuse his offer. And I shall rely on you to help me muddle through it."

"I suppose I must, but I confess I will not find it much fun either."

"Then what shall we do, Janet? We must look for amusement, for the life of an invalid stretches all tolerance."

Janet stood up and straightened her bodice.

"Perhaps we might take an outing in one of Mr. Knighton's carriages. I should so like to see the Royal Pavilion at close range," she said thoughtfully. "And perhaps we might swim in the sea, as we have longed to do from the first. Miss Hathawae tells me the water is tolerable enough for bathing and she will guide us through our first experience with the machines. Mrs. Gunn, for all her reputation as a dipper, can be rather abrupt, I am told."

"I wonder at what time of day we can expect to swim."

Janet giggled. "Do you mean, at what time are we quite likely to meet the young gentlemen who swim without their clothes?"

"You know we will not!"

"Even so," Janet mused, "would it not be a memorable experience?"

She walked past Lark to the closed window and pulled apart the draperies. The sun broke in on her, and she squinted as she looked at the brilliantly glowing sea.

"More so for us than for them, I expect. They may be altogether common rogues." She stood for several moments, gazing upon the spectacle. "And yet I believe one of them looks vaguely familiar to me."

Chapter Five

*T*hree days later, the badly battered body of a man washed ashore on Mr. Knighton's fine beach.

Lark knew something was amiss even as she lay in her warm bed, just awakening to the morning, for she heard the anxious shouts of men outside her window and a good deal of scurrying about in the hall. Bored enough to imagine that whatever disturbed her sleep was likely to be the most interesting event during her indefinite stay at Knighton's, she wished she dared throw on her bed jacket and simply dash out her door. Instead, she could only console herself by pulling on the bell and hoping someone—prepared to gossip—would come.

"Did you ring for me, my lady?" A young maid came so quickly that Lark knew she must have been just at the door.

"Indeed, Mary," Lark said sweetly and pulled herself to a seated position. "I am feeling very anxious, for I hear strange voices and loud shouting. It is very bad for my nerves, you know. If you would but tell me the cause of it all, I can put myself at ease."

The girl hesitated, and Lark guessed her inclination was at war with her orders.

"Do tell me, Mary, or else I believe I might faint with fear," Lark urged, grateful that no one else could hear her blatant manipulation of the poor girl.

"Oh, please do not, my lady! Or else Mrs. Jones will blame me, and I do not know what I shall do!"

"Calm down, Mary," Lark said, feeling guilty for tormenting her so. "No harm will come to me, or to you, if you confide the truth to me."

"Mrs. Jones ordered us to keep everyone in their rooms and the draperies drawn, lest anyone be disturbed. For it is a most dreadful thing, my lady. A man is drowned and is on our beach. Peter, who gathers driftwood for our fire, says he is very badly beaten and dreadful to behold."

Lark shivered, understanding why the information would be distressing for Mr. Knighton's guests.

"How awful for Peter to find him, to come upon such a sight unsuspectingly."

"But Peter did not find him. Two gentlemen were already there, examining the body. It is fortunate they are doctors and able to give their opinion on the matter."

Lark raised her eyebrows in mock amazement. "Surely, as the poor creature was already dead, one does not have to be a doctor to offer a very precise diagnosis on the case. I could do it myself."

"Oh, no, my lady! You must not look upon him!"

"I do not intend to," Lark said grimly. "In any case, I suspect he is already removed from the premises."

Mary put her hand to her brow and looked so ill, Lark wondered if Mr. Knighton had a vacant bed for her.

"He remains on the beach, along with others who are awaiting the magistrate. It seems the gentlemen found something on the man's body of some importance. Peter does not know what it is."

Lark's interest renewed, and she practically leapt from the bed.

"Do they think him a smuggler . . . a villain . . . a spy?" she asked eagerly.

Mary looked surprised, as if such thoughts never occurred to her. Perhaps they did not.

"Oh, Mary! You must bring me out onto the veranda so I can see it all, or else I shall die of curiosity! If you do not, I shall manage it myself."

As soon as Lark spoke, she realized her error. Anyone other than poor simple Mary would have been suspicious at once and wondered at so miraculous a cure. But Mary stood, dumbstruck, possibly more concerned with the consequences of doing as Lark demanded than with the enthusiasm of those demands. She looked away from the bed to the wheeled chair and then to the impossible narrowness of the door.

"You can do it, Mary," Lark whispered. "I have seen it done so many times, I could direct you. And I am not at all heavy. Once we release the catch on the wheel, it moves along easily. Miss Tavish manages it quite well."

"Could she not do it now, my lady?" Mary asked nervously.

"I will not wake her for such a reason, when you are perfectly capable of it! If you should help me now, I shall recommend you most favorably to Mrs. Jones," Lark said, certain she would get her way. "Will you help me dress?"

She saw the surrender on the girl's face and almost regretted her own willfulness. She would not allow Mary to be punished for disobeying orders, if she could help it, and would otherwise reward her handsomely. But as no one need know the part Mary played in Lark's outing, no harm should come of it.

Thus Lark reasoned as she allowed Mary to wash her and struggle with her simple dress and pin up her hair. The maid's inexpert hands fumbled with each task, but Lark could not imagine it to matter so very much, since she did not think anyone else would venture upon the veranda. The other guests, compliant, would remain in their rooms, and the staff would be concerned with more important things this morning. And she would dismiss Mary as soon as she was settled at the balustrade of the veranda.

Silently, Mary held up a mirror to Lark's flushed face. Inspecting her image, she saw her eyes looked too bright and her cheeks too rosy. The pink dress gave her color where none was desired, and she looked altogether too healthy. She glanced up at her companion but saw only a person unhappy with her own part in the business. Mary, it appeared, did not reflect on the apparent fitness of a seriously infirm patient.

Their entrance into the hallway was conducted with the greatest care. They waited until all footsteps and voices died away, and then they proceeded very slowly out the room, past the great room and dining hall and to the wide doors leading out onto the veranda. When Mary drew back the draperies, Lark had her first glimpse of the scene and was rewarded with a carnival of activity near the water's edge.

"The veranda is empty, my lady," said Mary, clearly relieved.

"It is as we hoped. You need only bring me to the edge, near the beach, and hurry off as if you had no part in it. You have my word I will tell no one and will accept all the blame for disobeying Mrs. Jones. It will be our secret."

Mary nodded and pushed open the door, shuddering when it squeaked. But elsewhere, all was silent. With a sudden burst of energy, she propelled the great awkward chair through the door and past the labyrinth of furnishings upon the wide wooden deck. Lark would have feared for her own safety, but for her confidence in the sturdiness of the balustrade. Within moments, the wheeled chair bumped up against it and, indeed, did not crash through onto the rocks below.

Lark caught her breath and sighed in relief.

"I dare no longer stay, my lady," Mary said urgently and backed away even before Lark dismissed her.

"Thank you, Mary," Lark said, straightening her bonnet. "I will not forget this kindness."

Mary looked as if it were already best forgotten and made a dash to the door. It closed behind her, its draperies cutting off any view from within.

Cheered by the success of her exploit, Lark tucked her woolen blanket around her knees and defiantly faced the stiff, cool breeze coming off the sea. In his selection of Brighton as a setting for a sanatorium, Mr. Knighton was surely to be commended, for the fresh air did much to restore one's spirit.

If, indeed, one's spirit desired restoration.

For now, Lark desired only diversion, something to break the endless monotony of life as an invalid. Unfortunately, today it came at the very harsh expense of another.

Gazing upon the scene, and once again wishing for a spyglass, Lark could not see the dead man, but she knew precisely where he lay. A group of men stood in a circle, all looking down at the pebbles and what surely lay upon them. Several horses were tethered nearby, and a small carriage stood poised at an awkward angle. Farther back, a black-draped hearse awaited its burden.

But no one seemed to be in any particular hurry. A gentleman broke through the circle and wiped his hands on a cloth proffered to him by one of the others. Someone else held something up to the light, and the crowd shifted as the men gathered around to study it. Beneath them, momentarily abandoned, a large figure remained sprawled on the beach.

This, then, was the dead man. Lark had never seen a

dead person, but she recalled very vividly the morning she
had discovered the lifeless body of a beloved pet dog and
knew how strange the experience.

She shifted her position and leaned closer to the balustrade. Snatches of the men's conversation reached her, but
nothing sufficient to draw any inference. They seemed
somewhat agitated, though none more so than a tallish
gentleman in mustard trousers. Something familiar in the
way he turned his head made Lark recognize him at once,
though why Gabriel Siddons should be so concerned about
the death of a stranger on their beach was something about
which she could hardly speculate.

Most likely, he felt responsible for the welfare of his
uncle, for the sight would surely distress the old man. Or
perhaps he recognized a colleague, for he did seem to have
some knowledge of the sea. She then realized she had no
idea what Mr. Siddons did other than visit his uncle. Perhaps he might be on the scene in a very official capacity.
If so, he would not have been very happy to learn that Mr.
Queensman had come upon the dead man first, for there
seemed to be no love between them.

Lark did not know why this was so, but some tickling
notion of her fancy wished it might have to do with her.
How difficult to abandon her old conceits, even in so deso-
late a place as a sanatorium.

Smiling, and quite forgetting herself, she sat up in her
chair and then rose to her feet, leaning on the balustrade.
She wore only slippers, the accustomed garb of Mr.
Knighton's invalids, and felt the rough wood beneath her
toes. As her toes explored the hard surface, the soft leather
caught a nail and ripped.

But rather than be distressed by the thought of the inevitable explanation for such damage, Lark laughed out loud,
feeling more mischievous than she had in years.

"I am surprised you could find the misery of another
such good sport, my lady," came a deep voice behind her.

Lark whirled about to face Mr. Queensman and wondered how he had come upon her. She had not heard the
door open or close, nor had she heard the sound of footsteps below. But here he was, looking very severe.

"You know I do not, Mr. Queensman. I was merely enjoying the pleasure of a private thought, and the wonder

of a glorious spring day," she said boldly and reached up to catch her ribbons as they blew around her face. "I am sorry to know of another's misery. I am sure it was quite unpleasant when you happened upon him."

As she spoke, Lark noticed his shirt was stained with something dark and, even at a distance, she could smell the salt water on his person.

"I am, unfortunately, too used to it in my profession. Even so, the discovery proved a nasty surprise, particularly when Mr. Warren and I realized nothing could be done."

"I understand," Lark said, and believed she did. Even so, it went quite against her spirit to gratify him in any way, and so she added, "It must be very frustrating when you are unable to work a cure on some poor soul. You necessarily know you have failed."

Mr. Queensman raised his eyebrow but said nothing against her unfair judgment upon him. He crossed his arms over his broad chest, pressing against something of bulk in his pocket, and studied her in silence. Lark returned his gaze, wondering if she should ask him to leave. He was trespassing, after all, and it seemed quite inappropriate he should be standing alone with her.

"My pride insists I can accept blame only if the patient is alive when I come upon him. Likewise, I will accept praise only when my own ministrations restore a subject to good health." He waited, as if expecting some response. "Of course, sometimes a patient recovers due to no miracle on my part."

"Perhaps nothing really ailed the patient in those cases," Lark snapped at him.

"That is precisely what I am thinking. Of course, I guessed it from the beginning."

Lark opened her mouth, ready to demand an explanation, when the light suddenly intruded on her cloudy brain. She cursed herself for being as simple and easily manipulated as poor Mary. Reaching blindly for the arm of her chair, she leaned heavily—and dramatically—upon it.

"But wait! Can I be mistaken?" Mr. Queensman asked as he came forward. "I thought I saw you standing quite unaided just now, looking as sturdy as an oak in a summer storm."

Lark sank down onto the chair a little awkwardly as her

dress twisted around her waist. She put a hand to her brow as she closed her eyes.

"It comes and goes, Mr. Queensman. It comes and goes. Suddenly I find myself with a strength I do not expect, and I seize advantage of it. And then, just as suddenly, I am fallen once again. It is a sad business, for I then must pay dearly for my little bout of exercise," she sighed, blinking away imaginary tears.

"My poor lady," Mr. Queensman said, without the slightest hint of sympathy. He came up to her chair and sat down beside her before he presumed the intimacy to tuck the wool blanket around her. "It is very noble of you to endure such pain, and all in the name of anxiety for a fellow human being. Did you know him?"

Lark felt herself grow warm where his hands met her flesh through the thin fabric of her gown. Though he did no more than brush his long tanned fingers against her arms and shoulders, it seemed as if he left an imprint upon her, for she could still feel his touch even after his hands moved on to settle innocently on the balustrade.

"Did you know him?" he repeated impatiently.

Lark was so flustered by her body's betrayal she did not know whom he meant.

"Mr. Moore? I assure you I waste no anxiety on that undeserving wretch! I—"

"I do not refer to your unfortunate choice in a husband, my lady. I mean the even more unfortunate fellow on the beach."

"The dead man?" Lark stopped short and frowned. "How on earth would I know him? I know no one in Brighton save Miss Tavish and yourself."

"And Mr. Siddons," Mr. Queensman reminded her quickly. "Interestingly, Mr. Siddons seems to be acquainted with the victim."

"Is he indeed?" Lark asked, genuinely curious. "I thought I saw him down with the others upon the beach."

"What else did you see?" There seemed a note of urgency in his voice.

Lark wondered why it should possibly matter to him, unless it was to get her to admit to spying on him and his friend. And though it should delight her to do so, she was surely enough of a lady to refrain from gloating over anything so indecent. Someday perhaps, when she was quite finished with him and his tiresome cousin Raeborn, she might enjoy hinting at the forbidden sights she had glimpsed.

"Nothing else I care to discuss, sir. As you have no formal hold on me, I do not see why it could possibly matter to you. My impressions of the sad scene are for my own keeping."

"It matters to me if the sight of such unpleasantness distresses you unduly."

Lark remembered she was supposed to be in a relapsive state, and she sank down deeper in her seat.

"You may rest assured that if I never recover it will have nothing to do with the events of this morning."

"On the contrary, my lady. On the basis of what I see this morning, I have every hope for your recovery."

He saw altogether too much.

"However, there will be much consternation here if it is discovered that one of the servants brought you out onto the veranda, so I had best bring you inside, lest Mary shoulder the blame."

Lark brushed his hand away—and was struck with the sense of some spark that flew between them.

"How do you know who brought me here, sir? I will not have you invade my privacy in such a way."

"I did not intend to do so, my lady. But, in fact, you invaded mine. I sat here on the veranda for more than an hour before your chair burst through the door. I did not require your company, but I do not regret it.

"Even so," he continued, "I think you had best go within. Miss Tavish may be wondering where you are."

"I wish to remain outside," Lark said stubbornly. "Miss Tavish can find me well enough."

"When you are recovered, my lady, you may make your own decisions about such matters. But for now you must trust my judgment on it."

Lark refused to dignify his arrogance with a retort, but as he turned her about in her chair, she caught a glimpse of the scene on the beach. Three men lifted the weight of the body between them, and a fourth caught the lolling head. Wet clothing hung wretchedly from the limp frame.

Perhaps Mr. Queensman's judgment was wiser than Lark

could admit. Even the brief vision she had just had would be sufficient to induce a month of nightmares.

"What do you make of it?"

Matthew Warren ran his fingers over the water-stained particles of wood and paper Ben had just unwrapped from the package hidden in his breast pocket.

"I hardly know," he admitted, and picked up one of the pieces to hold it closer to the candle. "This could be a section of a map. But why would the man bother to mount it on a board if he needed it for a journey? It seems a cumbersome waste."

"I am sure it is," Ben said quietly. "But I do not believe Monsieur Thibeau needed much help in direction. My sources tell me he spends a good deal of time along the southern coast and has been seen in Rye as recently as last week."

"The body had not been in the water very long," Matthew reminded him. "Just long enough to damage the contents of his pockets and wash the blood from his wounds."

"Of course. But whoever did this deed might have intended for him to be adrift a good deal longer, and perhaps never reach shore."

"I suspect whoever did this also knew nothing of what he carried."

"Unless anything that mattered was already removed," Ben said grimly. "And yet this should have aroused suspicion."

Matthew resumed his study of the refuse on the table.

"It appears as if we have a dissected puzzle, of the sort now being made in London."

"By Mr. Wallis?" Ben asked eagerly, remembering precisely where he had heard of the businessman and his cunning creations before.

"Of course. I suppose I am not surprised you know of them, for you are ever curious. But they are rather new on the market." Matthew, so fresh from the London scene, delighted in recounting the marvels of the great metropolis.

"I have never seen one myself," Ben admitted. "But I did overhear a gentleman promise to bring one to a lady."

"A charming gift," Matthew said with a touch of sarcasm. "The lady must be desperate to prefer it to chocolates or flowers."

"I believe she is. Lady Larkspur does not enjoy many diversions at Knighton's."

Ben continued to study the pieces of the dissected map upon the table, even as he sensed Matthew Warren studying him. He wished he had not mentioned her name, for he surely did so too often.

Matthew, to his credit, did not tax him on it.

"Was Monsieur Thibeau the gentleman who so promised?"

"He was not. Nor is it likely he intended to deliver this as ambassador for the other. But all the same, it is odd to come across a dissected map only days after one has heard talk of it. It is a very strange coincidence."

"No more so than that your cousin's promised wife should be residing within a mile of your home," Matthew teased.

Ben thought perhaps he deserved the pointed jest.

"I told you—it is no coincidence. I promised Raeborn I would look after his lady and return her to him as soon as she recovered."

"What precisely ails Lady Larkspur?"

Ben hesitated, for what passed for explanation or excuse among the uninitiated would hold no water with a physician as experienced as Matthew Warren. He could not blame a failing heart, for Matthew would recommend some treatment. He could not suggest a general malaise, for Matthew would scoff at such a notion.

In fact, bringing Matthew into the case would almost guarantee the return of Lady Larkspur to her anxious family. It was why he preferred to keep his friend at a comfortable distance.

"I believe she suffers from exhaustion of the spirit," Ben said carefully. "She has experienced some great disappointments recently, to the displeasure of her family. They, well meaning though they may be, sought to prevail upon her will, to no good end."

"I see. And is your cousin's offer the cause or the intended cure for her sad situation?"

Ben fingered the pieces of the map, aligning place names

and lines of latitude. He recognized the formal grid of property corresponding to the geography of Winchelsea, a small town not many miles distant. Of what use might such a picture be for such a one as Thibeau?

"Come, Ben. Will you not answer me? I would not concern myself with your affairs if not for the lady's possible connection with the dead man."

"Be assured there is no connection," Ben said with a touch of anger. "I will remind you her presence in the neighborhood is entirely of my own doing, in an effort to assist my cousin Raeborn in his suit. And he is not a bad fellow at all, though probably not the sort to appear in a young girl's dreams. But perhaps I speak with the conceit of youth."

"I shall remind you of it when we are sixty and plagued with the gout."

"Thank you very much."

"And when a young thing forty years your junior makes you wish to go out dancing every night."

"It would prove a fine thing, for I have not the time for such indulgences at thirty," Ben pointed out.

"Nor do you. But I daresay you might summon the energy for it if you were to find the right lady to inspire you. You managed to attend all the best affairs when you were in London, and seem to have come away with your heart unscathed."

Ben returned his gaze to the pieces of the map on the table, noting ink stains on the edges of several of them. Surely someone doctored his own notations onto the dissected map of Winchelsea, though the particulars would remain a mystery, as they had all but disappeared. He lifted one small piece to the light, hoping to appear so indifferent to Matthew's comment that he could not be bothered to grace it with a reply.

In fact, as he knew with perplexing certainty, he had not come away unscathed. He did meet a lady who provoked and fascinated him, and who had managed to spark the unbidden flame from wood that had seemed impervious for so many years. She resented and distrusted him, and insulted him to his face. And yet, he found he could not keep away, no more easily than on the night they first met, when he had dared to approach her and ask her to dance.

Of all the things he might confide to Matthew, this surely was not one of them.

"It is Winchelsea, certainly," he offered instead. "Looking at all the towns along the coast, I would have thought it of the least consequence."

"I have been there, and never thought to return. But we do not know if the king holds it in any special regard or, more specifically, if he holds one of the townspeople in special regard. I am sure the ladies there are as lovely as elsewhere," Matthew murmured. "Should we inform the king's men of our find?"

"I am not sure," Ben said, willing himself to concentrate on the business before him, and not on the tempting remembrance of a brief reel danced in London. "But as the royal entourage will not arrive in Brighton for many days, we have some time to make sense of Mr. Wallis' tricky map and prepare some sort of statement. With Thibeau and his message gone, there may not be any cause for alarm."

"In that case, I suggest we return to matters of more immediate concern. I have noticed, for example, we are nearly out of our supply of bandages."

Ben pushed his chair away from the table and massaged the back of his neck. He had been engaged in very intricate surgery the night before and had barely allowed himself time to rest.

"I already asked Mrs. James to have several cases delivered," he said and rose stiffly to his feet. "But you are right to remind me of our most pressing matters. I should like for you to examine Jed Parker, for the wound on his leg is not healing. And last night I stitched the mauled hand of a child bitten by a dog; the bandages ought to be changed. Did you ever have occasion to reset broken bones while you practiced in London?"

Matthew nodded.

"Excellent. A man is being brought to us this afternoon whose crooked leg prevents him from work. We may have to break the bone to repair it."

Matthew caught up with him as he walked to the door.

"What have you prescribed for the lady?" he asked.

Ben stopped suddenly, not knowing at first what his friend meant. Then, seeing the glint in Matthew's eyes, he realized his attempt to divert the conversation from the

subject of Lady Larkspur had not been altogether successful. He could do nothing but continue to feign indifference,
as if her person could be of only the slightest interest to
him.

"I have recommended a regimen of bathing in the sea,
eating only the freshest foods and declining any activity
that might prove too tiring. I believe it will repair the lady.
But as soon as Knighton returns, I daresay he will revise
such suggestions to accommodate his own form of
quackery."

"I do not doubt it." Matthew nodded sagely. "But have
you ever considered shock as a form of therapy?"

Ben looked with amazement at his colleague, thinking
him quite above any such suggestion, though guiltily remembering his own attempt at it in London.

"You cannot think I would inflict such torture on a delicate young lady, one who has been gently bred for nothing
more painful than aching feet after a dance? To abuse—"

Matthew interrupted the tirade by holding up his hand
in protest.

"Stop, please. I am not referring to medieval torture,"
he said impatiently. "If the lady is soon to be a part of
your estimable family, I do not doubt she is as fine as one
could wish. But she does suffer from a mysterious malady
of very indefinite characteristics. I merely thought if she
were to witness cases of genuine pain and suffering, and
understand something of neglect, she might be shocked into
realizing her own complaints to be of little consequence.
Such might be the strongest prescription for her recovery."

Ben immediately opened his mouth to protest, but within
a few moments grasped the wisdom of his friend's plan. The
thought of shocking Lady Larkspur's exquisite sensibilities
pleased him beyond measure. It might manage to squash
her macabre interest in dead men washing up on the beach.
Indeed, it might manage to convince her of something else,
though it surely was of no consequence. No consequence
whatsoever . . .

Lady Larkspur might be made to understand what motivated gentlemen to do something other than gamble in private clubs and spend their afternoons calling on young
ladies. She might even come to respect such endeavors.

But he dared not articulate such a thing to Matthew.

"I knew I would not regret bringing you to Brighton," Ben said instead, and clapped his friend on the shoulder. "I think it is an excellent plan, one likely to instill some sense into an impressionable imagination. In fact, I would bank on it, but for the fact the lady is a bit of a shrew and very likely to resist with all her strength."

"I see. And you will have me believe a great strapping fellow cannot manage to seduce a frail thing to join him for a few hours?"

"I will not kidnap her," Ben declared with a growing sense of frustration. Damn the chit—he might have to resort to such tactics.

"Nor should you." Matthew shrugged, seemingly unaware of his companion's discomfort. "But do you not think she will be happy for some diversion and will accept the offer of a carriage ride? You can, in all seeming innocence, manage to convey her to our very door."

"Removing splinters from a tongue might prove the easier task." Ben frowned. "But I have nothing to lose but my pride. And the lady threatens that with our every meeting."

"He wants to take the afternoon air with us," Lark said in a deep, mimicking voice. She threw the fine linen paper onto the table. "I daresay he is desperate to trick me into confession, and imagines his generosity sufficient to distract me!"

Janet Tavish reached for the invitation, scarcely able to contain her excitement.

"It is very well written, Lark, with no hint of divisiveness. I am flattered he wishes me to join you as well."

"He undoubtedly desires a witness to my forced admission."

"More likely he is aware of the proprieties and the need of a chaperone. But no matter! I should love to be free of Knighton's, if only for a few hours. I am amazed you do not feel the same."

"Do you not think it is like climbing out of the boiling kettle to fall into the fire? Who knows where he might take us?"

"You cannot accuse him of mischief when his behavior

must be accountable to Raeborn. He says he looks only to take us for a cabriolet ride along the beach road. It sounds like heaven."

"Heaven, my friend, is not a place, but a state of being among those you love and care about. With Mr. Queensman nearby, I should be in hell."

"Then forget his company, and leave him to me. I am not so hopeless I cannot manage to flatter and amuse him myself. We shall leave you to the scenery, the sun and the fresh sea air."

Lark looked at the glowing pleasure on her loyal friend's face and wondered how well Janet admired the handsome doctor. Perhaps she might manage to suffer a few hours in the detestable man's company after all. She would have to be very careful not to forget herself again, and she would have to manage a good show of her frailties for his benefit. It would be very difficult.

But to feel some sense of freedom! To come alive within, even while affecting disdain without, and allow oneself to be entertained by a gentleman of some intelligence and wit!

She was not certain it would be a pleasure to witness a flirtation between Janet and Mr. Queensman, however, and observe every look that passed between them.

"Well, Lark?" Janet asked breathlessly. "Will you answer Mr. Queensman?"

"I will allow for you to do the honor, for you must tell him I am too weak to pick up a pen. And while you do, I shall be engaged in other matters."

"Is there anything I can do to help you?"

"Indeed there is, Janet. I shall need your advice on everything. For I must decide what I shall wear and what will suit me best."

"If you hope to look ill, you had best select what will suit you worst," Janet reminded her.

Lark said nothing as she made her way to her large wardrobe closet.

Chapter Six

L ark nervously fingered the ribbons on her bonnet while Janet stood sentry at the window of the main hall. It would not do to appear too eager, and so, though the day proved gloriously warm and calm, they did not await their ride on the veranda.

"You need not fret so, girl," Miss Hathawae said suddenly, looking up from her small volume of poetry. "Mr. Queensman is a well-respected gentleman in Brighton and will not allow any harm to come to you. I do not doubt he is a very courteous driver."

Lark felt curious to know how this reclusive lady knew about a man who would not have been a familiar figure at Knighton's before her own arrival.

"And did you ever ride with him yourself, Miss Hathawae? On whose authority do you vouch for the gentleman?"

"I have it on very high authority, my dear. I am well acquainted with someone who has brought Benedict Queensman into his confidence," Miss Hathawae answered a trifle haughtily, and returned her attention to her book.

Lark looked away, wondering if she was the only person on earth who found Mr. Queensman's company so officious, so difficult to endure with any degree of equanimity. His eyes, far too bright and knowing, were capable of stripping away one's most precious delusions, leaving one completely bereft of any fond secrets. That he had almost immediately uncovered hers was to his credit, she supposed. That he did not yet choose to expose her to her family was not. She did not know why he was willing to sanction her deceit; she only knew she ought not trust him. Indeed, she ought not trust anyone who put her in danger of forgetting herself.

Perhaps he had this effect on other ladies. A gentleman with his rather obvious recommendations would hardly have been able to slip through the hands of anxious matrons if he did not have some compelling flaws. And Lark, who continued to receive letters full of news and gossip from her four sisters, would surely have heard if Ben Queensman had ever been married or promised to another. Indeed, his defects must be apparent to all.

Lark looked up to where Janet danced expectantly at the window, waiting for his arrival, and wondered when her good, honest friend would become aware of them.

"He comes," Janet said breathlessly. "At least, I suppose it is he, for I cannot imagine another such vehicle arriving at Knighton's."

"Does he drive a hay wagon or something of that sort?" Lark asked languidly.

Janet laughed out loud. "Indeed not. It is a painted cabriolet, of the sort we know well from our summer in Margate. But this one is infinitely more splendid. Its hood is bright yellow, and all four wheels are painted red and blue."

"Goodness. The man is certainly a peacock. I believe he must endeavor to mask the dullness within."

"Or to cheer our day? Come, Lark, you must not be so censorious. Mr. Queensman may drive a frivolous carriage, but I see nothing but modesty in his demeanor."

"Do you indeed?" Lark asked sharply. She saw Miss Hathawae look up from her book and felt a little reckless. "Do you consider it modest for a man to demand the attention of a lady who is already engaged to another?"

Janet turned from the window, and for the first time in all the years of their friendship Lark thought perhaps she had gone too far. The cool demeanor with which Janet customarily masked her deeper emotions melted away, and in its place a spark of anger flickered in her eyes.

"Are we still resentful of ancient history, then? Can you possibly continue to resent a gentleman who sought to do you homage and behaved with nothing but respect? And, if truth be told, Mr. Queensman's insight on that unfortunate evening proved more discerning than yours, my lady!"

Lark recoiled as if smacked in the face. When her oldest friend called her "my lady," the title was invariably hurled like some sharp-pronged weapon. She caught her breath and glanced towards their curious audience. Miss Hathawae quickly looked back to her book.

"He intruded wherein he was not invited. He persisted

when told to leave. And he remained when it was not his place to do so," Lark said slowly and clearly. "If such things are not sufficient for me to develop a dislike for him, I know not what else might be. Unless, of course, it is his continued persistence in interfering with our lives here at Knighton's."

"He comes with the approbation of his cousin, and your father, my lady," Janet said sternly, though her tone seemed less harsh.

Miss Hathawae cleared her throat. Her book slipped to the floor, prompting Janet to recover it immediately.

"It is none of my business, my dears, though your conversation well within my hearing demands my participation. If I may say so, Lady Larkspur, while you are a very lovely lady from an excellent family, your continued ill health cannot make you a desirable candidate for a young gentleman's attention. In addition, as you are intended for Lord Raeborn, a generous man apparently willing to overlook your faults, Mr. Queensman surely does not desire to come between you except in a professional manner." Miss Hathawae paused and looked from one girl to the other. "Is it not possible to believe his continued attendance is due not to any particular interest in yourself, but rather to a developing affection for Miss Tavish?"

Janet blushed like a fool, and Lark frowned in dismay. She truly, genuinely, absolutely did not mind if the fellow sought to connive his way into Janet's affections, she told herself. She felt disagreeable only because she preferred not to consider the possibility.

"My friend, Miss Tavish, enjoys an understanding with a certain Mr. Banlowe, of our acquaintance," Lark said, thinking it could do no harm to remind Janet of the fact.

Janet shrugged her soft shoulders. "It is nothing to prevent me from looking elsewhere. As well you know, my lady, I have not received a single missive from the gentleman since our arrival in Brighton. Nor do I expect one."

"Ah, then it is settled." Miss Hathawae hummed with pleasure. "But Lady Larkspur must endeavor to get well so Miss Tavish is no longer obliged to attend on her. Only then can she happily proceed with her relationship with the young man."

As Lark attempted to fashion a suitable retort, Mary came skipping into the room.

"Mr. Queensman is here, my lady," she said excitedly. Undoubtedly the sight of the absurd cabriolet had sent her into raptures.

"Do show him in, Mary," Janet said graciously, and gathered her shawl from a nearby chair.

Their visitor entered at once, proving Janet's point about his modesty by appearing in a well-cut dark jacket and gray trousers. His dark hair looked somewhat windblown, as if he rode without a hat, but it fell cunningly on his brow. His eyes, possibly brightened by the exercise, looked as brilliant as the sea as he glanced about the room, greeting the other guests before he settled upon Lark.

His smile vanished at once, and the habit of vanity made her wonder if her weeks of enforced misery had taken their toll. She winced, wishing it did not matter. Or that the notion of his favoring Janet could give her any sort of pleasure.

He continued to study her, without his usual intrusive arrogance, but as one who seemed as much in doubt as she. A mirroring of such feelings could not be possible, she told herself, and it was even less likely that her own good opinion of him should matter. He wished only to see her defeated in her ruse, exposed for the fraud she was, and returned in all triumph to his cousin Raeborn.

"You need not look so concerned, Mr. Queensman," Janet said gently. He turned to look at her as if he had quite forgotten her there. "Lady Larkspur is well dressed against the elements and is prepared for a lovely outing. I am grateful you were able to find the time to indulge us."

"The gratitude is mine, Miss Tavish," he said chivalrously. "It is not every day I can find such an excellent excuse to abandon my practice."

"Do you leave your patients quite alone?" Janet asked, on a note of concern.

"Not at all. There are several other physicians who work with me. My new partner arrived from London almost at the same time you did yourself. His name is Matthew Warren. I should enjoy the privilege of introducing him to you."

Miss Hathawae, who sat quietly all this while, suddenly clapped her hands with glee. "If he is the son of Gerald Warren, I know his family well. His mother is the daughter of the Earl of Allston, is she not? Wonderful! Perhaps, Mr. Queensman, you might consider sending young Warren here one day in your stead, so I also may greet him."

"I am sure he would be delighted, Miss Hathawae. We shall therefore contrive to bring you together," Mr. Queensman said politely, and then looked again at Lark. "But I am under very strict instructions from the lady's family to have the care of her myself when Mr. Knighton is not in attendance."

Lark bit down on her lip, wondering what it could mean. If he brought in a colleague, the man might well find nothing wrong and suspect her artifice. Would that not strengthen Mr. Queensman's case against her?

Or did he intend to blackmail her into some sort of defeat, and thereby accept all the credit when he triumphantly returned her to her family and his?

She did not doubt he played with some plan in mind, but as either seemed to contrive to keep her longer in Brighton, she needed to hold her cards carefully.

Miss Hathawae nodded thoughtfully, looking as if she quite understood what continued to elude Lark.

"You take your responsibility very seriously, sir, and it is an admirable trait. You would not have the ear of the king if you were not so respected."

From the corner of the room, where he seemed to be soundly sleeping, Colonel Wayland suddenly sputtered to life.

"The king is on his way here, you know," he said grandly. "I believe he plans to make several stops along the coast before his triumphant entrance into the Royal Pavilion."

Mr. Queensman laughed humorlessly. "I believe it can be said his majesty's entrance is somewhat less triumphant precisely because of the same pavilion."

"Do you mean because he beggared his colonies in America to finance it?" Lark asked, interested. The eyes of the others turned on her, and she silently scolded herself. "You need not look so surprised, sir. My life at Knighton's provides me with ample opportunity to read every scrap of paper that comes my way."

"What you read, my lady, sounds treasonous." Colonel

Wayland blustered from his corner. "To impute the rebellion of the Americans to the construction of a masterpiece—"

"Nevertheless," Mr. Queensman interrupted, "I believe the king himself is somewhat regretful of the folly of it all."

"Treason!" the colonel repeated. "The king will not meet with such disrespect in Rye, or Dover, or Winchelsea."

"Winchelsea?" Mr. Queensman asked softly. Lark could see that something particularly interested him, but he bit back additional comment.

"It is a town not far from here," Miss Hathawae volunteered. "I am surprised a native such as yourself does not know of it. The king considered it as a site for his palace before he settled upon Brighton."

"I am familiar with it, Miss Hathawae. It is only that someone brought the very place to my attention recently."

No one said anything for several minutes, and Lark wondered how such a lame excuse for conversation could go unassaulted. It should be obvious to the others that Mr. Queensman found something intriguing about Winchelsea, for if he did not admit it in his words, it revealed itself by the stiffening of his broad shoulders and the way in which he narrowed his eyes. She could not be the only one to notice the betrayal of his body.

"Do you know anything about the identity of the drowned man, sir?" Colonel Wayland asked, and Lark felt grateful for the change of subject. .

"He is a Mr. Thibeau of Calais," Mr. Queensman answered promptly. Lark realized, however, that the subject did not seem to be changed at all. Mr. Queensman still waited cautiously for something, looking ready to jump at the slightest provocation.

"A stranger to our shores," Miss Hathawae murmured.

"Apparently not, for there are many in the area who seem to know him," Mr. Queensman corrected. "But we English may no longer look forward to his company."

"A pity," Miss Hathawae pronounced.

"I wish it were so, madam. But I fear Mr. Thibeau did not come as our friend."

"Explain yourself, sir," Lark demanded, genuinely curious.

Mr. Queensman returned her gaze, and whatever matter had held him loosened its grasp.

"It is not for your delicate ears, my lady. I come here today to lighten the burden of your ailment, not add to it. And so I suggest we depart this place while the sun is still high on the sky and the winds calm. Miss Hathawae and Colonel Wayland will certainly excuse us."

"Oh, yes. Please do not remain on our account!" Miss Hathawae urged happily.

Colonel Wayland conspicuously said nothing.

"Shall I wheel Lady Larkspur to the foyer?" Janet asked as she tied her bonnet.

"Do not bother. We shall abandon this clumsy chair here, and I will carry the lady to the carriage."

Without asking her advice on the matter, Mr. Queensman came to Lark's side and gathered her up in his arms. As he had once before, he drew one arm beneath her knees and the other behind her back and balanced her body against his chest. It ought to have been an awkward business, and yet the only clumsiness seemed to be Lark's own inability to settle herself comfortably.

Too easily she felt his bone and muscle embrace and subdue her. The subtle scent of soap and something indefinably his lulled her into a sense of security, though she would no sooner rest against him than lean on a splintery plank. And yet how she felt tempted to put up a finger and trace the contours of his nose and lips, and make herself free with his body as he did with hers. It would put him in his place. And surely wipe the look of arrogance off his face.

He shifted his hold, and she gasped, thinking she would fall.

"Fear not, my lady," he said, as he whisked her through the wide doorway. "I will keep you safe, for I have certain things in mind that would require it."

Lark had never felt so helpless in her life. The assault on her determination seemed as keen as the one on her body and mind, and for the first time since her orchestrated collapse in London, she was tempted to abandon the ridiculous scheme. How lovely it would be to bask in masculine admiration again, to enjoy the pleasures of an outing without any of the pain of subterfuge, to engage in lively conversation without being warned of the damage it might do her frail nerves. What joy to dance again, with someone rather taller than Janet as partner. And what of all the other missed purposes and wasted energies of her current existence, wherein she accomplished nothing but persuading others of her helplessness?

And so, though she ought to have vigorously protested Mr. Queensman's impudence in carrying her away like an eloped bride, she did not. Instead, she gave herself up to sensation, closing her eyes and savoring the impressions of sound and scent assailing her.

She heard Janet gushing, "Your cabriolet is quite marvelous, Mr. Queensman." They stopped suddenly, and Lark knew they must be just before it. "I must confess, you always seem to be so full of common sense and practicality, I am surprised you would own so frivolous a vehicle."

Lark heard the laughter rumble from deep within his chest, a tentative sound at first, but finally strong enough to lend its tone to his voice.

"My sisters would be delighted to hear you say it. They have something of the same opinion of my character, and they insisted I buy a beachworthy carriage for those times I escort them around Brighton. None of them still live here, so the town is no longer their home, but rather an opportunity for adventure."

"Do you have many sisters? And do they quite overpower you?" Janet giggled.

"I fear they would if they did not have their own husbands and children to occupy their energies. The care of a bachelor brother, especially one who prefers work in a hospital to assembly balls, could prove a tedious task. They share responsibilities, however, as there are five of them."

"Five sisters!" Janet cried. "Just as in Lark's family! And you the only brother?"

"My sisters tell me they are grateful for it."

"Poor man," Janet said, and sounded like she meant it.

"Not at all. I live very comfortably," Mr. Queensman said teasingly as he hoisted Lark's unyielding body into the seat. Though she felt soft cushions beneath her, he still held her, and her head fell against his shoulder. "I was prepared to treat my sisters very generously, but they all managed to do quite well for themselves. They lack nothing but seeing me settled."

"Then you must not disappoint them, Mr. Queensman," Janet said artlessly.

"It is a subject I avoided for a good many years. But recently I seem to be of a mind to gratify them at last."

Lark opened her eyes and regretted it at once. His eyes, so close to her own, looked down on her, their lids masking their natural brilliance. His arms shifted, and though she could not have dropped more than a few inches, she felt as if she were falling, quite free of any limitations. Instinctively, she reached up to grasp his collar.

"Fear not, Lady Larkspur. The cabriolet looks frivolous but is, in fact, a very sturdy vehicle. No harm will come to you here," he said, but he did not remove her hand.

"I have driven them myself at the park," she answered, a little unsteadily. "But I have rarely seen one so well turned out. The salt air is reputed to damage the leather and wood."

Benedict Queensman's eyes opened wider, and as he turned to Janet, Lark's hand fell on the throbbing pulse at his neck. His skin, warm to her touch, was roughened by the shaved hairs of his beard.

"Miss Tavish, I believe your friend is of a practical frame of mind similar to my own. I do not recall any other lady of my acquaintance likely to discourse on matters of rot and corrosion. If it were not for her frail sensibilities, she really would be a very useful person to have about."

He pulled away to assist Janet as she stepped up to her own seat. The carriage shifted and shuddered even under her slight weight. She settled herself beside Lark and tucked the soft blanket about the invalid before she answered.

"Indeed she is, sir. We often attend on the poor in our own neighborhood and bring things that may comfort them. As you already know, Lady Leicester is very knowledgeable about greenery and grows many varieties of plants. Lady Larkspur has been permitted entry into the herbiary since childhood and creates her own medicinal potions, following ancient recipes. She is reputed to have the remedy for most ailments."

"A very impressive lady, though in another age she might

have been reviled as a witch. But it is a pity there is nothing in her text she might use upon herself, for I am certain I know of no modern cure," Mr. Queensman said, continuing as if Lark were not in their company. "I am surprised, for my professional ancestors were more likely to address matters of broken hearts and unrequited love rather than dog bites and running sores. Lady Larkspur's herbiary must be a storehouse of such remedies."

Lark straightened in her seat so she would lean on neither of her companions. Even Janet did not appear as reliable as she had the day before.

"For a provincial gentleman, you seem the worst snob, Mr. Queensman. You belittle my efforts if you imagine my potions produce nothing more useful than aphrodisiacs or other bits of artifice. Such concoctions went out with the Renaissance poets, I believe," she retorted.

"So long ago as that, my lady?" Mr. Queensman sighed as he picked up the bright braided reins and urged the horses on. "A gentleman—a particular friend of mine—is perplexed by the contempt heaped upon him by a lady he hopes to admire. Shall I tell him you can offer him no hope?"

Lark looked directly ahead, at the rise of the seawall as it protected the narrow road from the sea and wind. Mr. Queensman's talk of such things must surely be a trap of some sort, contrived to make her confess to her duplicity. He would like to send her home to Raeborn; of that, she must remain certain. But did he not already own enough evidence to do so? Why continue to bait her and test her endurance?

"There is no potion capable of making one person love another, Mr. Queensman," Lark said carefully. "There are sweet-smelling things capable of enhancing sentiments, but nothing so strong as to induce in an individual the divine pain of true love. I think it is a blessed affliction that comes quite unbidden and strikes the victim almost at once."

The cabriolet rolled along steadily, attracting the notice of a flock of gulls and at least two spirited dogs.

"You speak with conviction, my lady. I suppose you know of what you speak with firsthand experience?"

Lark thought of the dozen flirtations of her youth, and the several more serious affairs deemed by many to be of serious import. She thought of Hindley Moore with hardly a twinge of longing or regret, and the sterile and staid companionship offered to her by Lord Raeborn. And then, with an uncomfortable jolt, she thought of the handsome and industrious gentleman at her side, who had ignited some indefinable passion in her even before they met. And who now, most assuredly, looked upon dear Janet Tavish with the admiring eye of a suitor. She ought to wish only happiness for Janet, but the prospect of her dearest friend settled with the enigmatic Mr. Queensman left her agitated and unsatisfied. She felt an aching hunger to taste of some rare spice she had not yet sampled. She could not name what it was she lacked, but she rather thought he might provide it.

"I believe, sir, it will prove the saddest part of my elegy, for I believe I do," Lark said, and thought she would burst into tears.

"The building is not yet completed, for the king entertains a good many notions for its construction," Ben informed his companions as he brought the horses up close to the Pavilion. As he expected, the banners announcing George IV's arrival were not yet flying from the turrets, though there seemed to be a fair amount of activity in the drive and the courtyard. Perhaps Mrs. Fitzherbert, the king's devoted mistress, intended to ride out today or planned some frivolous entertainment for her lover's pleasure. Ben had not heard of it, but surely it was not impossible.

Ben Queensman knew a great deal about the comings and goings at the Royal Pavilion at Brighton, though he rarely revealed more to a confidant than that he had stood in the king's favor since the days of the Regency. So much could be accounted for by nothing more than the fact that he had been summoned to the Regent's chamber one stormy night after the court physician, in a drunken sweat, could offer no remedy for what ailed the royal heir. Curiously, for all his talents, it did not require much effort for Ben to determine the cause of the problem.

The king had been walking in the garden at Kensington several days before and had not taken the precaution of wearing any clothes to protect himself. A spider undoubtedly found his rather large Achilles' heel and attacked the royal flesh. Thus was Ben able to conclude from the round, swollen area on the king's foot and the rising fever elsewhere.

The conclusions of the royal advisors were not so simple.

After the fever passed, as Ben expected it would, it was reported to the king that an attempt had been made upon his life by a traitor who had brought poisonous spiders into the garden at Kensington. The more Ben argued that it was likely just a random act of nature, the more he unintentionally worked his way into the king's favor. And so it happened that Mr. Benedict Queensman, of Brighton, entered into the service of his monarch and became as trusted an advisor as any in the royal retinue.

His responsibilities were rarely arduous; playing whist with the king until dawn might be the most punishing exercise. But occasionally there came reports of treasonous plans and assassination plots. As they came now.

"I think it is a splendid structure," Miss Tavish said generously. "Do tell his majesty not to change a thing, nor add another turret. I think it perfect."

"And you, my lady? What do you think of the king's Pavilion?"

Ben glanced down at the lady at his side and admired her unusual beauty. She would blame him all anew if she knew their little journey had provoked the freckles to come out across her nose and induced color in her cheeks, but he felt willing to risk her wrath for the pleasure it gave him. Her dark eyes fell into the shadow of her bonnet's stiff brim, but the Oriental turrets of the Pavilion were clearly reflected in their unfathomable depths.

She opened her mouth, and her tongue wet her pink lips. The practical side of his nature wished to warn her that to do so in the salty breeze would likely prove irritating. But another, antithetical side felt tempted to bruise her lips with his own.

He looked away.

"I am not sure it is a very happy place," she finally answered, surprising him. "I imagine the king, frustrated with so many other things, must have sought solace with his architects and tried to buy satisfaction with such an awesome project. And why in Brighton? Before the king settled upon it as a site, it must have been a lonely place."

"You forget, my lady, I have lived my entire life here," Ben said.

"Was that fact sufficient to recommend it?" Lady Larkspur looked teasingly at him.

Something twisted in his heart, and he turned away.

"I hope not, for then my family and I would need to shoulder the blame for the changes done to our comfortable little neighborhood since the king's arrival. New townhouses have gone up everywhere, often displacing more modest dwellings. The roads are more trafficked, making them unsafe for children. And bathing machines have sprung up on the pristine beaches that were once open to everyone. The natives are not altogether happy with these improvements, although most are aware of the honor due them by the king's choice."

"And did you live in one of those modest houses, now gone?"

"I suppose you would like to have me admit to it. But I am sorry to disappoint you by saying I grew up upon and now own a rather large estate just to the north. My ancestors arrived on these shores with the Conqueror, and my cousin Raeborn still bears the original name: de la Reine. Sometime in the seventeenth century my branch of the family anglicized it to Queensman. Not as elegant, perhaps, but more solidly English."

"It is a very good name," Lady Larkspur said thoughtfully, "deserving of credit if it is earned. But how came you to Benedict? I know only a few of that name, and one is only a literary character."

"It also is a family name, one I share with Raeborn. But my parents were not unaware of the literary reference, and used it for their own pleasure. I suspect their nature is as playful as that of your own family. As you Leicesters are all named for flowers in the garden, my sisters and I are named for Shakespeare's heroes and heroines. I suppose I must count myself lucky their inclinations were not reversed, for I might have found myself called Petunia or something of that sort."

Lady Larkspur, forgetting herself, laughed out loud, and for a moment Ben could imagine he was escorting any beautiful young lady for a ride in his absurd carriage. But even in a fantasy, unencumbered by her obligations to his

cousin and by her determination to put off those obligations as long as possible, he knew she would never be
merely any beautiful young lady. Her beauty, original and
deliciously pure, was what had attracted him from the moment he first saw her at Southard's party. But in all the
weeks since, he had come to appreciate her revelations of
practical intelligence, bookish knowledge and cutting wit.
Her disarming beauty was as much a mask for her true
character as her feigned illness was a mask for her beauty.

"Well, Mr. Queensman? Will you not answer me? Or
are you so rapt by the display before us, you are speech-
less?" Lady Larkspur's sarcastic tongue laced into his rev-
erie, returning him to their business.

He smiled a little sheepishly. "I confess, I am rapt by the
display before me and did not hear your question. It is
unusual for me to be so distracted."

Lady Larkspur looked up at him with a gleam of suspicion in her lovely eyes, but wherein he expected a confrontation, she instead turned away. Her shoulders, shedding
the protection of the soft woolen shawl, were very straight
and rigid and would have been altogether uncompromising
but for a heart-shaped birthmark on the nape of her neck.
Ben wondered how many gentlemen knew of its presence.

"Lady Larkspur only asked about your familiarity with
the Pavilion, Mr. Queensman," Miss Tavish explained
clearly. "You have already told us you are welcome in the
king's company, which is a very fine thing. But have you
been within the building, admired its architecture and finery, dined in its hall, danced under the painted sky of the
ballroom? Met any of its other tenants?"

"Ah, Miss Tavish, you would tax me too much with your
curiosity if it were not for the fact I might answer yes to
each of your questions. But let me assure you, for all its
grandeur, the Pavilion seems to me to be a singularly unin-
teresting place. The same might be said for another tenant
in residence, though many people are curious to learn
about her."

"Do you mean Mrs. Fitzherbert?" Janet asked.

Ben shrugged his shoulders. "Of course. Mrs. Fitzherbert
lives very comfortably here and, I believe, provides a respite for our king when he wearies of court life in London.
She is, however, neither flamboyant in style nor exuberant

in speech. She is merely pleasant, gracious and seemingly honest in her manner."

Miss Tavish looked disappointed.

"I wonder if we might meet her while we are in Brighton," she said.

"It is not unlikely," Ben answered. "The king is expected in the near future and will surely provide entertainment. I am likely to be invited and am usually encouraged to bring several guests."

Miss Tavish clapped her hands. "Could it be possible? Would you truly take Lady Larkspur and me to a party at the Pavilion? It would be the most wonderful thing!"

"I am delighted you think so, Miss Tavish. But you misunderstand me. I did not think to bring the two of you. Surely Lady Larkspur might spare you for an evening so I might indulge your desire."

Poor Miss Tavish looked confused, so Ben glanced down at the exquisite termagant at his other side. The shoulders seemed a good deal straighter than they even were before, but the delicate birthmark had all but disappeared next to the blushing stain across the lady's skin.

He leaned over and spoke almost in Larkspur's ear.

"If your lady fancies an evening at the Royal Pavilion, I promise to indulge her as well. But I will do so under one strict condition: When Lady Larkspur is able to walk through the gates without any assistance, I will be her escort."

He waited for her to accept his challenge, and almost gave up on hearing it. But just as he lifted the reins again and snapped the horses into movement, he heard her clear her throat.

"When I am able to walk through the gates unassisted, I will neither desire nor need your cursed escort," she said.

He supposed it was precisely what he deserved.

Chapter Seven

*E*ven as Mr. Queensman deplored the rapid growth of the seaside town in which he lived, Lark thought there remained much to commend it to a discerning taste. With the notable exception of those responsible for the design of the Royal Pavilion, architects clearly designed new townhouses and shops with an eye to the sea and an ear to prevailing preferences in more sophisticated locales. They constructed neat rows of whitewashed buildings, enhanced by decorous awnings and umbrellas, and laid out streets in a sensible grid. The traffic so heartily condemned by Mr. Queensman did not seem so very arduous after London, nor did the proliferation of small shops in the vicinity of the Pavilion.

Brighton appeared, all in all, to be a very congenial place.

Nor could Janet Tavish have desired a more congenial guide. As the three meandered throughout the town, Mr. Queensman pointed out a good many local attractions of interest and answered even the most obvious questions. He paused to make introductions with fashionable sorts, of whom he seemed to know many, and to greet workmen and serving girls, who all seemed to know him. He told a dozen amusing stories and offered all the possible advantages for preferring this place over London. And he made Janet laugh at every street corner and exclaim at each sight.

If he asked Janet to abandon her father's home and live with him in a cave under the white cliffs, she most certainly would do it, Lark thought angrily. While the man disarmed her friend with his provincial ways, he surely was as experienced a seducer as any rake in town. She would have to lecture her friend on the subject if he ever returned them to Knighton's, for the poor girl clearly needed her protection.

After some time, the carriage turned into the wind, and there were no buildings nearby to protect them. They seemed to be heading in the direction of the sanatorium, and yet were on a road unfamiliar to Lark. A well-built stone wall marked a private drive, but they passed no gatehouse. As they came around a turn over the water's edge, Lark glimpsed the broad veranda of Knighton's on the hill above.

And even as she guessed at their destination, the low stucco building she had occasionally admired from afar came into view. Built to harmonize with the chalk cliffs and pebbly beach, it nevertheless had a certain grace and elegance. A grape arbor at the threshold to a garden drew the eye along a line of columns and down a stone path to the water. Broad windows opened to the light except where ivy draped too close upon them. And along the terrace bright flowers spilled out of Greek amphoras that looked ancient enough to have been brought to English shores by Alexander himself.

"Goodness, Mr. Queensman!" Janet exclaimed. "Could this possibly be your home? Lady Lark and I have ever admired it from the terrace at Knighton's and wondered who could be lucky enough to live within. It is a splendid place!"

Lark scowled at Janet's enthusiasm, which so thoroughly got the better of her that she should commit two offenses: first, that she should admit to admiring a man's private home, and second, that she should refer to her friend by a private name.

"I am flattered to hear it, Miss Tavish," Mr. Queensman said smoothly. "I regret it is not my home, for Seagate is not anywhere as original, as I expect you will see someday soon. But it is my consolation to spend even more hours herein than in my own library, for this is the hospital I have built. I hope it will be of interest to you and to Lady Lark."

If the man proved willing to cover Janet's embarrassment, he would only exacerbate Lark's own. Lady Lark, indeed! She recalled him giving her leave to call him Ben, but she did not grant reciprocal privilege.

"I do not see any great pleasure in visiting another hospital," Lark began, prepared to be thoroughly disagreeable. To be so went against her character, but she was becoming quite practiced at it. Indeed, a dislike of the kind she sustained for Mr. Queensman fostered it readily. "After all, do we not have enough of illness and infirmity and overwarm chambers at Knighton's? I doubt we will find anything to interest us here, Mr. Queensman."

"Who is that man?" Janet asked, cutting off Lark's retort.

"It is Matthew Warren, my colleague and friend who is already known to Miss Hathawae. He has heard much about the two elegant ladies I visit at Knighton's and is very anxious to greet you," Mr. Queensman said cheerfully. "Mr. Warren shares my plans not only for the future, but also for this afternoon."

"What plans?" Lark said tightly.

Benedict Queensman looked down on her and smiled. She would not be so easily seduced as Janet and tried to ignore him. But he lifted her hand to his lips and pressed it against them.

"My lady, a tour of Brighton could not be complete until you see, firsthand, the Queensman Hospital, established by an earnest young physician with a significant part of his inheritance and dedicated to the welfare of the poor and hopeless. Its residents are nothing to Knighton's, of course, but illness does not recognize class boundaries."

"You told me I would not be welcome at the Pavilion until I could manage to walk in myself, sir. Do I take it that similar restrictions keep me from your hospital?"

"My hospital turns no one away, whatever their limitations. As you suffer as sorely as any within, you will be allowed to enter."

"A pity we left my chaise on Knighton's veranda. I believe I must remain here, after all, for I have no access," Lark said and turned up her chin defiantly.

Unexpectedly and fleetingly, she saw in his face the reflection of her most urgent fears and unbidden imaginings. A great longing seemed etched upon his noble features, frightening her in its intensity. She knew then that she did indeed have access of the most intimate sort, bidding her to enter a private place with no barriers, from which there could be no easy leaving.

"You have access if you wish it, my lady," he said simply, though it had the effect of heating her soul. She tried to pull her hand away, but he only held it tighter.

"Welcome, ladies!" Matthew Warren called out, a trifle too cheerfully. "You have chosen an excellent afternoon to come for a visit."

"By which my good friend means you are not apt to see anything of a distressing nature," Mr. Queensman said casually as he released Lark's hand. He pulled the cabriolet up to the end of the drive and threw the reins to Mr. Warren. Two matrons immediately appeared in the open doorway, wiping their hands on their white aprons and looking more curious than expectant.

Mr. Queensman leapt from his perch with a grace unusual in one so large and hugged Mr. Warren cheerfully, as if they had not seen each other for days rather than hours. But Lark did not miss the quick exchange of words between them and thought perhaps all was not as harmonious as they would have her and Janet believe. Mr. Queensman shook his head briefly and glanced out towards the sea.

But the respite proved brief, for he returned almost immediately with introductions.

"Can this be Miss Tavish, then, about whom I have heard so much?" Matthew Warren asked. In the corners of his eyes, tiny creases marked his tanned skin, as if he were in the habit of taking too much sun. His straw-colored hair looked bleached, and the skin peeled off the very tip of his nose.

No longer separated from Janet by Ben Queensman, Lark felt her friend stiffen next to her on the seat.

"What have you heard, sir? You might very well be mistaken, as I am only a companion to my good friend, Lady Larkspur, and have only a modest history myself."

"You need not remain modest, Miss Tavish." Mr. Warren beamed at her and offered his hand. "A lady who is prepared to nurse a dear friend and sacrifice her own amusement for that of another must be hailed as the best of all women. Mr. Queensman often talks of your patience, and forbearance, and undying loyalty."

"Does he indeed?" Janet spared a glance for her unlikely admirer and then accepted Mr. Warren's hand with aplomb equal to that of accepting the apple from Paris. And why not? Lark reflected, feeling absurdly pleased. Mr. Warren looked nearly as handsome as Mr. Queensman. He was the sort of man one contrived to meet in London circles, only to find him married with four children.

"I am sure it is merited, Miss Tavish," Mr. Warren said and led her to the open door, now framed by the two maids. Patient, loyal Janet did not spare a glance backwards for her dear friend. Perhaps it was just as well, for she may have been disconcerted by what she saw.

Mr. Queensman said nothing, but turned to Lark as she necessarily remained in the carriage. Slowly, deliberately, he pulled the woolen shawl from around her elbows and from her lap, exposing her to the sea breezes. But the breezes were not nearly so titillating as his own appreciative gaze, as his eyes went from the tip of her bonnet to the soles of her untrodden slippers.

"Are you sure you can manage it?" Lark said slowly.

"Have I not already proven I can?" he asked, and swept her up as if she weighed nothing. Her arm, caught between their bodies, slipped out and came around his waist, visibly startling him. But his only response was to shift her position slightly higher, so she now caressed the small of his back. It was wanton behavior, to be sure, but she would not remain passive while he dared to take such liberties with her.

"Lady Larkspur, your health seems much improved," he choked out.

"Indeed, sir, it is not. I believe I may be suffering from a slight derangement. I . . . may do things I do not intend."

"On the contrary, my lady. I have the strongest hunch you know precisely what you do and the effect you have on others."

As he stepped through the doorway, they fell into shadow, and his pupils opened so wide one could scarce discern the blueness of his eyes.

"Will you send me back to Raeborn, then?" she asked recklessly.

He sucked in his breath. "I fear if I do you may kill him with such behavior. I believe you need a younger man, someone closer to your own age."

"Mr. Siddons, perhaps? I know he certainly admires me, for he flatters me at every meeting."

"A fool he is, then. Someone ought to tell him you have had too many such admirers, and flattery proves nothing.

You deserve a man who understands you and appreciates your talents.''

"Might not Raeborn be such a man?" Lark demanded to know.

Ben Queensman's chin tightened as he ducked under a low beam. His hand seemed to burn her through the fabric of her gown.

"No, he is not," he said finally, just as he dropped her into a large chair. Disappointed, Lark realized their strange confrontation was at an end, for they were now in a large room with a dozen curious faces around them.

"My good man"—Matthew Warren spoke up—"you look exhausted by your exercise, as if you had a hard time of it. I shall have to get you out more often."

"I am probably out too often as it is. And look what effect this day has had on me."

Lark did not dare meet his eyes, but looked around at her new surroundings instead.

She sat in an unusually curved room that seemed to emulate the prow of a ship as it fronted the sea. A dozen beds were lined up along the far wall, so every occupant looked out upon the water but was not bothered by the sun's bright reflection within it. Two of the windows stood open, admitting the stiff, fresh breeze that pervaded all of Brighton but was forbidden in the private chambers at Knighton's. Here, it did much to temper the odors of body and waste that were inevitable companions to disease.

"This is the children's room, my lady," Benedict Queensman said at her shoulder.

Startled, Lark returned her gaze to the beds and realized the tiny proportions of those who lay beneath the covers.

"Why are they not in their homes, sir? Surely children are happiest surrounded by those they love, who can best give them comfort."

"A very wise sentiment, my lady. But you are naive if you think every child has a home, or that he or she is loved by those who dwell within. Indeed, I am sad to tell you some of these children are here precisely because they are so unloved at home."

"Whatever can you mean?"

"Exactly what I say. You cannot be so sheltered as to believe children are not abused by whoever has the care of them, that many are not murdered every day only a few miles from your fancy balls and theater engagements."

Lark blinked, feeling a little stupid. Indeed, she must have been so sheltered. She knew nothing of the lives of the urchins in the streets—how could she?—and paid little attention to any but those few in the families she and her sisters took under their charitable wing. As for the others, she knew not where they slept nor how they lived.

"It is not possible," she whispered, and accepted Janet's linen handkerchief. She blew her nose.

Mr. Queensman dropped to one knee, so his face came very close to her own.

"I did not bring you here to distress you, but to show there is reason for hope. Children may be brought to us and allowed to recover their health."

"But why?" Lark asked bitterly. "So they may be returned to the harshness of their lives and similar abuse?"

"Your lady is a quick learner, Miss Tavish," Lark heard Mr. Warren say.

Mr. Queensman nodded his apparent agreement. "We endeavor to settle them safely elsewhere. Unless, of course, they wish to return to their homes."

"Why would they wish to do that?"

Mr. Queensman frowned before he answered. "Who can explain the vagaries of what passes for love?"

Lark had no answer to that, nor did she a half hour later when she had met all the children in the ward and knew she had somehow developed a profound affection for them. She found herself promising gifts and favors, and guaranteed she would return to visit them all.

"You would make an excellent politician, my dear," Mr. Queensman said wryly as he lifted her from her seat to bring her into another room. "You have managed to make everyone extremely happy."

Though possibly not as happy as he made her by his use of a simple endearment.

"Where do we go now?" Janet asked, just at her shoulder. But when they reached the doorway, she fell back in step with Mr. Warren.

"There are others I should like you to meet. I must warn you, however, they will take you very literally at your word and will not be appreciative of promises you will not keep."

Lark was stunned that Mr. Queensman should be so cynical of her, but a moment's reflection was sufficient to remind her why he would not trust a lady capable of such a massive deception as hers. Even as they moved down a cool corridor, she realized how very much she would like to walk beside him and enter the next room on her own account—not like some helpless invalid in his arms. But despite his cryptic words, she did not doubt he would promptly return her to Raeborn if her recovery proved suddenly complete.

"I have not broken a promise to anyone in my life, sir," she said.

"I would like you to say as much in my cousin's presence," he answered curtly.

"He can have no quarrel with me on that account, as he extracted no promise from me. My father negotiated an arrangement without my consent."

Ben Queensman's steady step faltered.

"That is not what he told me," he said gruffly.

"I am not surprised," Lark retorted bitterly. "I seem surrounded by a conspiracy of men who consult nothing but their own vanities. First I am jilted by a fickle suitor, and then I am bullied into submission by my father. Your cousin presents himself at my father's door, on the strength of a few minutes' meeting, and then commissions you to spy on me. Well, I have had quite enough of this. Put me down, sir."

Ben Queensman continued walking, tightening his hold.

"I said, put me down." Lark knew the danger of getting precisely what she wished, but anger made her reckless.

"I will not. You have not the strength to support yourself." Mr. Queensman perpetuated the charade even as she challenged him to abandon it.

"I do indeed, as well you know. I order you—"

"And I willfully disobey your order. You shall stay as you are."

She started to wiggle out of his arms, trying to escape.

"Lark!" The name slipped out in a sort of desperation, and had the effect of stopping her completely.

"Sir?"

He knew he had erred severely with the implied intimacy; she could see the regret on his face. It enhanced her growing sense of the power she held over him and strengthened her determination to provoke him while on her own two feet.

But her timing proved ill, as he brought her into another room and closed the door behind him.

"Will Mr. Warren not be joining us?" she asked, even though she already knew the answer.

"I believe he is showing Miss Tavish the drawing room."

"But Miss Tavish is my chaperone. It will not do to be without her."

"You need not fear for your virtue, my lady. We have chaperones enough here."

Mr. Queensman set her down gently at a table at which a man and a woman sat with a deck of cards between them and a tray of sweetmeats in each of their corners. They boasted neither the elegant dress of the residents at Knighton's nor the general look of refinement, but were neatly dressed and impeccably clean. The man rose shakily to his feet.

"Lady Larkspur, may I present Mrs. Bottles and Mr. Hill to you? They are temporary residents at the hospital, of course, but are both so helpful to me here, I may never declare them well enough to leave."

"You know I will do my job whether I live here or not, Master Benedict." The old lady laughed. But then, it seemed, she enjoyed her own joke too much, for the laughter turned into spasms of coughing. Mr. Queensman did not seem particularly upset, but massaged her gently on the back and offered her his own linen handkerchief. Lark noticed blood staining the fine fabric and winced.

"You need not concern yourself, my pretty lady," Mrs. Bottles told Lark reassuringly as she recovered. "These fits come and go, and are much improved since Master Benedict brought me here. I never thought to find him waiting upon me, and mean to enjoy it as much as possible!"

Lark looked curiously at Mr. Queensman and was amused by his sheepish expression.

"Mrs. Bottles was employed by my family at Seagate for over forty years," he explained, "until her condition made it impossible for her to continue. She moved in with her daughter in Dover, but a houseful of grandchildren did not encourage the sort of rest she needed."

"Still, I loved being with the babes. That is why you can often find me with the children here at the hospital, tending to them and doing what I can. I always loved children. Why, my happiest days were when Master Benedict and his sisters were all at home, carrying on so from morning to night. I remember when—"

"I am sure Lady Larkspur is not interested in our childhood exploits, Mrs. Bottles," Mr. Queensman said too quickly.

"Not at all, sir," Lark intervened, smiling wickedly. "I am sure Master Benedict must have been a regular tyrant to his sisters. He seems so experienced in the business."

"Master Benedict?" Mrs. Bottles looked befuddled. "Nay, if anything, it was young Juliet who carried the whip. Indeed, your gentleman was of a gentler spirit, always bringing home injured birds and animals and asking for leftovers from the kitchen so he might feed them. It surprised no one when he took up medicine."

"How very noble in character," Lark said loftily, but she admitted, to herself, the truth of it. "Nevertheless, Mr. Queensman is not my gentleman at all. I am no more than a patient, like yourself, Mrs. Bottles."

The woman looked quickly to her hero for confirmation, and Mr. Queensman nodded. But Mrs. Bottles looked singularly unconvinced and turned back to gaze upon Lark.

"What precisely ails you, my lady?" she asked, narrowing her eyes.

"Lady Larkspur suffers from a broken heart," Mr. Queensman said solemnly.

Mrs. Bottles sucked in her breath, but aside from that, the room seemed so quiet Lark thought she could hear the thumping of the aforesaid heart. How absurd it seemed in the very telling, how trivial her ruse proved next to the very serious ailments of all the others in Mr. Queensman's care! What would any of them give to have her health, her means and her future!

"Did you have anything to do with this, young man?" intoned a stern voice. Lark looked around her at the empty room before she realized Mr. Hill had spoken at last. He looked at least as old as Mrs. Bottles and slightly off balance. Several minutes passed before Lark realized he had but one leg.

"I plead my innocence, sir," Mr. Queensman said respectfully, as if addressing a schoolmaster. "I did no more than share a dance with the girl, wherein she rebuked me heartily for intruding on another's territory. But so little did the scoundrel deserve it—he ran off on the very night. Lady Lark has scarcely been the same since."

"And are you destined to be the one to mend her heart?" Mrs. Bottles asked with the candor of old age.

Lark thought Ben Queensman blushed under his tan. Whatever he expected by these introductions, he surely did not plan for a personal inquisition. Lark smiled at the sight of his discomfort.

"I regret I am not, sir. Again, I would be intruding into another's territory. My cousin, Lord Raeborn, claims the lady you see before you. I am charged only with protecting his interests."

Mr. Hill tapped long fingers on the deck of cards.

"Raeborn? Are you not his heir, Master Ben? Will you not gain his titles and estates if he does not marry?"

"Your memory is excellent, Mr. Hill," Ben Queensman said, "would that your health were as assured."

Mr. Hill grunted a response. "But you will explain to me how you came to be the one to protect the single obstacle in the way of your inheritance. If the lady recovers sufficiently to marry Raeborn, your hopes may be dashed."

Mr. Queensman's bright blue eyes seemed to darken, and he gave the appearance of being deep in thought. Yet, Lark realized, if either of these two knew him as well as she, they must know he had already considered every angle of the situation.

"I have invested very little in such hopes, Mr. Hill, for my cousin could have acted a hundred times to depose them. I have my father's estate and already live as comfortably as I could want. But as to the larger issue, the one seeming such a contradiction in your eyes, I can only say I will not intrude on my cousin's interests. It is a matter of honor, sir."

Lark looked up at Ben Queensman's face, reading the quiet determination there, and finally comprehended the ironies of the circumstances she herself had wrought. How devotedly she had once flung her expectations to one who ultimately proved to be without honor. And how now—

she finally admitted to herself—she found herself desiring another man whose honor was too great to offer her anything but pain in return. Already having a tantalizing glimpse of what might lie beneath the cool, solid facade of Ben Queensman's honor made her regret it all the more.

"Your father would have been very proud of you, my boy." Mr. Hill spoke first, and his dark eyes gleamed with moisture.

"You appear to be very familiar with Mr. Queensman's family, Mr. Hill," observed Lark. "Did you also live on the estate?"

"I worked in the gardens at Seagate for nearly fifty years, my lady. So I would remain today if Master Ben would have me."

"You make it sound as if I have cast you out, Mr. Hill. But would I not be censored by all the countryside if I still had you trimming the branches in the orchard?" Mr. Queensman clasped the old man's shoulder warmly. "Besides which, I am not sure we can spare you from the garden here at the hospital."

"They are very lovely. I often sit on the veranda at Knighton's and admire them," Lark said quickly.

"Lady Larkspur is fortuitously named, you see. She is a bit of a botanist herself. Her specialty is thorny roses," Mr. Queensman said, sounding very sincere.

"I am rather more interested in herbs," Lark corrected him with a withering look. "Perhaps you would like a strong cup of tansy tea, Mr. Queensman?"

"Oh, dear, no, my lady!" Mr. Hill cried out and put his hand protectively over Mr. Queensman's. "Too strong a dose of tansy can kill a man!"

To Lark's surprise, Mr. Queensman laughed out loud.

"I believe the lady might have something of the sort in mind," he said. "It is why I felt it important for her to meet the two of you, so she understands I have two protectors."

As the two elderly retainers looked critically at Lark, undoubtedly wondering how their darling boy could expose himself to such risk, Mr. Queensman leaned over her chair and once again lifted her into his arms. Over her shoulder, he clearly made some sign to the pair, for Lark heard Mrs. Bottles giggle. Aside from that, they remained silent as he carried her from the room.

"Why did you have me meet Mrs. Bottles and Mr. Hill?" Lark asked. "Did you feel you needed additional praise to recommend your character to me? Or did you merely desire to bolster your defenses? For all you say, you certainly cannot imagine you have anything to fear from me."

He looked down at her, his face so close, that his lips could have caught hers in an instant.

"Sometimes I think I have a good deal to fear," he said softly.

"Do you imagine me the vessel by which your lordly expectations might be supplanted?"

The muscle of his jaw tensed, making him look very severe.

"I believe you know me better than that. When I say I do not anticipate anything to come my way from Lord Raeborn, I sincerely mean it."

"And therefore you would not regret my marrying him?"

He said nothing as he carried her out onto a narrow terrace overlooking the sea. Lark glanced over his shoulder and realized they were not in the line of view of Knighton's veranda, nor of anything else. Before them lay nothing but the broad expanse of the water and a few playful gulls gliding over its surface. The same wind on which they soared whipped about her skirts, caressing her legs.

"You do not answer me, Mr. Queensman," Lark urged, emboldened by his silence.

"I think you already know the answer, my lady. I would regret it very much."

Lark looked into his face, hoping to meet his eyes. But they avoided hers, looking out to sea and narrowing against the reflecting sun.

Abandoning sense and all propriety, consumed by a desire so intense she dared not imagine what name to call it, Lark put her hand to his face and caressed the fine line of his jaw. Feeling it tremble, and knowing he would only speak to discourage her wanton display, she moved one finger to his lips so she might seal any protest within.

But suddenly she felt herself being lowered, and caught herself around his neck as she slipped out of his grasp. Beneath her thin slippers, her toes met the hard stone of the terrace, warm and supportive beneath her.

Still she held on to him, pulling his great height to meet

her more diminutive one and relishing the unaccustomed sensation of feeling the full length of his lean body pressed against hers. She arched her back, stretching her cramped muscles, and therefore encouraged him in a way she only partly understood.

She heard Ben's sudden intake of breath, and, in bracing herself for a rebuke, instead faced an assault of another sort.

His lips, smooth and warm, covered and caressed hers and made her respond in a manner neither practiced nor ladylike. She dared to open her mouth, wanting to taste more of the salty sea and of him, and he seized advantage of her vulnerability by plundering her with his tongue. His hands moved to her hips and pulled her against him; feeling his hard desire, she opened her eyes in astonishment.

He waited for her, watched her, though his lips did not leave hers. But in the bright blue depths of his gaze she saw the answers to questions she knew not how to articulate, and the unbidden longing she had only glimpsed before. Never before, in all the flirtations that had passed for love, had she known anything so achingly intense and so real.

Just as she thought her lungs would burst, Ben allowed her to take great gasping breaths as his lips began to wander over other parts of her body. She started to twist away, but he held her fast and caressed her nose and forehead and ears, exposing moist spots to the wind when he abandoned them. Tickled by sensation, she cried out with pleasure.

He stopped suddenly and held her apart from him as he looked into her face.

"Am I hurting you?" he asked.

Lark raised her brows, thinking a physician ought to know better than most men what effect he might be having on her.

"Yes. Most dreadfully," she gasped. "Please do it again."

His mouth twisted, making her wonder at his own pain. But then, seizing advantage of their several inches of separation, he bowed down and found the erratic pulse beating in her neck, pressing his lips against it to soothe its course. He traveled a light, quick path across her collarbone and down to the soft, untouched flesh of her breast.

"Dear, dear Ben." Lark felt herself sinking, her legs truly incapable of holding her. "This is impossible."

Without his lips leaving her body, he caught her as she fell and held her aloft in his arms again.

"And yet it is," she thought she heard him say against her aching heart.

Chapter Eight

"Something happened to you at Mr. Queensman's hospital, did it not?" Janet Tavish asked, looking up from a note that had been waiting for her when she awoke in the morning. Lark thought it might have come from Matthew Warren.

"If you mean did I come away with a greater appreciation of the nobility of the medical profession, you are correct. I am giving thought to the prospect of returning to the hospital and giving of my time to the children who live there. Certainly there is something I might do."

"How very charitable of you, my dear friend. But no, you misunderstand me. I am proud but not surprised you should be so affected. Yet you seem to be affected in other ways."

"Whatever do you mean?" Lark asked and quickly looked down at her own letter in her lap.

Janet laughed. "Why, your eyes are bright, and your skin is positively glowing. There is a transcendence about you I can hardly explain and certainly have never witnessed in all the years I have known you. You have not even the excuse of a brisk swim in the sea, my dear."

"Perhaps I am flushed by a fever," Lark said quickly.

"Tell it to others, if you may, but save your breath with me. If it is a fever, I daresay it is one of the heart."

"Janet!"

Janet Tavish lifted her small hand in protest and smiled. "I am neither stupid nor blind, my friend. And even if I were, I could hardly miss the look in Mr. Queensman's eyes when he talks to you, nor the way in which he waits upon your every word. You are accustomed to making conquests, but I have never before known a man deserving of you."

"You forget my circumstances, Janet. And his. I must despise him."

But in her heart, she knew it was already too late to

sound even remotely convincing in her often-repeated declaration. She did not despise him. She could only curse her own recklessness for settling on a course from which they could not escape with any degree of honor or dignity.

"And it is your hatred that has bestowed such radiance. A pity it does not work on several spinsters of our acquaintance. Think how they would be made beautiful by the exercise."

"You must know this talk does not make me happy." Lark pouted. "The last thing I wish is to look beautiful or healthy in the company of a certain visitor."

"Mr. Queensman? I am sure you have nothing to fear on that account. And Mr. Warren tells me they both will call this afternoon," Janet said, picking up the message.

Lark looked back down on her lap and wished her own letter had brought such tidings. It was not from one of her sisters, who wrote often enough, with anxious queries about her progress to recovery. In recent weeks she had managed to reassure them. But now it seemed she was destined for a complete relapse.

"I am speaking of another visitor, Janet. My letter comes from London, from Lord Raeborn. He begs to call on me in three days' time."

"Oh, dear. Does Mr. Queensman know?"

"I have no idea. But I expect he will be happy to expose my deception and deliver me triumphantly into his cousin's arms."

"You credit your suitor with too much strength if you think him capable of carrying you. And you credit Mr. Queensman with too little if you believe he will let you go."

Lark looked at her friend in surprise, wondering what had happened to the girl who until recently seemed to take special delight in Mr. Queensman's company. Perhaps she had made too much of it, filtered as it was through the lens of her own unbidden desire. And perhaps Janet understood the situation from the very start, for she seemed to transfer her affections very readily to Matthew Warren, and she seemed perfectly happy. Lark admitted to herself that she was happy about that, if nothing else.

"It is not a question of strength, dear Janet," Lark said sadly. "It is purely a matter of honor. And Mr. Queensman will not have what has been promised to another."

*   *   *

"She is the most delightful lady I have ever met," Matthew Warren said as he finished bandaging the leg of a sleeping child. "I do not understand how I never met her in London."

Ben elevated the child's head and pressed his ear against the small back. Satisfied that all was well, he glanced across at his bemused friend.

"Perhaps you were never able to get close enough. She was accustomed to a host of gentlemen climbing over themselves to get near her and her father's fortune, and enjoyed several brief engagements. I believe she rarely set her sights on anything lower than a baron."

"Miss Tavish?" Matthew looked nervous. "She seems so steady, so sincere. She never would have—"

"I was speaking of Lady Larkspur," Ben interrupted.

"Lady Larkspur? Please reassure yourself that while she might be ever on your mind, I myself have scarcely spared a thought for her. Oh, I grant you she is beautiful, with hair likely to turn the head of any man. And her breeding is excellent, as are her connections. But I do not think she has the gravity to make one a pleasant wife or a temperate helpmate. She is likely to invoke excited passions. I do not know how your elderly cousin will manage."

"Nor do I. However, he writes to tell me he will be visiting in several days' time and would like for me to put him up at Seagate. I have no objection, but must warn him I spend very little of my time there."

"But surely he does not come to visit you, my friend. He must make the journey to cheer up Lady Larkspur. As such, you should find him more often at Knighton's than in your drawing room."

"So I fear."

Matthew looked at him in surprise.

"You do not like the fellow?"

Ben knew he deserved that question, for he asked it often enough of himself. He knew almost certainly that he resented Raeborn and wished him away from Brighton. Let him marry ten times over and produce a hundred heirs, if he would but abandon his suit of Lady Lark.

But he did not dislike him.

"I have no objections to his company. But I fear he will

be very disappointed in the lady's poor progress, which will not be made any better by his presence.''

Matthew placed a doll into the child's arms deliberately and gathered up the discarded bandages from where they had fallen on the floor.

"He may be encouraged to abandon his suit," he said evenly. "Would that bother you very much?"

Ben stood up and stretched his weary arms.

"I desire it above all else," he said.

At midafternoon, when all the guests at Knighton's were assembled on the veranda for tea, a great cheer rose up from the drive. Lark looked anxiously at Janet, hardly believing that their two gentlemen friends would enlist such a response and wondering if it could be the great man himself who came to the sanatorium. Mr. Knighton proved as elusive as Queen Caroline of England.

But when the uproar moved through the halls and emerged upon the veranda, Lark saw only a great muscular woman as a stranger among them. In gray gown and stiff bonnet, the woman stood expectantly, waiting for deference.

Indeed, she received it.

Miss Hathawae was the first to speak.

"Goodness, is it you, Martha? However did Mr. Knighton steal you away from Margate?"

"He bribed me plenty," the woman said bluntly, and then bowed slightly when she added, "Miss Hathawae."

Miss Hathawae smiled delicately and turned towards Lark and Janet.

"Martha Gunn is the most famous of all the Margate dippers, and truly the most accomplished. Why, I remember one afternoon she rescued a poor horse from drowning."

A gasp of awe rose up from the others, but Lark could scarcely suppress her laughter.

"I am like a fish," the woman growled.

More like a whale, Lark thought to herself, unable to dismiss the image. "What is it, exactly, you do, Martha Gunn? We are very curious to know how the bathing machines work."

"It is most simple, miss. The ladies enter the cart while the machines are still on the beach. Once they are inside, they find a cozy bench to sit upon and hooks upon which to hang their gowns and shawls. The quarters are very tight, but that is a good thing, for if a lady should lose her footing while the machine is moving, she is not likely to fall to the floor." Mrs. Gunn laughed, a little too heartily. "She may be a bit bruised about the elbows, however."

"It sounds very dangerous," Janet said nervously. "Why is the machine moving?"

"Dearie, how do you expect to get into the waves? The horse, led by old Martha, makes his way down the wooden track and into the water. He knows to stop when the water laps about his neck, for then the water is at a height with the door in the cart. I rap on the door, and wait until the lady is ready for me. When she opens the door, we put my hoop around her, and she steps down into the brine. She'd best hold tightly, for I then push her down into the water and up again."

"You must be very strong," Janet murmured.

"That I am, miss."

"Why are the ladies not capable of submerging themselves in the water?" Lark asked, wide-eyed.

"It is not an exercise for them. A lady does not know how to manage the waves," Mrs. Gunn insisted.

"But I do. I have been swimming since I was a little girl," Lark argued.

From across the terrace a man's laughter rang out. Gabriel Siddons sat there with his boorish uncle, fingering a dissected map.

"You must not admit to it, my lady," he said. "You may be very fashionable in London, but you must remember the particular rules of our little society here. Ladies of quality neither swim nor sail. Nor, with capable men about, and the likes of Martha Gunn, are they ever required to."

"How very humbling, Mr. Siddons, to discover that one may not reckon among one's accomplishments what one has practiced for so many years. I suppose you would not like it very much if you were told you could no longer ride, but must be carted about in a carriage," Lark said playfully, for she knew she would not win her point in company such as this. Aside from anything else, she was believed to be an invalid, and so the old rules of behavior could no longer apply.

"I would not, to be sure. But we all of us make sacrifices for society."

Lark wondered at the change in his tone, at the implication that they were speaking of something other than fashionable mores. She smiled a little tentatively.

"You speak with some authority, sir."

Martha Gunn cleared her throat with all the delicacy of a cannon shot.

"Swim or not," she said, "I have orders to do my job. Mr. Knighton wants me to inspect the bathing machines and try the horses in the water. If all is well, I expect to see the ladies on the beach tomorrow."

"Not too early, Mrs. Gunn. There are several gentlemen who make it a habit to bathe in the morning," Lark said, affecting an air of innocence.

The renowned dipper coughed. "Let them bathe. They have nothing to show I haven't seen before!"

Miss Hathawae gasped in an appropriate show of delicacy. Mr. Siddons flushed a deep, dark red.

But Lark looked with a growing admiration on the newcomer, wondering what she knew of which she herself was only imperfectly aware.

"Do not get any fine ideas, Lark," Janet whispered curtly.

"Would you not like to get a closer view, to see if Mr. Warren is as . . . ah . . . amiable as you presently believe?"

Janet looked shocked, and Lark regretted her teasing words at once. What did she know of it after all? A few stolen moments with a man she thought she detested until moments before he dared to kiss her did not qualify her as a woman of the world. If, in fact, she was destined to marry the fossilized Lord Raeborn, she might have already shared more passion with a man than she should ever expect again.

By the time Martha Gunn marched from the veranda, Lark felt thoroughly disheartened.

"You look very weary, my lady. Should you enjoy some diversion?"

Lark opened her eyes and looked up into Gabriel Siddons' pleasant face. His moment of embarrassment apparently behind him, he now dared to approach her.

"I should love anything that allows me to forget my sad predicament," she said truthfully. "But I feel I must warn you: Mr. Queensman and Mr. Warren are due to arrive at any time."

A spark of sudden interest glinted in Mr. Siddons' eye.

"You do not feel they might be tempted to go for a swim first?" he asked pointedly.

Lark wondered how he knew so much about it.

"Indeed not. They prefer the morning hours, as I have already told Mrs. Gunn," she said daringly.

"Several of my acquaintances have met them there on occasion. I myself do not take to the waters unless absolutely necessary."

Lark wondered if this was an indictment against his cleanliness, and then realized she never desired to know if it was. Unlike other gentlemen, he never came closer to her than considered polite, and she preferred to keep it that way.

"In fact, one of them has brought me the very thing I promised you," he added, almost as an afterthought. "Do you recall? We spoke about Mr. Wallis' dissected maps."

Lark exchanged a glance with Janet, who rolled her eyes.

"Of course. You promised they would provide an excellent diversion. I hope I might manage it, for I have very little experience with such things."

"You will be marvelous, I am certain," Mr. Siddons said, with a good deal more confidence than Lark felt herself. "My uncle now works on a map of this very region, but I am certain he will interrupt his progress to guide you as you puzzle out the pieces of a map of America."

"America! You mistake me if you think I know a single thing about that savage place! I certainly do not expect to ever travel there!" Lark protested.

"Do not be distressed," Mr. Siddons said, though he did not look in the least apologetic. "It is only of the northeast, near the Canadian provinces, and most certainly relates to things you might have heard or read about. As you are a friend of Mr. Queensman, you have probably heard of his adventures in the army."

Again Lark wondered why he seemed to bring Benedict Queensman into every turn of the conversation and how he knew so much about him. If Mr. Siddons considered Mr. Queensman a rival, it might explain the first. But she could not guess at the answer to the second.

"As a matter of fact, I have not," Lark said warily. "Indeed, your own uncle reveals a good deal more about the subject of the American campaign."

"So he does!" Mr. Siddons laughed. "It is a subject of endless fascination for him! But so I suppose it must be to every hero."

Janet moved restlessly. "What, precisely, did Colonel Wayland do?" she asked.

Mr. Siddons hesitated, not enough to discredit him or his uncle, but surely so much as to cast a slight doubt on his heroism. Lark was quick to seize upon it, though she did not know why it should matter.

"Why, he—he surely already told you about it a dozen times. He speaks admirably for himself." Mr. Siddons smiled so brightly, Lark thought his face would crack. "Should you like for me to bring over the map now? You need not be in the least bit intimidated."

"Dear Mr. Siddons, how very kind of you," Lark said, reflecting his own smile. "And with your help, and that of your excellent uncle, I should fear nothing."

Mr. Siddons' eyes darted to the elderly gentleman, and he nodded briefly. Colonel Wayland rose shakily to his feet and picked up a wooden box from the table before him. While he made his way across the veranda, Mr. Siddons hastily removed drinking glasses and a book from the round table between Lark and Janet.

"We shall set it up here, where it can easily be moved within," he said.

"We have no intention of retiring on such a splendid day," Lark said, trying to sound encouraging.

"Ah, but the progress of work upon a dissected map may take days to achieve. If we leave the pieces outside, a curious gull may make off with a critical clue and leave us quite helpless to finish."

Lark looked at Janet, who shrugged. But there was no hope for them, as they were the very model of a captive audience.

Mr. Siddons removed a seal from the box and upset its contents upon their small table. Janet quickly retrieved the few pieces that tumbled to the ground, and Lark spread her fingers to prevent any more losses. The pieces of the map were cunningly cut at odd angles and seemed impossible to restore to any order.

But Colonel Wayland assumed command of the troops.

"First you must turn them all to face upwards and line them evenly along the edge of the table. When that is accomplished . . ."

Lark and Janet had no choice but to obey, and their fingers darted about the surface, making some sense of the chaos before them. Mr. Siddons deigned to help, but after his hand came into contact with Lark's, he settled back into his chair and watched at a safe distance.

"I do not understand how we might assemble this map if we are indifferent to the place names," Lark protested.

"The only geography one needs to know is the topography of each separate piece. They must fit into one another, like clasping hands."

Lark had a sudden remembrance of her body pressed close against Ben Queensman's contours and thought that a more intriguing analogy.

"Of course, if one does know, say, that the Hudson flows southerly, or that Canada is to the north of Albany, one's task is greatly facilitated," said a voice to the accompaniment of the scraping of a chair across the veranda.

"Mr. Warren! Mr. Queensman!" Janet cried with transparent—and radiant—pleasure. "How good it is to see you again."

Lark looked quickly at Gabriel Siddons' face before acknowledging her guests, and confirmed her suspicion that she would see dislike upon it. While she did not understand the cause of the enmity, she knew how strongly it was felt, and had a growing need to investigate it further.

"Lady Larkspur?" Mr. Queensman's voice demanded his share of attention, but remained pleasant and almost caressing. "Are you so rapt in the mind teaser at hand that you will not notice us?"

He knew very well why she would not rush to face him again, Lark thought, but she could not be censorious. After all, she had asked for his intimacies as much as he, and he had done nothing she did not desire. But it was, rather, the unaccustomed circumstances in which they found themselves that proved so unsettling, coupled with the almost absolute certainty that it should all come to nothing.

She looked up at him. His eyes studied her as if there were nothing else to see, and she caught the reflection of her own red hair in them. A smile teased the corner of his mouth even as he tried to be very serious, and she caught a glimpse of his straight white teeth.

As she watched him, his hand came up to straighten his cravat—as if that were the infraction—and she saw a bandage neatly tied across his palm.

"Whatever happened to you?" she cried, and realized, too late, that she sounded far too anxious for the professional relationship they espoused.

Ben Queensman caught her concern at once, and she could see it gave him pleasure. He held his hand aloft, like some banner of truce.

"A minor mishap on the beach this morning, that is all. Lucky for me, I am usually in the company of this fine physician at my side, so the damage proved minimal."

Matthew Warren beamed, and Janet sighed in appreciation.

Strangely, this bit of information proved disconcerting to Gabriel Siddons.

"You are incautious to be on the beach at such an odd hour, sir," he said sternly. "There are any number of dangers that might threaten you, and few people around to come to your aid if something were to happen to you both."

"I thank you for your advice, Mr. Siddons," Ben Queensman said icily, "but I need not remind you I am far better acquainted with these waters than you are. Or are you aware of some peril yet lurking? Are we to expect another invasion? Or a smuggler's plot?"

Gabriel Siddons grew very red, taking far more offense at Mr. Queensman's teasing than surely was justified.

"And how do you know about it, after all?" Mr. Queensman continued to provoke and antagonize.

Mr. Siddons glanced at his uncle, who seemed more engaged by the map than the sparring match.

"I know enough to say you were not caught in a crab's claws this morning, sir. I have information from those as canny in these waters as you yourself."

The jab hit its target or, at worst, was deflected. Mr. Queensman's eyes opened even wider, and he gestured silently in Lark and Janet's direction. Lark did not need a sixth sense to understand that he did not wish to discuss his affairs in the presence of ladies—and that those affairs might prove even more embarrassing than having feminine witnesses to his morning swim.

"How fortunate for you, sir. Your network of spies must also have informed you that I found a boot and a very fine piece of driftwood," Mr. Queensman said dismissively, and deliberately put his injured hand in his pocket.

"But we did not come to talk of our paltry finds." Mr. Warren broke in suddenly. "We have come to discover if the ladies have quite recovered from their outing into town."

"Oh, indeed, we have, Mr. Warren. We can hardly wait to go again," Janet said excitedly.

But Lark did not feel so recovered, nor did she think she ever would be. Remembering the things she had been doing with Mr. Queensman could provide no balm to her spirit, nor afford her any peace.

She glanced up at him and thought he must know what she was feeling.

"Do sit down," she said politely. "Our interests this day are rather sedentary, and you might prove helpful to us."

"It is our only objective, my lady," Ben Queensman said. He settled himself upon the chair he had pulled up when he first greeted them.

"Of course," Mr. Siddons felt compelled to add. "As you are the lady's physician, it can be your solitary concern."

"Have your spies also given you that piece of information?" Mr. Queensman asked rudely.

"We admitted a new patient this morning, Miss Tavish, someone you may enjoy meeting someday," Mr. Warren said, changing the subject. "Like yourself, Mrs. Jasper professes a great interest in Asian arts."

Lark looked at Janet in surprise. In all the years of their friendship, she never recalled anything particular about Janet's taste for the Orient. Of what could she have been speaking while Lark discovered other delights on the terrace at the hospital?

"It would be a pleasure to meet her. I hope she is not so very ill?" Janet said smoothly.

Mr. Warren glanced at Mr. Queensman, who seemed

more interested in the pieces of the map. "As to that, we cannot yet say. She is here on vacation, visiting her daughter, and we know little of her history."

"But that she likes Asian arts," Lark interrupted. "Perhaps that is why she is drawn to Brighton. The sight of the Royal Pavilion must provide some gratification."

"I am glad it does to someone," Mr. Queensman said distractedly. And then, to Colonel Wayland, "I believe you are mistaken, sir. The fort at Mount Hope is not down near Kingston. A man of your experience ought to know it."

Lark, confused at first, realized he had turned his attention to the dissected map. Colonel Wayland had been busy on it, but now it seemed Mr. Queensman took issue with some of the placement and was set upon rearranging the pieces.

"I say, sir, I did not have these brought for your enjoyment. I hoped to entertain the ladies with the little puzzler," Mr. Siddons protested.

"Ah, surely they would not mind if I set them upon the right course," Mr. Queensman said, and snatched up one piece.

"I hold the city of Albany in my right hand, Colonel Wayland. Where would you have me put it?"

The colonel made some vague gesture at the table, and Mr. Queensman held the piece aloft expectantly.

"I believe the bathing machines will be available for use tomorrow," Mr. Siddons said, demanding their attention.

"I can hardly wait." Janet clapped her hands.

"You must be very careful, Miss Tavish," Mr. Warren said. "As practiced as Mrs. Gunn is, the whole business is not without its mishaps. I understand there were several drownings in Margate."

"You sound almost as worried as Mr. Siddons," Lark said easily, though she continued to be drawn to the little drama between Mr. Queensman and the colonel. "We shall be very safe. I, for one, look forward to the lovely freedom of dancing in the waves."

"Are you very fond of dancing, Lady Larkspur?" Mr. Siddons said, on a note of sympathy.

"She may profess to enjoy it, but I, for one, found her resistant to its appeal when we first met in London," Mr. Queensman said, though he still looked at Albany in his hand. "I finally prevailed upon her to dance with me and can report she has a very fine step."

Lark would have liked to knock the map piece from his hand, and the complacent smile from his lips.

"Did you know each other in town?" Mr. Siddons asked, scarcely disguising his curiosity.

"Yes," said Mr. Queensman.

"No," said Lark at precisely the same time. Mr. Queensman allowed himself the indulgence of looking away from his hand to gaze upon her.

"That is, hardly at all," Lark amended. "Mr. Queensman is acquainted with my brother-in-law, as they were together in America."

"Did you know Southard, Colonel?" Mr. Queensman asked pointedly.

"An elderly gent, well past his prime, as I recall. Widowed two or three times."

As the description did not fit John, or any of his immediate relatives, Lark felt ready to correct the colonel. But a look from Mr. Queensman made her reconsider, and she looked down at the map again. She was coming to think Mr. Queensman's affairs as much a puzzler as the dissected map before her.

And she may not have been the only one to think so, for no one said anything for several minutes. They each sat around the table, studying the map as if it held the key to eternal youth, and pushed the little wooden pieces around on the smooth surface. Mr. Warren's fingers trifled with Janet's, and Mr. Siddon's rather thinner ones tapped impatiently on the arm of his chair. Mr. Queensman and Colonel Wayland seemed engaged in some sort of contradance, as one placed a piece only to be corrected by the other. And Lark, too aware of everything going on around her, tried to concentrate on the tiny letters imprinted upon the map.

Suddenly Colonel Wayland tossed a piece over the side of the veranda, sabotaging all their efforts.

"There is no such place," he said angrily.

"I assure you, sir, I have been there myself," Mr. Queensman said, looking as if he were the victor of some major battle.

"I wish to have my tea indoors," Colonel Wayland insisted. "Gideon, you must come with me."

If Mr. Siddons noticed his uncle mistook his name, he gave no sign of displeasure. Instead, he rose slowly and came around to assist the old man.

"I will return tomorrow," he said to Lark.

"And I shall welcome you," she responded politely. As he led his uncle away, she said to Mr. Queensman, "I do not understand why you dislike him so."

"Someday, I may be in a position to better explain it," he said simply and returned his attention to the map.

"Would you like to walk upon the beach, Mr. Warren?" Janet asked sweetly. "If the dangers are as great as you say, I should appreciate your advice as to the currents and rocks in the water before Lady Larkspur and I venture out into the waves."

Matthew Warren looked momentarily flustered and almost ready to dismiss Janet's fears. But then, apparently realizing the great opportunity she offered, he collected himself.

"It would be a privilege, Miss Tavish," he said. "Would Lady Larkspur and Mr. Queensman be so good as to excuse us?"

"We shall be engaged in completing the map," Mr. Queensman said before Lark could protest. And, in fact, he looked as if nothing could interest him more.

Finally, but for Miss Hathawae dozing in the corner, they were alone. After his unconscionable behavior on the terrace of his hospital, Ben did not dare imagine Lady Lark would ever allow herself to be unchaperoned with him again. If her contempt for him had managed to sustain her for so many weeks, it could only have multiplied many times over since he had ravished her.

And yet here she sat, quietly focused on the very same thing as he and acting as if she had not a care in the world.

He glanced at her and recognized his mistake at once.

She did not look upon the map, nor did it seem to matter to her at all. Instead, she waited on his notice and stared into his face with unnerving intensity.

"You do not like Colonel Wayland?" she asked.

His heart sank with disappointment that she thought not of him but of another man.

"I am reasonably indifferent to him as a gentleman. He

seems pleasant enough, if a bit of a bore. But I do not trust his recollections and wonder why he insists upon them when they are so imperfect."

"Perhaps he has nothing else," Lady Lark said. "Sometimes the imagination is more satisfying than real life."

"I suppose you believe the more we can satisfy our dreams, the happier we ought to be."

She seemed to contemplate his words, and he thought she looked vaguely troubled. "I have not thought of it that way, but I believe you may be right. It is a fault of yours."

He sat back, confused. "That I wish to satisfy my dreams?"

She smiled briefly, and her deep brown eyes looked wistful. "That you are so often right."

He looked down at the table again, wondering what game she played. Ironically, at the very moment he uncovered her deception, she seemed in every other way enigmatic and subtle, and ultimately far more complex than he could have guessed. And, even more unsettling, he had the feeling she enjoyed having the upper hand.

"I have had a letter from Raeborn," she said suddenly.

"So have I. He intends to bless us both with his presence," he added, wishing it did not sound so sarcastic.

"You have the ability to shorten his stay if you but pronounce me well."

"But you insist you are not well, my lady, and a gentleman must always believe a lady. Your unexpected insistence on standing on your own two feet back at the hospital might well have been inspired by the other patients you saw there. We both know you are not yet ready to be returned to my cousin and the rigors of married life."

"With your cousin they might not be so rigorous," he thought he heard her say, but then knew such indelicate words were impossible. He pushed some errant pieces of the map to the corner near her, wishing he dared touch her again.

Perhaps she did believe in the transference of dream into reality after all, because her own hand slid across the half-completed board to rest on his. Her thumb rubbed over the white bandage Matthew had applied so neatly, and she turned his hand over to reveal his palm.

"Have you ever had your fortune told?" she asked.

"At dinner parties when the company proved dull. And occasionally at a fair, at the insistence of one of my sisters. Gypsies seem remarkably single-minded, however. They all seem to think there is nothing in my future but marriage to one lady or another." With startling clarity, he recalled a turbaned crone of ten years ago telling him he would marry a lady with fiery hair. He looked across at Lady Lark, at her hair and eyes, and thought he himself would burst into flames.

"How unimaginative they are. Anyone could see you have more things on your mind than marriage."

Indeed he did, but he did not think they could be accomplished with one such as Lady Larkspur unless he already held a signed license.

"Do you propose to tell me what they might be?" he asked, a little roughly.

She looked up, a bit dazed, but she smiled. "I shall have to remove your bandage, sir, as it quite interferes with my reading. Will I hurt you?"

He shook his head, and she started to unpin what Matthew had worked so hard to achieve. Slowly, delicately, she unwound the fine linen cloth, hesitating only when an underlayer revealed the stain of his blood. He thought she would back down then, but she displayed the nerve of a physician.

Finally, his injury, still raw and deep, lay exposed to the sun and wind. He thought he heard her gasp.

"It was only an accident, my lady."

"It was not an accident, sir. One does not get this sort of cut unless one beds down with a knife. The edges are smooth and the cut quite deliberate."

"You are mistaken, Lark. It was indeed an accident, for my attacker hoped to slash my throat and necessarily settled for my hand instead. He did not aim for it."

"Your attacker?" she asked sharply.

When he only nodded, she returned her attention to his hand, though he knew she considered his admission very carefully. She ran a gentle finger over the cut, examining it with precision and tenderness and showing no signs of disgust or revulsion. He was right to think her compassionate enough to be an asset at such a place as his hospital. He wondered if she would also offer a prescription for care, or other professional advice.

"And this you received while swimming at our beach this morning?" she asked.

"I did."

"I shall heed your warning, sir," she said slowly. "Indeed, it seems a very, very dangerous place."

And then, quite unprofessionally, she lifted his hand to her lips and kissed it.

Chapter Nine

*L*ark felt deliciously wanton as the heat of the day warmed her exposed shoulders and bare arms. She did not remember the last time she had ventured outdoors without wearing a corset and knew her bright gypsy gown revealed more than could be considered modest in ordinary circumstances.

But today's circumstances were anything but ordinary, for Martha Gunn pronounced the weather fortuitous for the inauguration of the bathing machines, and all the ladies were advised to wear dresses that they could easily remove in the cramped quarters of the water-bound huts. They all required bathing costumes, of course, but as the thin cotton fabric made the garments hardly decent in mixed company, they would not be donned until the swimmers were well out of sight of anyone on the beach.

Lark knew it for the pretense it surely was, for she understood perfectly what a fine view of the water could be had from the oceanfront windows at Knighton's. She guessed that Mr. Queensman's hospital, perched comfortably on the nearly cliffs, afforded a pretty congenial view as well. But the machines themselves did something to obscure the direct line of sight and, in any case, one's head and shoulders were likely to be the only things visible.

"We were warned about sunburn—will you take no heed, Lark?" Janet asked scoldingly. From her vantage point at the back of the wheeled chair, she thrust a parasol between Lark's face and the offending sun. "If you will be careless, you will be as brown as a gypsy and will surely scare Lord Raeborn off."

Lark twisted in her seat but could not turn quite enough to confront Janet. No matter, she knew precisely the expression she would find on her friend's face.

"Is that not the point of this entire wearisome exercise, my dear?" she asked. "In fact, I am of a mind to take far too much sun and greet my suitor wearing a spray of freck-

les across my nose and in this very costume. He will be so
appalled, he will never darken the Leicester doorway again.
And then I shall be able to return home with some degree
of immunity."

"And never again attract the attention of a respectable
gentleman?"

Lark thought of Mr. Queensman's impassioned kisses
and bold caresses and shivered even in the heat of the sun.

"I am not sure a thoroughly respectable gentleman is the
man for me. Oh, certainly I should hope he is of good
family and does nothing to disgrace himself. But the more
I think of it, I believe most gentlemen of my acquaintance
bore me. I cannot imagine what Hindley Moore and I might
have found to talk about in five years' time."

Janet paused at the wide ramp leading from the veranda
onto the wooden walkway of the beach itself. The incline
proved rather steep, and Lark knew she did not trust herself to control the heavy chair. But within moments one of
the valets appeared, and he seemed to have no difficulty in
steering the chair down to the level surface of the pebbles.
He offered to continue, but Janet graciously resumed
command.

"It is lucky he jilted you, then," Janet said tartly. "Boring
company is even worse than no company at all."

Lark pushed back the brim of her bonnet, which had
slipped forward during the descent, and reflected how Janet's words, which would have struck a sensitive nerve only
weeks before, no longer held the power to disturb her.

"Do you think I might find a profitable life as a spinster,
then?" Lark asked lightly. "I should grow accustomed to
being quite alone. Unless, of course, I might always rely on
your excellent company."

Janet said nothing, and Lark knew she, herself, now
touched upon a sensitive nerve. Janet was several years
older than Lark, and had received only one offer in her
second season, and that from a most undesirable gentleman. But Lark sensed something recently changed in her
friend as much as in herself, and she did not believe her
casual comment would cause any undue distress.

"I do not think either of us will need to rely upon the
other," Janet said softly, and Lark knew her own supposi-
tion well founded.

A shadow fell across Lark's legs before she could ask anything further.

"Indeed you must, girls," came Miss Hathawae's cheerful voice. "It is essential that we rely upon each other and not just upon Mrs. Gunn when we are in the water. If one sees another in distress, it is necessary to cry for help."

"Thank you for your advice, Miss Hathawae. It is a relief to know we may benefit from your wisdom," Lark said without irony. She smiled at the elderly lady, who seemed a good deal more spritely than one expected at her age and whose eyes still glinted like a girl's. Briefly, Lark wondered what might be the lady's medical complaint.

"I have been coming to Knighton's for years and surely know my way about better than most."

"From our experience thus far, I daresay you may know your way about better than Mr. Knighton himself," Lark laughed.

Miss Hathawae seemed to ponder this before breaking into a smile.

"You may be right, my lady. He is a most indifferent landlord."

"Then why do you continue to come?" Lark asked, genuinely interested. She felt if she herself were truly ill, she would not bargain her health against such negligent care.

"I do not come for Mr. Knighton, but for another who resides in the vicinity. Our meetings are necessarily quiet affairs, but Brighton is one place where we can be assured of privacy. And I am quite comfortable here while I await his notice."

Lark considered Miss Hathawae's words while noting there seemed not the slightest note of resentment. The lady appeared quietly consigned to her fate and cheerful about her prospects. One could only wonder about the gentleman who deserved such allegiance. He must be a man of singular compassion, unusual talent or unsurpassing position. Lark glanced up at Miss Hathawae, but the lady's eyes seemed intent on the distant Pavilion.

"I think Mrs. Gunn is impatient for our company," Janet said a little timidly.

Down at the water's edge, Martha Gunn stood, arms akimbo, garbed in something resembling nothing so much as a tent. Its black fabric looked stiff, as years of use in salt water might ensure, and it stood away from her body in a wide triangle. She wore a little black lace cap on her head, providing no protection from the sun, but giving just the hint of gentility. Aside from that, she might have been a laundrywoman.

Lark laughed at the image, thinking the woman's role in dealing with the bathers not much different from that of a servant kneading her linens at the side of a brook. Indeed, the swimmers would be thrust up and down and eventually hung up in the bathing machine to dry. It was an absurd analogy, but not altogether inappropriate.

"You laugh now, my friend, but the woman looks as if she would like to drown us. I never met a more humorless person in my life," Janet said.

"Quite right," Miss Hathawae chimed in. "Old Martha takes her role very seriously, and she will find a way to punish any miscreants."

"However does she continue to find employment?" Lark asked resentfully.

"You cannot imagine there are many out there willing to satisfy a lady's indulgence to swim in the waves. Even though physicians now advocate the advantages of saltwater bathing, there have not been enough dippers to fill the demand. I feel once Brighton is established as the king's residence of choice, acquiring a dipper will be all but impossible," Miss Hathawae explained. "Then what shall we do?"

"Swim by our own strength? Like the gentlemen?" Lark smiled at the thought.

"Whatever do you know of men's bathing, child?"

An hour ago Lark would have thought the dear spinster too modest to entertain improper thoughts, but now she looked at Miss Hathawae with sudden respect. Propriety, it seemed, could be nothing more than a well-polished veneer, masking a host of passions and illicit deeds. Just as Lark was not at all what she seemed, neither, she guessed, was Miss Hathawae.

"Enough to know I should enjoy it very much," Lark said softly.

Miss Hathawae looked down at her. "Then I should advise you to do what I do when faced with such a need to strike out on my own. I swim beyond the reach of Mrs.

Gunn, keeping at a safe distance. When she growls at you, pretend the sound of the lapping waves is too noisy for you to hear her. She will be most displeased, but will do no real harm."

"I will take your advice," Lark said and reached out to squeeze her friend's hand.

"Who have we here, then?" boomed a deep voice ahead of them. The great dark tent loomed very close.

"Good morning, Martha, dear," Miss Hathawae said sweetly. "Surely you have already met Lady Larkspur and her excellent friend Miss Tavish? I encourage them to share a bathing machine, as this is a new experience for both. And the lady will require some help, as she cannot stand."

"No matter here, my lady. In the water, all cripples are like mermaids, free to move about and ride the waves," said Mrs. Gunn as she approached the chair.

"How very poetic of you, Mrs. Gunn. I shall take heart by your recommendation."

Suddenly Lark felt herself lifted into arms almost as powerful as those of Ben Queensman. She wondered if she should think less of the gentleman because of it or respect Mrs. Gunn the more. But there would be time to reflect on such things later, for the woman had already hauled her to the door of the bathing machine and unceremoniously kicked it open. Behind her, revealed by the tapping of her slippers on the pebbly beach, Janet struggled to keep up.

"Will you not join us, Miss Hathawae?" Lark asked over Martha Gunn's burly shoulder.

Miss Hathawae laughed. "You will not invite me so readily once you see the size of the interior. As it is, I do not know how two young women can manage without hitting against one another's elbows and knees. It will be very awkward."

Miss Hathawae's last words were nearly drowned out as Martha Gunn lifted Lark into the bathing machine. At once the air felt cool and a little fetid, for nothing of the fresh sea breezes penetrated the space. Lark quickly took in the sight of two wooden benches at either side of the enclosure and a line of pegs along the wall. A tiny mirror provided the only indulgence, and even that seemed hardly enough to do more than inspect one eye at a time. The glass suddenly went askew when Janet hoisted herself up next to Lark.

"I have our bathing costumes in the bag here," Janet explained. "Good heavens, we cannot change into them in such a place!"

"So Miss Hathawae warned us. But I fear we have no choice, for I believe the horse is already leading us into the sea."

Even in the dim light, Janet's complexion already looked quite green, and she clutched the edges of the narrow bench. "I hope you are appreciative of what I . . ."

"I am. I truly am," Lark said and stood upright. If nothing else, at least the ceiling was reasonably high. "I suppose we must disrobe now, or risk being thrust into the waves with all our finery."

She untied the ribbons of her bonnet and shook out her curls as the hat fell from her head. Though she and Janet knew each other well, she noticed her friend turned away as she slipped the gown off her shoulders and pulled the fabric down to her waist. Her breasts trembled as the machine started to rock slightly in the waves, and, she imagined, they looked fuller than usual. They fell forward as she leaned over to step out of the pile of fabric at her feet, and when she straightened up, she was fully naked. How unaccustomed and glorious a feeling to be in such a state of nature anywhere but in one's own dressing room! And how tempting to dive into the waves without a stitch of encumbrance weighing her down.

Lark's thoughts shocked even herself, but she would neither suppress them nor scold herself. For once in her life she dared to imagine things beyond the high walls of society's rigid mores, and it gave her distinctly unladylike pleasure.

"If you would but put on your bathing costume, I can get to the business of mine," came the voice of common sense. Janet held out the unlovely blue-and-white-striped dress with its attached capelet. Lark eyed it with unexpected resentment. The sleeves would become uncommonly heavy when wet, preventing her from any real movement, and the cloying skirt would tangle between her legs.

"I hate it," she said.

"A fine time to decide as much, my dear, as we have no other choice. You either wear it, or jump into the waves as naked as . . . oh no! Do not even think it!"

Even in the dim interior, Lark saw the flush spread across Janet's face and smiled as she pulled the costume out of her hands. Raising her arms, she wiggled into it and laced up the bodice.

"You cannot think I would do anything to endanger my one opportunity for freedom. Of course I shall wear it, as cumbersome as it is. I should not want to shock Martha Gunn into retirement."

"Indeed, you would earn the wrath of a good many ladies if you did," said Janet. She stood up and quickly started to change into her own costume. Lark tried to give her the same degree of privacy she had enjoyed a few moments before.

But Martha Gunn proved not nearly so gracious. The bathing machine came to a sudden halt, although it continued to rock back and forth, and a great deal of splashing could be heard outside. The door, meeting some resistance from the waves, was thrust open, and the woman's head appeared.

"Here we go, dearies. You needn't fret. Old Martha's never lost a lady. Nor a horse." Behind her back a large hoop appeared, and as Lark came to the top step of the bathing machine, she saw the hoop was attached to a lengthy handle and heavy twine. It looked like an instrument of torture, of the sort displayed in the Tower.

However, refusing the use of the device would undoubtedly gain her return to dry land, and that should make no one happy, least of all herself.

Lark stepped out onto the top step and felt the water swirl around her bare ankles. Martha Gunn dropped the hoop over her shoulders until it rested against her waist, and started to pull her out into the sea. Unresisting, soothed by the waves and the scent of salt water, Lark allowed herself to be drawn away.

The sensation was divine. She felt the water saturate her costume and tickle every part of her body, and she spread her arms in complete surrender. She opened her eyes to the vast sky and marveled at its exquisite blueness. Though she recalled another spot in nature to rival its color, she preferred not to think of Mr. Queensman's eyes just now and quickly put away the thought. To imagine him would tempt her to look up at the hospital, and she would not wish to see him standing on the stone terrace enjoying the show.

"It is not at all like Margate," Janet said as Mrs. Gunn thrust her into place. "It is so much less civilized."

"Indeed," Lark answered. She did not need to know exactly what Janet meant, for she felt something of the same herself. "We might as well be off the shore in America."

Janet did not laugh, as Lark expected. Instead she seemed intent on something, as if trying to decipher a riddle.

"I wonder: Do you think Colonel Wayland really participated in the American campaign?"

Lark, startled, turned to her friend. "He tells us he did. He certainly speaks of it often enough. Why should we doubt it?"

"It is not so much for us to doubt him as to wonder why Mr. Warren and Mr. Queensman apparently do. Did you not notice how Mr. Queensman disputed his placement of every map piece and questioned him about others? I do not think the colonel answered a single question without evasion."

"Now that you mention it, I see your point. I merely attributed it to Mr. Queensman's perfect disagreeableness."

Janet smiled knowingly. "I see through your dislike, Lark, as readily as you see through his. You surely do not continue to despise the man. I know you too well."

Lark looked away, fussing with the ribbon on her bodice. If her friend knew her that well and could read her thoughts, Lark should drag her out of the water and return her on the next stage to London. But Lark could not, for reasons nearly as selfish. If Janet suspected anything of the growing attachment between her friend and Mr. Queensman, she would be the only person who might provide some measure of comfort.

"It appears as if you do, dear friend," Lark answered, though she did not look up. "Perhaps you know me better than I know myself."

"I doubt it. Are you not ever admired for your keen insight into the human character? Surely your own is not exempt."

Lark abandoned her twisted, wet ribbon. "And yet it appears that it is. How came I to forget myself when I accepted . . . ah . . . friendship from this man? He is commissioned to unmask me, to deliver me into circumstances both humiliating and hurtful. He witnessed the disastrous end to one betrothal and promotes another equally doomed. He has seen through my frailties and undoubtedly has closely examined an embarrassing amount of others. No good can come of my knowing him, and yet—stupidly— I only want to know him better."

Janet cupped her hands and filled them with the salty blue sea. She closed her eyes as she splashed her face and then licked her lips with satisfaction. Though tempted to do the same, Lark only glared at her, wondering why her heated confession met with such casual indifference.

"Well? Do you not agree with me?" she asked. She attempted to stamp her foot, but nearly lost her footing on the pebbles beneath them.

Janet smiled, her damp face glistening in the sunshine. "Your indictments against the man are heavy indeed. One might think him the worst of men, a happy conspirator against you. But do you not think your argument is inconsistent?"

Lark sighed. "I already told you it is. He cannot both repel and attract me at the same time—"

"I am not thinking of your feelings, but of his, Lark. If he is the agent of your downfall, why does he not return you to the waiting arms of Lord Raeborn?"

It was, of course, the question Lark had asked herself a hundred times. And, for the first time, she dared to think she knew the reason why. But she could scarcely admit it to herself, let alone say it aloud.

"He will not let you go, Lark." Janet answered her own question. "It is both as simple and as complicated as that. Once he pronounces you well, you are lost to him. He shall be invited to your marriage to his cousin and will dutifully send you a crystal vase. When your first child is born, he shall advise you on matters of the measles and daily regimens of exercise."

"What if no child is born?" Lark said hopefully. She thought she should like to be a mother, but if it meant sharing a bed with Raeborn, she would sacrifice this wish along with all the others. "Mr. Queensman would not be so very unhappy, for it would mean he would be Lord Raeborn himself someday."

"Did you ever meet a man more indifferent to such lofty expectations? He does not even use his professional title in an introduction."

"Do you think him modest?"

"No," Janet countered readily. "Do you?"

A modest man would not have accosted her on the terrace and assaulted every bit of her mind and body. Nor would he have dared to hold her close to his heart as he carried her about the hospital of which he was so proud. Lark smiled, remembering the day, and their delightful interview with the two aging retainers.

"Well, you were never as sweet or shy as your sisters," Janet observed knowingly. "There are those who think your red hair must have something to do with it. As to that, I cannot say. But I do know I never imagined you would be happy with a husband who was not your match in temperament."

Lark opened her mouth, ready to protest. It was, after all, a bit of a stretch to go from having an acknowledged friendship with a man to considering him as a husband. She scarcely dared to imagine it herself.

But her argument was swallowed in a mouthful of salty water as a wave nearly submerged her. The flash of a white sail not too far away suggested they bobbed in its wake.

"Have a care, dearies!" Martha Gunn called out and tugged on their connecting line.

"Come join me!" another voice sang out. Lark twisted to see Miss Hathawae a little distance away, close enough to lie within the protective arms of the little beach but surely too far out to still be attached to her dipper. Her partner, a frowning Lady Crawford, remained close to the bathing machine.

"Let us go," Lark said hurriedly. "We are all wet in any case."

She heard Janet's cry of protest just as she dove out and under the ring that circled her, and into the swelling roar of the sea. Daring to open her eyes, she thought the underwater view surprisingly clear and could plainly see the green pebbles beneath her and Janet's kicking feet. As she arched her back to head for the surface, she marveled at the shafts of sunlight illuminating every bubble of air and drawing tiny sea creatures out of hiding. It seemed a mystical world, one she had not visited since her girlhood days in Margate.

But it was not a world to hold her for long, for she thought her lungs would burst. As she broke the restless surface, she faced seaward and saw the grinning face of Miss Hathawae.

"You naughty girl!" her experienced friend admonished, though her tone seemed all encouragement. "I hope you will not blame me for such misbehavior."

Lark smiled as she approached Miss Hathawae with a few firm strokes and clasped her outstretched hands when she reached her.

"I surely will never blame you for anything, and certainly not for this delightful respite. Whatever choices I make, I take full responsibility for them. Such is my nature," Lark declared, to a chorus of shouts behind her.

"Dear girl. I only hope your instincts serve you well," Miss Hathawae sighed.

Lark thought more might be forthcoming, but Miss Hathawae leaned back into a backstroke and allowed the buoyant waves to set her on her course. Beyond her, at some distance, the sailboat passed them again.

Lark glanced towards the scowling face of Martha Gunn and prayed those instincts would serve her very well indeed. The dipper looked like she would like nothing so much as to drown her recalcitrant charge and surely had the muscular strength to accomplish it. She raised her fist in a gesture of anger, but then, quite unexpectedly, seemed more intent on the men in the sailboat.

Fascinated, Lark turned back to the intruders, but flinched as something whizzed by her face. A bee, surely, or some other insect daring enough to risk its safety as it skimmed the waves. Then another, so close Lark could feel the breeze as it passed her nose. The white sail turned abruptly into the wind and set upon a new course.

Lark began a dive, but caught herself up shortly. Martha

Gunn was still shouting, but her tone took on a new urgency and her hands clutched her forehead. Squinting against the glare, Lark saw something red spreading across her splayed fingers just as the stout woman began to topple, like a felled tree. Janet, caught in the hoop, struggled to release herself.

Lark hesitated no more than a moment before changing her direction and diving for the direction of the bathing machine. She only briefly considered the danger of her own heroics, for she knew she could not live with her guilt if any danger should befall those who were responsible for her safety and whose advice she had decidedly disobeyed. She did not at all consider the probability that what had befallen Martha Gunn had nothing to do with her.

She came to the spot where she had last seen the downed woman and plunged into the sea after her. She did not have to go very far, after all, as her hand immediately fell upon the knot of Mrs. Gunn's grizzled hair. Pulling upon it, Lark then leveraged her arm under the woman's ample breast and thrust her to the surface. Gasping for air, but entirely single-minded in her purpose, Lark fell onto her back, hoisting Martha Gunn's weight against her, and attempted to backstroke to shore.

Several minutes of hard work played out as an eternity as Mrs. Gunn slipped twice from her grip and waves of water washed over their faces and into their mouths. Lark gagged on the salt and on another taste, most surely that of blood.

But then firm hands gripped her shoulders and relieved her of her burden. Miss Hathawae's dipper and Janet acted in unison as they pulled Mrs. Gunn to the steps of the waiting bathing machine. Lady Crawford, usually incapable of doing so much as adding sugar to her chocolate, held tightly onto the reins of the horse and barked her orders to the other two women.

Lark stood, both astonished and relieved, in breast-deep water and took painful breaths of fresh air as the enormity of their danger finally struck her. Shocked and suddenly bereft, she started to tremble as great sobs racked her body and threatened to topple her anew into the ceaselessly churning waves.

Suddenly she was caught again from behind and pulled

against something hard and solid. Strong arms held her just as she had held Martha Gunn only moments before, but she was nether indifferent nor unconscious to the hands of her protector. She allowed him to turn her half towards him and found a safe haven in the circle of his shoulder.

"Should you not attend to Martha Gunn?" she asked against his neck. "She is injured, though I do not understand how or why."

"I know the how of it, and I suspect the why, but that is a discussion for another day, my lady. Matthew is with her just now, so you are my only care."

Lark pulled away from Mr. Queensman and looked suspiciously at his body. Indeed, he would have been properly dressed if he were but dry, but the water made his trousers and linen shirt all but nonexistent. She could feel every muscle of his chest with her hand and other parts of his anatomy against her own wet skirts. Plastered against his head, his dark hair glistened in the sun.

"And yet there is no reason for me to be in your care at all. I am quite unharmed and perfectly capable of returning to shore unassisted." She chose not to allude to her recent moment of weakness, and neither did he.

"Indeed, I know it as well as you, Lady Larkspur. But did your adventure so much distract you that you do not recall no one else is aware of the fact? If you manage to walk out onto the beach unassisted, you will attract as much notice as a mermaid. And astonish them all."

Surely the excitement of the moment completely distracted her senses, for she thought she would enjoy it immensely. She smiled, wondering what great credit the invisible Mr. Knighton would demand when the success of his cure would be published and how she could not dispute it. Mr. Queensman, reading the open book of her face, gently touched her chin, and raised her face to his.

"Do not even think it, Lark."

She blinked, blinded by the sun and the brilliance of his eyes.

"I have feared the great moment would belong to you, Mr. Queensman, when you would expose me for all to see. Do not deny you have thought of doing so, even from the beginning of our acquaintance, and have taunted me with your knowledge. Why do you not choose this moment your-self and amaze the whole beach with your cleverness?"

"I would not steal anyone's praise, for surely everyone awaits us to applaud you as the day's heroine."

"Your honor is inviolate, it would seem."

"I prefer to leave a discussion of my honor out of this."

A wave pushed her forward, and she once again found a stronghold on Mr. Queensman's warm body. He bent slightly and scooped her up.

"And why is that, sir?" Lark asked huskily.

"I have other things on my mind at the moment. And none of them are particularly honorable."

"Please tell me what they are, Ben." Lark closed her eyes, wanting nothing so much as to hear his confession, his admission that he wanted her as much as she wanted him, his protestations of love. She opened her lips, ever so slightly, and waited for what must surely come.

"There is an intent of evil here," he said.

Lark's eyes opened at once. "You recognized the men in the sailboat?"

He nodded briefly.

"Martha Gunn has been struck down, and any one of the rest of you might have been injured. Someone hoped to do mischief—or worse—and it would greatly satisfy my curiosity to know the reason for it."

"Why does it matter?" Lark asked bluntly. "The stone whizzed just under my nose, and yet I am not half so inter-ested as you in the matter."

He looked down at her, and his expression softened. He raised one dripping finger to trifle with the tip of her nose.

"Perhaps I am feeling proprietary."

Lark squirmed to free herself. "Though you regrettably exercise some power over me, no part of my body belongs to you, sir!"

"A pity," he said, angering her more. "But I was speak-ing of my hospital and beach, not of your beautiful self."

"And yet neither seems in any danger. Nor, come to think on it, do I. You may release me, sir. I shall make my own way to the beach, even if I have to crawl all the way to get there."

"My dear lady. I ran through bramble and over rocks to

reach you. I abandoned a perfectly good worsted jacket and new cravat on the wet sand and have ruined my favorite pair of boots in the water. I have also been standing here clutching your immodestly dressed person, compromising my integrity as a physician and yours as a respectable lady. At least allow me the privilege of rescuing you so I might make some attempt to redeem myself."

"I do not need rescuing."

"I did not say you did. I said only I needed to rescue you."

"You are utterly selfish, sir, and completely self-serving."

"Perhaps I am. But I should think a lady who has managed to deceive her whole family and a very concerned fiancé ought to consider such remarks carefully."

During the course of this nasty interview, Mr. Queensman managed to make a good deal of progress towards shore. Over her shoulder, Lark heard the excited cries of those already on land and knew she wished to say a good deal to this arrogant man, but did not have the time to do so.

"I have done nothing but consider my actions in recent days, sir. In fact, I am of a good mind to give myself up to Lord Raeborn, if for no other reason than to thwart you in your lofty expectations."

Amazingly, Mr. Queensman broke into gleeful laughter, and his body shook with it.

"Excellent idea, my darling! Your timing is fortuitous. When Raeborn arrives, in two or three days' time, I shall hand you over myself."

Lark struggled again. "It is not your place to do so," she retorted angrily. "When I accept the man I shall marry, I shall walk directly into his arms."

As other hands caught her from behind and wrapped her in warm, dry blankets, Mr. Queensman managed to get in the final word, for she thought she heard him say, "Then I hope for his sake it is not Raeborn, for you will surely knock him over."

Chapter Ten

Lord Raeborn put down his empty sherry glass and reached for the half-filled bottle before Ben could serve him. With a shaking hand, the elderly man poured out his portion and then settled back into his comfortable chair, apparently intent upon the draperies.

"I had no idea the family was so comfortably settled here at Seagate," he admitted. "When my cousin—your worthy father—abandoned life in London to take up with his little missy here at Brighton, we thought him making a considerable sacrifice in the name of love."

"Do remember you are speaking of my mother, my lord. And my maternal grandfather was the Earl of Doverfield, a considerable landowner in these parts. The lands and house you see here were given to my parents as a wedding gift, and my father spent the rest of his life improving upon it."

"There now, I meant no offense, boy. But you must see how unfavorably Brighton compares to London."

"I am afraid I do not, my lord. Nor, I believe, does our king."

"Ah, yes. I am invited to the Royal Pavilion this week, did you know? The king requests your presence as well."

Ben put his glass down on the mantelpiece, though he had hardly touched the drink at all.

"Did he ask for me specifically, my lord?"

Lord Raeborn looked confused. "I am not at all certain. Just said to bring my young cousin, or something of the sort. He cannot know you, can he?"

"Only slightly," Ben said. He usually was very discreet about his relationship with those at the Pavilion, a preference the king shared. "Perhaps he meant your lady."

Raeborn laughed. "Indeed, we are somewhat related on her mother's side, though I am not certain of the particulars. But I am sure he meant you."

"Very well, my lord. We will wait upon his word."

Raeborn grunted his assent and finished what remained in his glass. As Ben came forward with the bottle, his elderly cousin waved him off.

"Enough. I have drunk too full of it already, and we have much to discuss."

Ben felt a dull, aching pain in his breast, as if the weight of a hundred bricks rested upon him.

"Indeed. I know you have not journeyed all this way for the sole purpose of admiring my properties."

"And yet it does me well to see them, my boy! I feared you had not already married because you did not possess enough to tempt a good woman. I am happy to see you so settled."

Ben felt the gentle slap of his cousin's reproof.

"I am very busy with my work at the hospital, my lord. If I have not married, it may be because I have not tried very hard to find someone."

"Then I am right to worry about you. I would caution you not to make the same mistakes as I have. Dallying about while all the prime maids are sacrificing themselves to other men and stocking their nurseries."

Ben did not like to think of beautiful, spirited Lark in such a mercenary role, though for the last few days he felt she deserved some sort of lesson. But marriage to Raeborn ought not be it.

"I have hardly been dallying, what with all my endeavors at the hospital. And I should not wish any lady to sacrifice herself for nothing more than the perpetuation of the family name."

Raeborn said nothing for so long that Ben thought he might have fallen asleep. Or worse. But he suddenly looked up and studied Ben, allowing him to glimpse a weariness and longing.

"I would have liked a son," Raeborn surprised him by saying.

"I think it is the fondest wish of every man."

"If I had a son, I fancy he would have been very much like yourself."

"I am honored you think so, my lord. The newness of our relationship would ordinarily preclude such a judgment."

"And yet everything I now know about you is very encouraging. I am somewhat worried about your unmarried state, to be sure. But if you succeed in improving upon that situation anytime soon, I should be very proud and satisfied to have you as my heir."

Ben coughed down his sherry. Surely Raeborn had not come to Seagate to discuss his expectations, slender as they were. The woman Raeborn intended to marry sat not three miles off, waiting to know her fate.

"My lord, is it not your intention to marry Lady Larkspur and produce an heir of much closer relationship than I? I am flattered you consider me in such a light, but I truly own no designs upon your title or properties."

Raeborn gave a snorting sound and shot Ben a look of pure disbelief.

"You may believe me, my lord," Ben said quietly.

"If I do, it is only because you have not been brought up in town. Such sentiments there are rare, and never believed," Raeborn pronounced and tapped his head. "But you are right to wonder as to my intentions regarding the lady. I hope, by the way, she still lives?"

If Ben ever doubted his cousin's affections towards Lark, he knew he now understood the situation as well as she.

"She not only lives, but is being hailed as a heroine in local circles. Not three days ago she saved the life of Martha Gunn, the famous dipper. She risked her own life to do so."

"Then she is well . . . and healthy?"

Ben knew he stood at the edge of a precipice. Nothing ailed the beautiful lady but a waspish tongue and a willful disposition. But to pronounce her well would be to condemn her to a loveless marriage to a man who would barely begin to understand her. Her spirit would be stifled, her soul burdened.

And he could not bear to be the agent of her unhappiness, for to do so would be to bring the same punishment upon himself. He loved her, more than he had ever loved anyone or anything in his entire life.

"She is not, my lord," he lied. "She may display a burst of uncommon energy and always has her wits about her, but she does not leave her chair. I have accompanied her on several outings and have had to carry her about."

Raeborn looked him up and down, and Ben wondered if he had already revealed too much.

"Have you, indeed? Even a tallish thing like the chit should pose no burden for a great strapping lad like yourself. But is my lady comfortable with the arrangement?"

Ben put a hand up to his neck and loosened his cravat.

"She is uncomfortable with her frailty, my lord. Nothing more. She is indifferent to me as anything but an attending physician."

"I see. Then perhaps I shall take her as she is."

Ben's hand froze in midair. "Is that not contrary to your hopes and expectations? Or have I misunderstood your feelings in that regard?"

"You misunderstood nothing, my boy. But I have had a considerable change of heart in recent weeks. I realize I am satisfied in naming you as my heir and am not entirely happy with the notion of a tiny Raeborn bawling at all hours of the night and getting underfoot. And if I might mention a subject to you entirely in your medical capacity, I am not at all sure I retain the . . . ah . . . energy to beget an heir."

Ben cleared his throat. "If such is the case, why is Lady Larkspur's health of importance to you, my lord? If you set her aside now, no one will think ill of you for doing so. And the lady will bear her disappointment as she must."

Raeborn nodded thoughtfully. "Yes, I suppose it would break her heart. After all, recall her agony when that Moore fellow abandoned her. I could not be so indifferent to a lady's feelings."

"You are very honorable, my lord."

"Of course. But I am not without vanity. Therefore, I have decided I would very much like a wife to mourn me after I am gone, to see to the appropriate pomp at my funeral. Though you are a good boy, I cannot expect you to remain in gloom when you have just come into a title and a fortune. Most men would consider it the happiest day of their lives."

Ben waited to hear more, some explanation of what all this meant. But Raeborn settled back again, obviously satisfied that all was clear.

"I am sorry, my lord. I am not certain I understand."

"Has the sherry gone to your head? I hope you do not drink before a surgery or examination! There is nothing so complicated about it: I wish for a wife to provide comfort for me in my old age and after I am gone. I am quite settled on you as my heir and care not if my lady provides one." Raeborn emphasized each point with a slap on the arm of his chair. Outside, in the hall, footsteps passed at the door; surely the housekeeper thought the furniture was being dismantled.

"You reveal a very practical nature, my lord. You wish for a lady who will be as excellent a widow as she would be a wife," Ben said thoughtfully. "Then why, under such circumstances, do you remain fixed on Lady Larkspur? Surely another lady—possibly even an older lady—would do as well."

Raeborn waved his hand dismissively. "Perhaps as well, but not nearly so convenient. I already have Lady Larkspur in hand, and she suits me. She is of excellent family and amuses me. You may not have noticed her form or features, but she owns a stirring sort of beauty."

"I have noticed, my lord."

"I am glad to learn you are not entirely absorbed in your books and work. Therefore, you can appreciate my next concern. When you are head of the family, I should like for you to guide her. She will be attractive to fortune hunters, and may wish to remarry. You must convince her of the sacred responsibilities of widowhood."

Ben raised a questioning brow.

"Is that not your job, my lord?"

"As her husband, my job is to make her happy. As my heir, your job is to make sure she is not."

Ben studied the carpet, not wanting his cousin to see his smile. If his job was only to make Lark unhappy, he should do very well. He had so much practice at the sport already.

"When will I see her?" Raeborn demanded.

"On the morrow. She rises quite early to study the scenery and should be ready to receive you by late morning."

Lark put down her twice-read letter from Del and gazed out towards the stormy sea. A strong wind had blown up in the late hours of the evening, bringing a good deal of rain with it and playing havoc with the furnishings at Knighton's.

It seemed a pretty apt reflection of her own feelings, and though she searched through her sister's letter to find some scrap of sunlight to alleviate the darkness of her mood, there was little save her family's concern about her uncertain health. She was a fool to perpetuate this myth and cause them such dismay when there was every reason for the Leicesters to otherwise rejoice. In other letters, she heard that Del was in excellent health, and Rose and Columbine thought they might be increasing as well. Lily expected to travel to Rome in the fall, and their mother hoped to have her paintings exhibited at the Royal Academy. Her father sought to purchase an estate in Scotland and intended to fish a good deal. They all seemed very settled.

But Lark was as tempest-tossed as the sea. In the morning, when she would have preferred to see Matthew Warren and Benedict Queensman taking their daily swim, she saw instead workmen pulling the bathing machines up onto higher ground and folding up their bright-colored hoods. The machines, only days before promising unfettered freedom in the sea, now seemed a sad reminder of the injury done to Martha Gunn. She would recover, they all were reassured by Mr. Queensman, for the bullet had delivered only a glancing blow.

But why there should have been a bullet fired, or for whom it was intended, was never answered. Lark recalled the small sailboat on the waves that moved past them at least twice. And she thought of the remarkable coincidence that Matthew Warren and Ben Queensman happened to be nearby when they should have been with their patients. What were they doing on the beach?

Lark shifted restlessly in her seat and told herself it was only because she was bored and shuttered in for the day that such things bothered her so. It was not because she had sent Janet off to visit Matthew Warren at the hospital. And surely it was not because her rescuer had neglected, even with four days' time, to send over so much as a note to inquire after her health.

Rather, she felt anxious and edgy because she knew Lord Raeborn had already arrived in Brighton and had been closeted away with his cousin all the while. If only she had not left off so badly with Mr. Queensman or had had the discretion to remain fixed in her guise as an ailing patient. But she now understood, belatedly, how she had trusted him with too much and how such trust was likely to be abused. His loyalty to Raeborn was familial—and might even have been bought—and he had undoubtedly already exposed her for the hopeless fraud she was.

"What time do you expect the gentlemen?" Miss Hathawae's soft voice was comforting and warm.

"I know not, Miss Hathawae. But I am growing ill in anticipation."

"There now, you need not fret. I remember Raeborn well, as we traveled in the same circles. He is a good man and a kind one. His young cousin has something of the look of him, with his dark hair and blue eyes. I remember when all the girls would swoon in his company."

Lark tried to keep her lips straight. "It sounds as if you may not have seen the gentleman in some years. Time has taken some toll, and you may not recognize him."

Miss Hathawae smiled. "I may not look the same as I did forty years ago either, but I surely will recognize him. As he will me."

"Let us hope your reunion is joyous, dear Miss Hathawae."

The good woman's smile promptly faded, but the glint in her eyes remained. When she answered, it was to do so quietly, so no one else could hear. "Indeed, I have the impression I am a good deal more happy to see him than you are yourself, my dear. Is it possible the company of your fiancé will not give you pleasure?"

"No, it is not possible, Miss Hathawae," Lark began, with an effort at indignation. But it sounded frail, even to herself. "I am honored Lord Raeborn found the time to wait on me here in Brighton. It is so far out of his accustomed circle."

"But his circle necessarily must be wherever you are, Lady Larkspur. Your two worlds must meet as one. It is the very definition of love."

Lark said nothing, wondering how this apparently innocent speech could weigh so heavily upon her soul. Miss Hathawae seemed to understand her plight better than her own mother and sisters, perhaps even better than Janet. How tempted she felt to confide all to this dear lady, to cry out her confusion, her longing, her absurd hopes. But she bit down upon her lip and said nothing.

"You do love your fiancé, do you not, Lady Larkspur?"

Lark shook her head, trying to hold back tears.

Miss Hathawae tactfully averted her eyes and studied a sapphire ring upon her third finger.

"And yet you show the unmistakable signs of a woman in love. If it is not Raeborn who has put the glint in your eye and the bloom upon your cheek, you are surely about to marry the wrong man."

"I have little choice, Miss Hathawae. My marriage to Raeborn is all arranged, and the man I . . . the other gentleman is entirely inappropriate. It is impossible to marry him."

"Oh, dear. Is he a laborer, perhaps? Or a foreigner? Might he be the king himself?"

Lark giggled and wiped away some of her tears. "Oh, nothing so dreadful as that," she laughed, and was surprised when Miss Hathawae did not join her. "It is only that he does not want me. Indeed, he has endeavored to show me how very much he despises me. He is the last man to wish to marry me."

Miss Hathawae slipped the ring off her finger and studied the elegantly cut stone by candlelight.

"My dear, I believe you are only partially right. He is surely the last man who would dishonor himself and you by advancing an unwelcome suit. But I believe he would desire nothing so much as to be your husband."

"You speak with conviction, Miss Hathawae. Is it possible you enjoy the confidences of the man I will not name?"

"I enjoy only the role of observer. I consider myself quite an expert at it. But I would have to be blind not to see the fire burning between you and Mr.—"

"Hush! I beg you not to speak of it, for it can only give me pain. I am quite resigned to marry Lord Raeborn, and you yourself confirm he is a good man. The rest must come to naught."

"Do not allow yourself to be sacrificed in such a way, dear girl. I know something of it myself, for I have endured a lifetime of deprivation in the name of honor. But there is a great difference in your situation and my own: The man I once loved, the father of my only child, could not marry me under any circumstances. I know the definition of impossible, and your situation could not be so wretched. I pray you will not allow it to become so."

"I beg your forgiveness, Miss Hathawae, for I did not know—"

"No one knows but he and I. I did not speak so forthrightly to beg your sympathies. I would only have you saved from heartache and forever yearning for what your pride prevented you from having."

"Just now, my pride is even more bruised than my heart," Lark confessed.

Miss Hathawae stood back and appraised her, as if she were an artist coping with a difficult subject.

"It looks perfectly healthy to me, Lady Larkspur. In fact, you look—" Her voice broke off and she looked over Lark's head to the door beyond them. "How would you say Lady Larkspur looked, Colonel Wayland?"

Lark sighed at the approach of the heavy footsteps. The bubble of confidences broke, and the moment of intimacy was lost. When the man spoke, Lark felt the weight of his pomposity was even more apparent than usual.

"She looks entirely too robust to remain an invalid. Her heroism in the cold sea, while distinctly unladylike, was something I have not seen since my days in America. There, Indian women work the fields, carrying one or two children on their backs, and manage it without complaint. Add this to their daily cooking and organizing the camp, and you have a fairly good view of their hardships."

"And I should only desire to walk again, Colonel," Lark said dryly.

"A modest expectation, but a good one. In America I once—"

"Do you know any news of Martha Gunn, Colonel Wayland?" Miss Hathawae interrupted, winking at a grateful Lark.

"Why, I have only just left the woman and am happy to say her recovery will be swift. Mr. Warren has changed her bandage, and there is very little bleeding. Of course, she speaks of nothing but her gratitude to you, Lady Larkspur, for your excellent rescue and suggests you might consider a profession as a dipper yourself."

Miss Hathawae's already rigid back stiffened perceptibly.

"Lady Larkspur is a lady, sir. What Mrs. Gunn suggests is impossible."

"No offense meant, miss. It was said in good fun."

"Lord Raeborn will not find it so funny, sir. And his arrival is expected this very day."

Colonel Wayland gave the illusion of surprise, but Lark could see he somehow knew of Raeborn's presence in town. Well, it could not be very surprising, for Raeborn had been received at Seagate some days before.

Though it was surely irrational, Lark despaired of the fact she had not already been a visitor to Mr. Queensman's estate by the sea. And if Raeborn scooped her up—figuratively, at least—and carried her home to London, she might never see it at all.

"Then we shall have a pleasant little party," the colonel said at last. "My nephew, Gabriel, will be joining me here this afternoon."

Miss Hathawae looked down at Lark and smiled, making Lark wonder if the good woman somehow thought it was Mr. Siddons who captured her heart. The thought made her shudder, though truthfully, she knew no ill of the young man.

"We have missed him here, Colonel, and the cheerful little diversions he brings us."

"He has been in France. He has very important business there, you realize."

Miss Hathawae raised her eyebrows. "You must watch what you say, Colonel. It is not well regarded these days to have either business or friends in France. Of course, your nephew could not possibly be causing any mischief," she said artlessly.

For a moment Colonel Wayland looked panicked and glanced quickly at Lark. It was only an instant, but enough for Lark to wonder at her own connection to this and to begin to share Miss Hathawae's apparent belief that, indeed, Gabriel Siddons was involved in some mischief.

"My nephew is a distinguished negotiator, a man trusted in the highest circles of diplomacy. His many travels to America were all in the name of peace."

"How very noble a profession, Colonel Wayland," Miss Hathawae said sweetly. "But, pray, whose side did he support?"

The poor man opened and closed his mouth several times, and Lark feared he was having an attack of some sort. But Miss Hathawae, whose own mischief clearly prompted this response, had no such concerns. Instead, she raised her brow and smiled knowingly at Lark.

Before the colonel could seize upon a convenient answer, the door behind them opened once again, and a woman cleared her throat.

"Lord Raeborn," came the solemn announcement, as if they sat in a formal drawing room and not the common hall of a sanatorium. "And Mr. Queensman."

Lark knew precisely what she would see if she turned around, and she wished to delay the pleasure as long as possible. Instead, she studied the faces of her two companions.

Miss Hathawae sighed and smiled as if her face endured great strain to do so. Her bright eyes darted from one man to the other, and by the look in them Lark guessed where Lord Raeborn stood in relation to Mr. Queensman.

Colonel Wayland also studied the two men, and his smile of greeting seemed equally strained. If Lark had to guess, she might have said just the slightest bit of fear cast a shadow across his features. But she could not guess why it might be so.

"My dearest lady, my own love. I have endured much anxiety while worrying about your condition," exclaimed the wavery, refined voice above her.

Lark pressed her eyes closed and held her breath, and then looked up to face the inevitable. But she miscalculated, and instead of gazing into the eyes of her fiancé, she confronted Benedict Queensman. He seemed somewhat chastened and utterly serious, and looked as dispassionate as he had when he first came to her in her father's home, obliged to do a job somewhat distasteful to him. But they had shared much since that day, and Lark felt she knew him a thousand times better. Which was why his expression pained her so much; she knew what he was about to do and why he would do it. Miss Hathawae's well-meaning advice could only prove false currency in circumstances such as this.

"I . . . I bring you your cousin and mine, Lady Larkspur," Ben Queensman said quietly. Something flickered in his blue eyes. "Though he has been very anxious to see you, there were matters of business we needed to discuss at Seagate, where Lord Raeborn has been my guest."

"Enough, boy!" interrupted an impatient voice. "A lady knows nothing of business and certainly could care little about our arrangements."

"Even if it concerns her, my lord?" Ben Queensman asked somewhat aggressively.

"What concerns my lady is of no concern to you. That is, until after I am dead," came the rejoinder. Suddenly small hands were on the arms of Lark's wheeled chair, abruptly turning its direction. "And I will greet my lady properly."

Lark finally looked directly at Raeborn, wondering if he meant he would kiss her. But, oddly enough, he stepped back when he saw her, as if he expected someone else. Had she changed so very much since her carefree days in London?

"My lord," she said politely and bowed her head slightly. "I am appreciative of the honor you do me."

"It was not an easy trip. My stomach was not as it should be, and we stopped at every posting house," Raeborn reported, as if his bodily functions were of paramount concern to her. Well, perhaps they ought to be.

"You must remember to eat in small quantities, my lord. Did I not mention it in London?" Mr. Queensman said sternly, in the voice of Raeborn's doctor.

"I am not about to start to change my habits just now, my boy, whatever you say." Raeborn patted his stomach contentedly. He looked around the small circle, and his expression changed to one of unexpected pleasure. "I declare, it cannot be Betsey Hathawae, now can it?"

"Of course, Lord Raeborn. I told Lady Larkspur we were old acquaintances."

"But you did not tell her we were . . ." Lord Raeborn paused, looking acutely uncomfortable.

"Lovers?" Miss Hathawae supplied. "And that you wanted to marry me? I did not, though surely there is no harm in it. Lady Larkspur is too wise to fear a rival of over thirty years ago."

"Indeed. It is nothing to a rival of the present. Especially if one is a young man vying against rank and wealth," Raeborn said.

Lark felt the warmth leave her face and dared not look at Mr. Queensman. What had he said to his older cousin when they were closeted at Seagate? He could not have been so indiscreet as to confess to a certain interest in the young lady entrusted to his professional care. As her heart started to beat erratically, Lark knew a flush began to spread across her features, and she looked to Miss Hathawae for guidance.

But Miss Hathawae just smiled beguilingly, looking ever so much younger than her years.

Mr. Queensman cleared his throat. "Would you not like to accompany me to the game room, Miss Hathawae? I understand you are remarkably proficient at billiards."

The lady laughed out loud. "I must not admit it in the presence of a gentleman. Lord Raeborn will think very ill of me, I am sure."

"That, my dear, is quite impossible," Raeborn said graciously. "But I would like very much for you to teach my young cousin a lesson. He is altogether too complacent about his talents."

"So he should be, Benedict. He has the trust of the—"

"Let us away, Miss Hathawae," Mr. Queensman said hurriedly. "I am sure Lord Raeborn would like the luxury of a private interview with his beloved."

Raeborn rubbed his hands in satisfaction as the two departed and he did not speak until their footsteps could no longer be heard along the polished floors of the corridor.

"My dear," he began, "I must first inquire after your health."

Lark had rehearsed her answer many times over, for although she challenged Mr. Queensman's authority at every turn and would have liked to take the wind right out of his sail of disclosure, she still could not bear the thought of returning to London on the arm of her aged suitor.

"It remains faulty, my lord," she said in a whisper. "I am still quite weak and unable to leave my chair."

He did not seem so very disappointed.

"And yet all the town is singing your praises. I understand you have acted bravely and altogether worthy of the Raeborn name."

"But I am not a Raeborn, my lord. Am I not able to still give credit to the Leicester name? Surely it is as worthy."

"It is an excellent name, or else I would not have thought to align myself with it."

"Do you prefer the name to the person?"

Lord Raeborn looked stupefied.

"I cannot understand why else you would wish to marry me," Lark went on. "You know me not at all."

"I know you as well as I wish," Raeborn said gruffly. "It is not for you to question it."

"I have been jilted by other men. Do you suppose they had a reason for it?" And before he could answer, "I am known for my willfulness and temper."

Raeborn seemed to consider this, though not nearly long enough.

"You will learn to do as I say when you are my wife."

"Do you propose to beat me, or starve me? It would not serve you very well, my lord. An unhealthy woman is likely to have unhealthy children." Lark nearly choked on the words, but Raeborn looked apoplectic.

He grasped the edge of a table and bowed forward, as if recoiling from a blow. What remained of his thinning hair fell forward and dangled before Lark's eyes like string edging a shawl. She knew then she had gone too far, but she could not help but wonder if too far was yet far enough.

"My lord?" she asked, more gently.

Raeborn looked up at her, his face very close to her own. Lark expected to see anger, frustration, and even cruelty. Instead, she was surprised to see something resembling sadness.

"You do me wrong, Lady Larkspur. I am no villain in this piece, only a gentleman who seeks to make up for what I could not achieve in my life. I would have you honorably and would treat you fairly. Those who know me know no wickedness in me, nor can they discredit me in any way. You have painted a very black picture of me, and perhaps of yourself as well. By all reports, you would make a very desirable wife."

Lark swallowed and looked away, unable to meet his eyes. Perhaps she had wronged him, in all her indignation and desperation to avoid her arranged marriage. Indeed, her own dear father was as much an accomplice against her as the man who made a respectful and even chivalrous offer. She realized that she resented Raeborn purely for what he was, rather than for who he was.

And he apparently was no more than a lonely, somewhat dissipated old man who hoped to make one more bid for immortality.

Lark was chastened, and momentarily regretful, but caught herself before her better nature could entirely overwhelm her stern resolve. Raeborn might be a decent old soul, but that did not make him qualitatively more desirable as a husband. She did not love him, or desire him.

And in her moment of new insight and understanding, she also realized she had not even understood what those two words meant until she came to know Benedict Queensman.

"I cannot do as you wish, my lord. I am not well enough to marry."

"You were well enough to pull Martha Gunn from the water and dare a rescue of which many men could not prove capable."

"Reports have surely been exaggerated. I did hardly anything. Miss Hathawae and Miss Tavish were as much involved."

"But I do not wish to marry Miss Hathawae and Miss Tavish."

Lark said nothing, reflecting on the brief but bold reunion between the former lovers. They had been startlingly frank, and yet something remained elusive. She could not help but wonder what it might be.

"I wish to marry you, Lady Larkspur."

"I am not well enough to marry," Lark repeated, emphasizing each word.

Lord Raeborn settled back in his chair, with a smile of great satisfaction upon his face. Lark felt a moment of distress, unable to pinpoint what she had said to make him so happy.

"Perhaps you did not understand me, my lord," she began.

"My dear, darling child. I understand you well enough," Raeborn said and rubbed his hands together. "If the state of your health remains your only objection to this marriage, the decision is entirely out of your hands."

Lark bit down on her lip, remembering that the decision never was in her hands. Indeed, she would not have had to revert to such a deception if she had ever been given any power to determine the course of her own life.

"I am not sure I understand, my lord."

"It is no complicated affair, my girl. You tell me you are not well, and I am no expert to understand it one way or another. Therefore, we both must defer to my young cousin." Raeborn looked over her shoulder at the open door and the sound of approaching footsteps. "Let Benedict Queensman be the judge."

Lark swallowed, and tasted the blood of her cut lip.

Chapter Eleven

"*Y*ou have allowed me to best you this day, Mr. Queensman," Miss Hathawae said knowingly as she put down a cue nearly as tall as herself. "Are you not aware every lady is sent out into the world with the admonition to defer to gentlemen in all games of skill? I shall surely be reviled by all if it is ever known I proved myself a worthy adversary for you at a gentleman's game."

Ben laughed as he replaced the balls in their rack. "I daresay your reputation is strong enough to withstand such criticism, Miss Hathawae. And in any case, I have the feeling it would not be nearly as troublesome to you as you make out." He paused, thinking of his own talents for a moment and realizing how strongly they had been compromised by his distraction over Lord Raeborn and Lady Larkspur. It would not be fair to say he had allowed Miss Hathawae to win, but neither did he put up a very strong fight. "And, in any case, would it not be my own reputation suffering if word of this match ever came out? There are those who would be amused to learn I could not prove myself more skilled than a smallish woman of questionable health. I daresay I would be considered unmanly."

"Dear Mr. Queensman," Miss Hathawae began and slipped her slim arm through his elbow, "the consequences of a game of billiards could not possibly matter to you or me or anyone else. You would be considered unmanly only if you let something of great value or importance to you slip from your fingers. What was then lost could not be easily replaced, and the deprivation could plague you for the rest of your life."

Ben glanced down at the small woman at his side and wondered what she knew of his tumultuous passions and desires. He did not think Lark would be so indiscreet as to compromise her own schemes, nor so innocent that she would discuss certain intimate events with a near stranger. And yet, of what else might Miss Hathawae be speaking?

He put his hand over hers as he led her from the room, taking comfort in her warmth. She was right to challenge his strength, for he had never felt so indecisive in his life as he did this moment. He would have liked nothing better than to prolong their return to the large social hall, or to avoid it altogether. For, like a desperate commander in he midst of battle, he knew he could not win, whatever his action.

If he pronounced Lark well, her anxious suitor would have her away from Brighton before the sun would rise again. If he pronounced her ill, the result would be very much the same, though Raeborn would exercise more caution in the moving of his beloved back to London. Then Ben might continue to see Lark, though never dare touch her again and be driven mad with wanting her. For Raeborn would have her, either way.

If he pronounced Lark well even as she remained in her chair, Raeborn would come to understand how she had deceived him and how she would have continued to do so if her masquerade had not been uncovered. And if he pronounced her ill, and her ruse was later discovered, his own integrity as a doctor would be severely compromised. And Raeborn, who had already confessed his admiration and plans for Ben's future, would abandon all confidence in him.

"You are very quiet, Mr. Queensman. Are you considering my words?"

"Indeed I am, Miss Hathawae." Ben did not quite lie. "I daresay you are speaking of my hospital. It has been the most important thing in my life for many years."

Miss Hathawae waved her hand dismissively.

"It is a very noble endeavor. You will ever be admired for the good work you do there. But I do not believe you are in any danger of losing it. In that regard, I was thinking of something else. Someone else."

They continued down the long hallway, their footsteps echoing eerily in the silence.

"She does love you, you know."

"I do not know," he said firmly. "Nor does it provide any comfort to hear you say it, even if it were true. I will not take what is not mine, no matter how desirable such a thing is. It is purely a matter of self-respect."

"I do not see it purely a matter of anything, sir. The important things in life rarely are." Miss Hathawae slapped his arm, like a demanding governess. "And I would not be so quick to dismiss the lady's affections. Remember, she is as much caught in a spider's web as you."

"But it is not of the spider's making. In truth, it is the lady herself who has designed her own trap. If not for her cursed cleverness, she would not have required the services of a physician, nor would she have been in Brighton to weave him into her plan."

Miss Hathawae drew back slightly. "Now you are most certainly being unmanly, sir. Need I remind you that the spider's web is made only of gossamer? You are quite free to pull out whenever you wish. The lady cannot hold you unless you wish to be held."

And, as they walked through the double door into the large hall, Ben realized Miss Hathawae was perfectly right.

Lark looked up as soon as she heard the pair of footsteps at the door, anxious for a reprieve from her ardent suitor and even more anxious to know what might be Ben Queensman's pronouncement on the matter of her health. But what she saw disconcerted her.

She knew Mr. Queensman for his arrogance, his superior confidence, his ability to plot a course through uncertain waters. Indeed, she loved him not only in spite of it but perhaps because of it. And yet none of those qualities were evident upon his face when he returned to the room.

He no longer looked like the cool, dispassionate physician who was obliged to examine her in London, nor the dutiful visitor to Knighton's who greeted her close upon her arrival. He scarcely resembled the man who consistently challenged the authority of Colonel Wayland and Gabriel Siddons or who proudly showed off his hospital to his visitors. He did not look like the man who had once held her in a passionate embrace or who had held her steady against the rolling sea.

He looked troubled, uncertain, as if he wrestled with an unhappy truth. Lark knew better than anyone what it might be, and longed for the chance to reach out and touch him and bring the confidence back into his eyes. Indeed, she needed something of it herself.

But before she or anyone else could say anything, the door opened again without ceremony, and Mr. Siddons burst upon them, awakening his dozing uncle by doing so.

"Oh, I am sorry," he said. "I did not realize there was a private party in here. I came only to see my—"

"Come in, come in, my boy. Have you brought your friends with you? The men I met—"

"I did not," Mr. Siddons said, too quickly. "They do not enjoy the same luxuries of time as I."

The colonel chuckled. "No, indeed. No gentlemen they, but the sort who spend their days industriously."

Ben Queensman cleared his throat. "Might I point out there are gentlemen who are rarely idle with their hours?"

"Ah, Queensman, are you already returned? You are correct to point out my error, but I am sure you need not expound upon your virtues in the presence of this young lady. She is already quite set upon you."

The colonel's words had the effect of a bucket of icy water thrown on the company. No one answered, and no one dared to meet another's eyes. After the initial shock, Lark felt the blood returning to her face, but rather too quickly, so she felt herself aflame. She realized if she did not dispute the point, no one else would.

"I am betrothed to Lord Raeborn, sir. If Mr. Queensman, as my physician, pronounces me well enough to marry, we shall only then be related as cousins."

The answer seemed to satisfy almost everyone, but Lark could not bring herself to look up and meet Ben Queensman's eyes. She knew not if he planned to expose her deception, but it appeared that in other matters she had already revealed herself far too plainly. She was foolish to do so and would probably be made to regret it all the rest of her life.

"What have you brought for us, Mr. Siddons?" Miss Hathawae asked softly, and Lark was instantly grateful for the diversion. "If you have not brought your ungentlemanly friends for entertainment, might we hope for some other small pleasure?"

Gabriel Siddons laughed nervously. "Indeed you may, dear lady. But I hope you will not be disappointed to learn it is yet another dissected map. Knowing how difficult the maps of America proved, I decided on one a lot closer to home. It is a map of the coastline, from Winchelsea to Brighton."

"I believe you already once picked Winchelsea as your subject, Siddons," Ben Queensman said. "I remarked on it as an odd choice, since so few people are familiar with it."

"And yet, the king himself will embark from there to arrive in Brighton on the morrow. It is why I thought this dissected map an excellent choice, so the ladies and my uncle could visualize the route he sails."

"How very clever of you," Ben Queensman said dryly. Lark wondered if he was still smarting from Colonel Wayland's thoughtless comment about his ungentlemanly labors. "And are you quite sure the king travels by sea?"

The tension between the two men was palpable. Lark had never understood the animosity between them, though she had once flattered herself into believing it might have something to do with her. She finally appreciated her own foolishness in that regard, as ill conceived as her determination to avoid an arranged marriage to Lord Raeborn. For it was perfectly clear that whatever made Ben Queensman and Gabriel Siddons go at each other with tipped foils, it was not anything so frivolous as the love of a lady.

"I am quite sure, sir," Mr. Siddons finally answered. "The royal barge is decorously prepared and is being loaded with provisions."

"Have you seen it yourself? Or do you rely entirely upon the word of your good friends? You do know the ones I mean, of course. They own a rather sturdy sailboat and seek to discourage those who stand—or swim—in their way."

Miss Hathawae chose that moment to sit down upon one of the chairs in their small circle, prompting the gentlemen to do the same. Lark looked at her gratefully, knowing she had moved so some of the tension could be diffused. But the two antagonists would not be so easily diverted.

"As a matter of fact, I have only just come from Winchelsea," Mr. Siddons said. "The king went to visit with friends, but the whole town celebrates his attention and the honor he bestows upon them. I am sure there are those among them who wish he had settled upon their neighborhood as the site for his Royal Pavilion. It would have greatly enhanced the local markets." Mr. Siddons paused, no doubt reflecting on his words, and the well-known fact of the many people in and around Brighton who despaired of the hundreds of city folk now summering in their once quiet town. But then he narrowed his eyes at Ben Queensman. "But what do you know of my friends and their boat?"

Colonel Wayland made a slight noise, but Mr. Queensman ignored him.

"Why, everyone knows it is my habit to take the waters in the early morning, before the beach is host to other bathers and clammers. I see a good deal in those quiet hours, including furtive meetings between those on shore and those sailing through."

"Such meetings are innocent enough, sir. A man might greet strangers to these shores."

"If a man is confident those strangers are friends."

"Why would you ever suspect they are not?"

Ben Queensman gave a short, humorless laugh.

"You have apparently forgotten, as your uncle will not, that I am the local physician in these parts. Not very long ago, a man turned up dead on the beach. And several days ago innocent women were attacked by men in a sailboat. Such matters necessarily come to my attention."

"A dead man is not in great need of a physician." Colonel Wayland laughed too loudly.

"Unless one wishes to know how he came to be so," Ben Queensman said with a certain flourish.

"And do you have such knowledge, sir?" Mr. Siddons asked.

Ben Queensman looked at him with barely concealed contempt. "We are in the presence of ladies, my good man. As we are all gentlemen here . . ."

Lark knew she was perfectly right about the offense he took at Colonel Wayland's stupid remark. Despite the abundance of uncertainties surrounding everything else, Mr. Queensman's pride remained perfectly intact. She studied him with unabashed interest, considering how quickly his look of uncertainty had passed and how he managed to maintain control of a conversation in which he ought to have been the least integral participant. Lord Raeborn, their most honored guest and certainly the loftiest among them, might as well have been absent.

It seemed impossible to imagine Ben Queensman so invisible in a group. His physical bearing and interest in all things made him instantly noticed by those around him; as soon as he spoke, his audience was fully engaged. And possibly enamored. Lark remembered how she had felt ever so long ago, when he had entered the door of her sister's home, and how she could scarcely comprehend Delphinium's words, distracted as she was by an unbidden and certain unseemly fascination with him. He was a stranger then, but how quickly the fates had conspired to change that.

He glanced down at her, his eyes glinting with mischief, and Lark wanted nothing more than to rise out of her chair and stand up beside him. If he still stung from Wayland's barb, she wished to apply the balm to his wound. If he waged some private war, she wished to fight with him. Her love for him, so painfully strong, would never be requited, but neither would it be put aside.

"Do you think the king in any danger, sir?" Lark asked. "Is it possible the two events in question were not accidents?"

Mr. Queensman's blue eyes widened, but nothing else in his countenance changed.

"I trust our king is safe, surrounded as he is by so many who would protect him. And no, I do not believe Martha Gunn was attacked intentionally, but only stood in the path of another."

Of the dead man, he said nothing. And while the rest of the company gave a collective sigh of relief, Lark realized the obvious implication of his words. It was a question she had already asked herself. That is, if Martha Gunn was the accidental target, for whom was the missile intended?

She looked up quickly and met his eyes, and intercepted his brief, meaningful nod.

"Then we shall greet the day cheerfully," Miss Hathawae said graciously. "When the Royal Barge arrives in Brighton Harbor, we shall join the crowd and sing out our praises as loudly as the next person. Our carriages can accompany the escort to the Pavilion, and we shall wave to people in the street. You are quite certain the king arrives by sea?"

"I have it on the best authority, dear Miss Hathawae," Mr. Siddons said with very much the air of having the last word.

Indeed he did, for Mr. Queensman, so quick to dispute him and wonder at his information, only nodded.

Gabriel Siddons, grasping his moment of triumph, withdrew his little offering from its brown paper wrapping and scattered the many pieces of the dissected map onto a broad table. Lark saw far too many pieces of bright blue paper, indicating the sea on the map, and wondered why he thought such diversions would be amusing. She would have much preferred a new book, or several tubes of watercolor paint so she might devise the same color on a canvas.

But Colonel Wayland, of a different disposition, hastened to the table and began to arrange the small pieces in some sort of order. He gave the appearance of having greater familiarity with the English landscape than with his earlier attempts at the American. But then, it seemed perfectly natural.

Miss Hathawae soon followed them to the table and pulled up a small chair, apparently engaged. Lark wondered if her move was more out of politeness than interest in the map, for she certainly must be sensitive to the fact that Lord Raeborn might wish to spend some time alone with his beloved.

If her action was intended to be a guide, surely Mr. Queensman would take the hint and remove himself as well.

But it was Raeborn who stood up next and stretched his creaking joints.

"I have never amused myself with a dissected map," he said. "And yet it appears to be just the thing for a day's diversion. I should like to try my hand at it."

Ben Queensman promptly rose to his feet, and Lark wondered if she would be entirely abandoned at her seat by the window. But as soon as Raeborn moved off, Mr. Queensman sat down again.

"Are you not fascinated by Mr. Siddons' little puzzler, Mr. Queensman?"

He settled back into his chair and ran his fingers through his thick hair.

"I am more fascinated by Mr. Siddons himself than by a map of the countryside I have known all my life. Indeed, Mr. Siddons appears to be more of a puzzle than anything he has yet brought here."

"And yet I consider him a very thoughtful, kind man. He is deferential to his uncle and always pleasant with the rest of us. Indeed, I have found him a more agreeable companion than I usually find you, sir."

Mr. Queensman's hand stopped in midair, and for a moment it looked as if he might reach for her.

"But it was never my intention to be pleasant or agreeable, so I had nothing to gain by assuming such a stance. Mr. Siddons, on the other hand, plays his part very nicely."

"You do not consider him the genuine article?"

"I consider only that the most glowing veneer might be of the cheapest varnish. One does not necessarily see the quality of the wood underneath."

"And I suppose you are an expert in such matters?"

"I believe I hold a certain degree of authority there."

"I see," Lark said, and doubted it not. "Is there any matter on which you will not prevail? Any prize you will not attempt to claim?"

His hand came down slowly to his knee, where Lark watched it knead the firm muscle around the bone.

"I am afraid there is one. A month ago I believed with absolute confidence that none existed, but circumstances have proved me a second Bonaparte. It appears that, like the little general, I am not infallible."

"You must not blame yourself, sir. After all, you did not ask to be in this war."

"Of course. I resisted it mightily. But then, I was not told to embrace it as well as I did."

If his pun was intentional, it aimed to sting her heart. For how else would they endure through the remainder of their lives, but through veiled allusions and metaphors? And what else could this be but his justification for their brief affair, and his gentle valediction? She now knew, with painful understanding, that this day he would return her, outwardly healed but inwardly dying, to his elderly cousin.

"You are a man of strong convictions, Mr. Queensman. I believe you feel things more strongly than most. It is not a defect in your character, but an asset."

"I might say the same of you, Lady Larkspur."

But that is where it must end, Lark thought to herself. A nod to mutual integrity and spirit and determination. A suggestion of what might have been if only they had met under different circumstances and at a different time. But whatever else they shared, the very things that would make them a whole from two separated selves must remain forever unspoken.

Their awkward, unnatural silence went unnoticed by the four companions who seemed to be expending too much energy on the dissected map.

Lark would have gotten up and walked away if it were possible, but she remained a captive of her own making.

"You seem very confident that Martha Gunn was not the intended victim of this week's mischief, sir. May I ask how you concluded as much?" Lark wished, for her own sake, to return to a conversation that did not affect her quite so personally.

Mr. Queensman, rather than appearing grateful for the door she opened, seemed somewhat distrustful of what lay behind it.

"It is not so difficult to conclude, my lady. Who would wish to do Martha Gunn any harm? She is a bit of a celebrity, if a little stern and forbidding. But she is an honest woman making an honest wage. There are few who would fault her for it."

"Perhaps her enemies might be those who resent the current popularity of Brighton," Lark said thoughtfully. "But then, I suppose they would have more quarrel with the king than with poor Mrs. Gunn."

She saw Ben Queensman sit up straighter in his chair and thought he looked suddenly wary.

"Nevertheless, even if I concede your point, and Martha was an accidental target, for whom might the missile have been aimed? Only Miss Tavish, Miss Hathawae, and I were close by. Anyone else would have been very far off the mark."

"Where were you only minutes before the shooting, my lady?"

Lark thought carefully before she answered. She had just escaped the hoop of Mrs. Gunn's protection, diving mischievously below the surface of the sea so she might meet up with Miss Hathawae. Anyone setting her in his sights would have been surprised by her unladylike move.

She looked across at Ben Queensman and saw the face of a stranger.

"Had you just removed yourself, albeit unintentionally, from the line of fire?"

"How would you know, sir?" Lark asked, though she had a fairly good idea how it was possible. His next words confirmed it.

"I was watching from the terrace at Knighton's. Why else do you suppose Matthew and I arrived on the scene so quickly?"

"It was very rude of you to be watching ladies at a time when we were assured of privacy."

"I will not argue about the temptations of such a scene, but, in truth, I was more intent upon the men in the sailboat."

"Mr. Siddons' friends?" Lark asked with belated, but clear, understanding.

"Precisely." He nodded.

"I see. But why would Mr. Siddons' friends want to injure Mrs. Gunn?"

Mr. Queensman made an exasperated gesture, perhaps entirely justified.

"You think they wished to hurt me?" Lark whispered. "But I have done nothing, that is, I mean . . ."

"Mrs. Gunn is a good sort of woman, my lady, but you must realize I would have had no real interest in the bathing scene unless I feared for your own safety."

"But why would anyone want to hurt me?"

Ben Queensman hesitated, and Lark thought he was gathering his words very carefully.

"Perhaps they thought that by injuring you they would be momentarily disabling me and might then proceed with their scheme. I do not believe they intended to do you serious harm. But there are others, myself included, who stand too much in their way."

Lark would have asked a million questions at once, starting with who were the villains, and what was their scheme, and why would they think Benedict Queensman would be standing in their way. But only one thing seemed to matter just then, and its answer was worth all the rest.

"Why would they believe my welfare would be of any consequence to you, sir?"

The bright eyes glinted. "Someone must have told them it was so."

And by that one simple sentence Lark knew it was so.

"Of what can you two be speaking?" Raeborn's thin voice interrupted them. "Are you making plans for the king's entrance on the morrow?"

"I am sure, Benedict, that there is very little we need do to prepare." Miss Hathawae came up beside him. Lark glanced towards the table, where the other two men were still engaged in their activity. "But we may come out to meet the king, and perhaps join the entourage. What say you, Mr. Queensman?"

"You are quite right, Miss Hathawae, for you understand the routine very well. The king's carriage will be approaching on the eastern road, where the way is very narrow. He will pass through several small villages on the outskirts of Brighton, and we might as well give the townspeople a good show. I think we could safely join him about five miles down the road."

"An excellent plan, my boy," Raeborn said happily. "He knows I am to be here, and will be delighted at our early opportunity for a reunion."

"I hope I might ride in your carriage, my lord," said Miss Hathawae, "for I have none of my own here. I usually rely upon the kindness of friends."

Raeborn patted her hand comfortingly. "Then I consider it a privilege to call myself the very oldest of friends."

Miss Hathawae laughed girlishly. "Oh, dear, Benedict, you are not so very old as all that!"

"In truth, you make me feel like a man of thirty again."

The genuine man of thirty caught Lark's eye and shrugged in apparent disbelief at the most blatant flirtation going on right before them.

Lark smiled, sparing enough of her attention to be amused by the goings-on. But, in truth, something else nagged at her imagination and would not be dismissed.

Did no one else notice that Mr. Queensman—who had earlier agreed with Mr. Siddons that the king would be arriving by sea—was planning their reception of the royal entourage on the road leading to Brighton?

"Would an outing to see the king give you pleasure, my dear lady?" Lord Raeborn asked and put his face very close to Lark's.

Ben knew his cousin was in the habit of assuming this stance because his hearing was faulty. But Lark, not knowing her fiancé nearly as well as a young lady ought, looked troubled by the intimacy and pulled away as much as her captive position could allow. She looked from side to side, but there remained no one to rescue her but himself.

"Yes, I suppose it would, my lord," she said a little unsteadily.

"Of course. I do not need to be a physician myself to prescribe it as a remedy for what ails you, my dear. What do you say, Ben? Does our king bestow a healing blessing on all those who behold him?"

Raeborn, on turning to look at him, removed himself from Lark's face. Over his cousin's thin shoulder Ben saw the lady's look of gratitude.

He smiled, absurdly pleased that he could give her even this little respite.

"I am sure our Princess Caroline would not have felt so blessed. In fact, in my professional opinion, I believe the sight of her husband made her positively ill."

Raeborn grunted. "They were ever a poor match," he admitted.

Lark clasped her hands together, and Ben noticed how she twisted her fingers nervously.

"I have no complaints against the king, but I am sure he possesses no healing powers, sir. One studies endlessly, and cares a good deal for one's patients to claim such talents. Your cousin demonstrates this every day. In fact, Mr. Queensman proves himself so proficient, I can—"

"Of course, you are partly right, my lord," Ben rushed in. He neither liked nor trusted the look on Lark's face, whereby she gave all the appearance of a prisoner seizing a newly discovered avenue of escape. "If not the king's society, then surely the outing itself will do some good. The sea air greatly restores Lady Larkspur's spirit."

"Excellent! My lady's retirement to Brighton has proven wonderfully beneficial, then!"

Ben wished he could say the same.

"In fact, my lord, it has restored me so much I can—" Lark began, but Raeborn put a silencing finger upon her lips. Benedict envied him more in that moment than he had ever envied anyone before.

"Hush, my dear. As you yourself have just extolled the virtues of physicians, I am sure you would admit that the sole decision maker on the matter must be our only impartial judge," Raeborn said with unintended irony as he glanced up at Ben. "What say you, Doctor? Is my lady well or not?"

Ben heard Lark suck in her breath, but dared not look at her lest he falter in his path.

"Well, Doctor?" Raeborn insisted. "You must have some opinion on the matter."

"Indeed I do, my lord," Ben said, feeling the rush of blood to his face. "Your lady remains an invalid, in poor health and unstable spirit."

Lark gave a little cry, attracting the attention of those still busy at work on the dissected map. Miss Hathawae looked as if she would come forward, but Ben gently waved her off. If there was anyone who could reassure the lady, it was he himself. But not in this place, nor in the company of others.

"I protest, Mr. Queensman. I most heartily do. My health has made considerable improvement since the first sad days of my confinement here. Much of that is largely due to you, sir, and the benefits of this excellent society. Lord Raeborn already knows of my recent triumph in the waters. But neither he nor you knows of my first tentative steps on dry land. In fact, I should like to demonstrate . . ."

As she flung her blanket off her knees and gripped the sides of her wheeled chair, Ben comprehended in an instant what she intended. He knew not why she insisted upon revealing herself just now, or how much she hoped to prove, but he felt almost certain she did not guess what Raeborn intended.

He bent down and caught her by her tensed shoulders and pressed against her soft flesh. The temptation to circle her with his arms and bury his face in her sweet-smelling curls was almost unbearable, but reason immediately prevailed. He needed to set her back down in her chair and preserve his cousin's illusions about the woman he hoped to marry under any circumstances. If in doing so, Raeborn would no longer have any illusions about himself, then it was a sacrifice Ben felt resolved upon making.

The lady's indignation was patently clear. Her glorious

shoulders, covered by silk still bearing his imprint, shook with frustration, and she glared up at him as she once again shifted to the edge of her seat.

"I am quite fit, sir," she said firmly.

"And, as your physician, I say you are not," Ben said, yielding nothing.

The heavy silence between them was broken by Raeborn himself, who seemed to take great pleasure in the battle of their wills.

He laughed too heartily. "But it matters little, my dear, darling wife. You need not protest so."

Lark turned so sharply that one of her curls whipped Ben's cheek. Her mouth formed a small *O*, looking hungry for whatever offerings Raeborn would serve her.

Raeborn cleared his throat.

"I know you would come to me healthy and whole, my darling. But I am here to tell you it no longer matters." He smiled a little tentatively. "Healthy or not, it is of no consequence to me. I will take you either way, and joyfully."

Raeborn surely considered his words carefully, and with every expectation of receiving gratitude. But Lady Larkspur promptly closed her lips, refusing to sup, and closed her eyes as she settled back against her invalid's cushions.

Chapter Twelve

"*I* suppose you will be happy to know, after all these weeks, that you finally manage to look nearly as ill as you profess," said Janet, though she scarcely looked away from her own image in the glass before making her judgment. "I daresay the sight of several rugged young men taking the waves this morning did not sufficiently restore your spirit?"

Lark untied the ribbons on her bonnet and threw the frivolous bit of finery on her bed.

"How could it?" she demanded. "Especially as I am now condemned to marry a man so old he insists he wants me for little more than a companion. What will I ever know of strong arms and sturdy bodies?"

"What do you know of such things already?" Janet asked.

Lark looked sharply at her friend, and thought she could fairly ask the same question herself. Though no man could compare to Ben Queensman, Matthew Warren was not a bad specimen.

"I have spent this whole night, tearful and awake, comprehending only too well how sterile and cold my life shall be. The man I shall marry wishes only an ornament for his home, a doll he may display as a treasure in his cabinet. I mean nothing more to him than any possession, and even less than his own pride. And there is no one who will save me from such a fate."

Janet finally turned away from her own reflection. "What would you have me do?" she asked gently.

Lark moved restlessly to the dressing table. "You have done more than any friend, endured my rants and inconsistencies and only sought to help. You shall be my only comfort when we return to London."

Janet's face changed so suddenly, Lark comprehended her mistake at once.

"You will not return to London?"

Janet's mouth twisted with her indecision of expression. "I did not wish to tell you, for fear it would make you most unhappy, dear Lark. But when I return to London it will only be to select my wedding clothes. Matthew Warren has asked me to marry him, and even now prepares to meet my father. To think such circumstances have produced such a happy result! I only wish you could know such joy!"

Lark willfully lifted the great burden that had settled upon her heart and smiled tearfully at her dearest friend.

"But I do! I do!" she cried, hugging her. "To have you so happy is to give me the greatest pleasure! Mr. Warren is an excellent man, a gentleman truly worthy of you. I cannot imagine you with another."

"Can you not? I once recall you saying you would not have either of us settle for anything less than a baronetcy. And now I shall be a doctor's wife."

"Perhaps I have matured in my sensibilities. I believe I do not consider marrying a physician or a barrister or a banker any worse than, say, marrying a man who swims naked in the sea. At least you know precisely what you are about to get."

"Lark!" Janet blushed mightily, but Lark easily saw through her maidenly modesty. Their stay in Brighton had educated them about a good many things, not all of which would meet the approval of their parents.

"I am being absolutely truthful, Janet—which is an experience quite rare for me in recent weeks. So when I say I am delighted for your great happiness and wish you every wonderful thing, believe it is quite from the heart." She paused and then added, with a trace of wistfulness, "When do you marry?"

Janet turned back towards the mirror, but not before Lark could decipher the look of discomfort on her friend's features.

"Janet? Whatever is the matter?"

"I long to marry Matthew and settle in this lovely place with some degree of permanence. I truly do. But I will not be agreeable to such a plan until I have fulfilled my promise to you, dear friend. I will not leave you alone. I wonder, now that you seem to have Mr. Queensman as an ally, would you feel comfortable if Delphinium or Columbine joined you here? Rose and Lily are far too silly and would drive you quite mad."

"And yet they found husbands with very little difficulty," Lark said ruefully. "But you are right about the effect they would have on my sanity. Rose and Lily are increasing, you know, and Columbine would not be happy without Edward. And Del—but it is no matter." Lark shook her head.

"Why on earth not?"

"I shall be leaving this place soon enough, and not altogether to my regret. Raeborn will have me either way, so it appears I have done nothing by my masquerade but buy myself a little time. But even that is now sand through the glass, and I have not even managed to meet the great Mr. Knighton."

Janet laughed. "I suspect he does not exist."

"Oh, he does. I have it on Miss Hathawae's authority. But whether we meet him or not, he surely is more real than any of my hopes or dreams."

"What are they, dear Lark?"

Lark looked closely at her oldest friend and saw the radiant skin and bright eyes of a woman in love. She also recognized loyalty and contentment and the calm satisfaction of someone who knows she is to have everything she ever desired.

"I believe you have the answer to that already. The sea air of Brighton has changed us both, making us so much more than the insipid misses we were upon our arrival. Your own story will end happily, triumphantly. Mine will not be anywhere as gratifying, ending just where it began. I may have grown and gotten wiser, but it is to no avail. I will still marry Lord Raeborn."

"When you would rather marry another." It was a statement, not a question.

"Of course," Lark admitted and looked at her friend. "But where I once thought him the very last man I would marry, I now believe him the very last man I *could* marry."

"What can I do to help you?" Janet asked again.

Lark looked up in surprise. "What can you do? Have you not already done everything in your power to help me? No, I believe there is no one who could act on my behalf.

And, suddenly alone and my own champion, I do not see what could possibly be done."

"There is still hope."

"I doubt it."

"Perhaps Lord Raeborn will realize he prefers Miss Hathawae. Have you not noticed how much they seem to take delight in each other's company? If he jilts you, your parents will be quite inconsolable, but I doubt if you will be very much upset."

"Dear Janet. I should dance in the streets."

"But not in his presence. Or else he will surely reconsider his suit when he finds you so healthy."

Lark, feeling a great need to throw something, flung her abandoned bonnet at her most loyal friend.

Two well-dressed carriages glistened in the afternoon sun gracing the circular drive at Knighton's, and several of the patients peered from their shaded windows to behold the spectacle. Lark, settled as comfortably as possible in her chair, glanced up and waved at them, unintentionally making them duck back within their rooms. But of course she was not the object of their attention or admiration, for she was as sickly and as helpless as they.

Or so they thought.

Their eyes may have been on Lord Raeborn, who looked as pompous as a peacock, in a blue military suit with gold braid. Lark, who believed his young cousin the only soldier in the family, gave credit to a bold London tailor who had likely assured Raeborn of the appeal of such garb.

In any case, Miss Hathawae seemed quite taken by it. And he by her lovely blue sailor dress. They perfectly complemented each other in style and, seemingly, in temperament. Lark considered Janet's acute observation and wondered if she dared hope for the truth in it.

Probably not. Raeborn remembered all the niceties in addressing both Janet and herself and showed Lark the respect her unique position deserved. He preened and bowed before her and gave every appearance of the attentive fiancé.

But he proved not nearly as persuasive as Matthew Warren.

"I have convinced Ben to divide our party unequally, but to everyone's satisfaction," he said. "I shall ride alone with Miss Tavish and allow the four of you the pleasure of each other's company."

"I do not see how everyone is to be satisfied by the arrangement, Mr. Warren." Lark spoke up quickly, before she quite realized how happy Janet would be to have Matthew all to herself. "I am not certain Mr. Queensman is ready to abandon his own carriage."

Ben Queensman, who seemed concerned only with the placement of the luncheon hampers upon the carriages, turned away from his chores.

"I hardly think Mr. Warren will run off with my vehicle, my lady. And by moving into Lord Raeborn's carriage, I might attend upon you. Someone will be needed to set you up in your seat and carry you back down."

"I am sure my fiancé will manage without you," she said tartly.

Raeborn looked nervous and cleared his throat.

"But we should be delighted to have you ride with us, Mr. Queensman," Miss Hathawae said quickly and shot a meaningful glance at Lark. "You shall be our guide to the coast and the beautiful sights along the way."

"I am glad I might make someone happy," Mr. Queensman said, looking pointedly at Lark.

At this rate, she thought to herself, I might as well ride by myself in a pony cart.

"Well, then, as it is all settled, why not be off?" Raeborn said quickly, perhaps concerned that Mr. Queensman would change his mind.

"An excellent suggestion," Mr. Queensman said gaily. "The king's entourage should come to the great salt marsh in less than an hour's time. They will undoubtedly stop there, as the king will want to shoot a duck for his evening's meal."

"Judging by his girth when last I saw him, I believe he may desire two or three," joked Raeborn in a rare moment.

Laughing, Ben Queensman agreed. He helped his two elderly companions into the carriage, and when he turned to face Lark, his face suddenly sobered.

"With your permission, my lady, I shall lift you to your seat."

"You never asked for it in the past," she said nastily.

"As your doctor, it was perhaps not necessary for me to do so."

"I do not recall dismissing you, sir."

"It is not for the patient to dismiss the doctor. It is for the doctor to determine there is no more to be done."

"And is that your determination?"

"Would you have it otherwise?" he asked as he leaned over her and slid his arm beneath her knees.

It was a question she could not answer, for to do so would be to admit too much and to gain nothing but pain by it. Instead, she used her few private moments with him to address something else on her mind.

"You seem to know the king's business very intimately, sir."

It was not her intention to surprise him, but she saw immediately that she did. Perhaps it was because she evaded his probing question and he was accustomed to confrontation. Or perhaps it was due to the fact that he was guilty of some overzealousness on behalf of the monarchy. Lark had often noticed that those with no illusions of nobility were strangely drawn to its trappings.

"It is my business to know his when he comes into the neighborhood," Mr. Queensman said simply.

This time it was Lark's turn to be surprised.

"Your interest seems to extend beyond a mere physician's authority."

"Do you still imagine my patients and hospital my only concern?"

Her eyes met his, and she read there the invitation to take what liberties she might. Once, not very long ago, she would have accepted it with a sense of discovery and delight. But so poised in his arms between the wheeled chair that brought her here and Lord Raeborn's carriage that would take her away, she could do little but say, "I know they are not."

And very briefly, driven by nothing more than the desire to be close to him for perhaps the last time, she pressed her hand against his heart.

They might as well have been all alone. All sounds and sights and smells suddenly fell away until the only things that existed were the two of them and the warm vibrating space between their bodies. What a mistake to have let this man enter her life, to create such standards that no other man might compare! How she had been tempted, and how she would be forever punished.

"Up with her, boy!" Raeborn's voice broke through the bubble, and Lark felt hands grabbing at her shoulders. "Can you not manage it?"

Ben laughed, or at least gave the sound of it. "I am not sure Lady Larkspur will ever be managed by anyone. I envy you the challenge, my lord."

He placed Lark very gently on the seat next to his cousin, and Lark saw immediately Raeborn's consternation. But she did not know if it was for being told he might have a difficult wife, or if he had seen her brazen handling of their mutual friend. When Raeborn took her hand and held it tightly between his, she felt as if he sought to tame her and knew not how to go about it.

Feeling pity, she gently smiled at the man who would marry her.

"You make a charming couple, my dears," Miss Hathawae said from her seat across from them. "You have each found the best of mates."

The carriage lurched to one side when Mr. Queensman stepped into it and settled himself next to Miss Hathawae.

"And would you not consider me a good mate, ma'am?" he asked her teasingly and then gave the order for the groom to move on.

Miss Hathawae waited until the two vehicles moved out of the circle of the drive and were set upon their course before she spoke.

"Are you proposing to me, sir? For we seem to be the only two people in this company who are not already attached to another."

Ben Queensman smiled broadly at the elderly lady at his side, and Lark could have kissed him for his generosity of spirit.

"I would consider it, but for our recent experience at billiards. I must confess it left me feeling very inadequate."

Miss Hathawae laughed, a sweet, musical sound—a girlish sound.

"I thought we were never to talk of it, sir!"

"What, my boy? Has she bested you?" Raeborn boomed.

"I should have warned you. She beat us all mercilessly in our day, and scared off more than one suitor with a well-placed prod of the cue. I remember it well. Why, my dear, do you remember that night in Windsor—"

Raeborn returned Lark's hand to her lap and leaned forward to pat Miss Hathawae's knee. Surely it was the bright sun that made her face so red.

"Hush, Benedict! And it certainly would not do to remind the king of that evening. There were things on his mind other than the balls on the table."

Lark caught Mr. Queensman's eye and shared his amusement. There was something very charming in the delight Lord Raeborn and Miss Hathawae took in each other, surely making them a more appealing couple than Lark and her elderly suitor. Mr. Queensman raised an eyebrow but did not comment.

Indeed, there was nothing to be said. Lord Raeborn finally removed his hand from Miss Hathawae's knee, and the four of them settled back into their seats, assiduously avoiding looking at each other, each to his or her own thoughts.

The passing scenery, with the broad expanse of the sea on one side and a changing fare of cliffs, hills and open meadows on the other, was fascinating unto itself. Where once Lark imagined the stench of the Thames to be the natural condition of moving water, and the hothouse flowers her mother grew the veritable definition of natural beauty, she now owned a greater appreciation of the countryside and the pleasures to be derived from it. She could not vouch for the efficacy of sea air as a cure for all ailments, nor for bathing in the waves as a redemptive act, but she could understand why Janet would be perfectly happy to live here for the rest of her life.

She would be delighted to do the same.

"These marshes are situated on my estate, though we are some miles off from the house," Mr. Queensman said suddenly.

"Are these the ones where you expected the king to amuse himself?" Lark asked suspiciously. They had not gone very far.

"Not these, but ones very like. There is much wildfowl here, but I also have farmers at work and should not like the king to practice his marksmanship upon them. He is, you know, a notoriously bad shot."

Lark sniffed something sweet, almost fruity, in the air.

"But did you not say the marshes were salty, sir? I know enough about foliage from my talented mother, and do not believe there is much to be farmed here."

Mr. Queensman smiled.

"Perhaps your mother, more concerned with the splendid show of such plants as the columbine, larkspur or delphinium, does not bother with the humble blossom of the fenberry. The little plant thrives in the salt marsh and produces a small red fruit, very bitter in taste."

"Such an indictment surely confirms my comment. Why would one wish to farm a bitter fruit?"

"There are some who add sugar to a boiling pot of fenberries and consider it an excellent preserve. I, however, am more interested in the healing value of the fruit. It seems to aid intestinal disorders. And eases the pain of childbirth."

"My lad," cautioned Raeborn. "I will remind you there are ladies present."

"And are we not the ones to be most interested in such a discussion, my lord?" Lark asked impatiently. "Besides, you yourself assigned your cousin to be my physician, and I feel obliged to take his professional advice."

Raeborn's protest died on his lips, and Lark wondered again if he doubted the advantages of having an outspoken wife. Perhaps, she thought a little ruefully, she had gone about it all wrong. Her boldness might have been a stronger deterrent to their marriage than her feigned illness.

Ben Queensman looked uncomfortably at his cousin. "Forgive me, my lord. I have grown too accustomed in recent weeks to speaking to Lady Larkspur as if she were a friend. I hope I may remain so, even though I am no longer her physician."

"Of course, of course," Raeborn said generously. "Things will be more comfortable that way when we meet as family, as we are apt to do."

"And yet, my lord, you may remember you and I saw nothing of each other for ten years," Mr. Queensman said.

Lark felt a wrenching pain in her chest, realizing the truth of the situation. When she and Raeborn married, she would not be likely to see Ben Queensman until friends or circumstances conspired to allow it. And, she realized all too keenly, she had rather come to rely on his provocative conversation to keep her own wit keen and insightful.

"Perhaps we might correspond, as friends," Lark quickly suggested. "My interest in your fenberries is not merely polite, sir. I have already spoken of my study of garden herbs and their medicinal powers, an education I have, ah, cultivated despite the protest of my painterly mother. She, of course, prefers large blossoms with heavy perfumes. I am more intrigued with the subtle gifts of our gardens, for I believe they yield greater power."

"Not unlike many women," said Mr. Queensman and leaned forward in his seat. "But you are right to admire the quiet greens so rarely noticed by others. I recall you noticed my own humble efforts at the hospital."

"I did indeed, sir. I will confess, after our visit not long ago, I asked that my sisters send down my books and notes from London. I did not recall, for example, the value of the parsley growing in your garden."

"Parsley?" Mr. Queensman looked mystified. "I believe it is best used as a garnish for my broth."

Raeborn laughed, which Lark thought made him as ungenerous at her expense as Mr. Queensman. She frowned and looked towards the sea, where a small flotilla of boats bobbled in the waves.

"Parsley sweetens the breath, Lady Larkspur," Mr. Queensman said quietly. "It provides my patients with some measure of comfort, particularly if they are afflicted with a disease of the lungs."

She turned back to thank him silently for this bit of information, and knew how much she would have enjoyed tending his garden.

"And I should be very happy to answer any questions you may have about my professional concerns," he added.

Raeborn laughed again. "I should not want you to make a physician of my lady, Ben. It would be most inappropriate."

"And yet, my lord," Miss Hathawae interjected, "before the days of our great universities, women practiced the medical arts almost exclusively. In some quarters they still do."

Raeborn looked across at Miss Hathawae, and Lark felt the warmth of the connection between them.

"And yet, dear lady, I would not have you do such a thing," he said.

Lark braced herself for some retort from Miss Hathawae, some reminder to Raeborn that what she did or thought was no concern of his. But the lady only smiled secretively and reached out to pat his blue-veined hand. Doubting the veracity of what she witnessed, Lark looked quickly at Ben Queensman, who seemed very thoughtful.

And so they rode along in silence for some time. The great salt marsh was soon supplanted by a chalky cliff, and the road, strewn with the loose rubble of the lime, grew rougher. Lark gripped the side of the carriage to balance herself, and thereby afforded herself a better view of the water. More boats appeared, several flying the king's colors. Gulls flew overhead, though probably in greater anticipation of a meal than of viewing the monarch. And, in the distance, the strains of a band could be heard.

Suddenly the ground shook with thunder, and Lark looked worriedly at the sky.

Mr. Queensman, who, she sensed, watched her the entire time, quickly reassured her.

" 'Tis the noise of cannon fire, a sound I know only too well. But here we need not fear the enemy as we did in America. We need only worry about the great cloud of smoke arising from the artillery of an overzealous welcoming troupe. The cinders could easily soil the ladies' dresses."

"That would be most unfortunate," Raeborn murmured.

"But we may take consolation in the fact that the king already approaches. The militia would not waste gunpowder for nought," Mr. Queensman said, as if he knew.

Lord Raeborn looked puzzled.

Lark sighed and then turned a little impatiently to her suitor. Would her good sense and intuition be constrained to providing explanations of the obvious throughout her married life?

"It is a valuable commodity, my lord," she said quietly. "It is best used against our enemies. Or if, as Mr. Queensman says, there are none nearby, to impress the locals in the presence of their monarch."

Mr. Queensman scowled at her, a rebuff she undoubtedly deserved, inasmuch as he numbered himself among the locals.

"Oh, look. He comes!" cried Miss Hathawae, sounding something like a local herself.

Lark could not help but be fired by her enthusiasm. She pulled herself up to survey the scene before them, and believed them truly at a vantage point, for the Royal Entourage still seemed somewhat distant. But from their windswept bluff, all the colors and pageantry, if not the king himself, were readily apparent. She could see the lines of red-coated militia, and the glint of their golden buttons in the sun, and the burnished brown of well-brushed horses. A large carriage, festooned with flags and ribbons, moved slowly between them, and one could just make out a wigged figure in a bright yellow jacket with one arm uplifted to the crowd. A great cheer went up from the hundreds of people who lined the dusty road, and the figure stood up unsteadily as the carriage continued to move.

"Perhaps we might stay here for a while, and enjoy the view?" suggested Miss Hathawae.

Lark turned to agree with her, but was instead distracted by Mr. Queensman's sudden movement. He did not dispute Miss Hathawae's vote, but Lark could see he was not altogether comfortable with it. He looked from one side of the road to the other, as if expecting to defend himself from some attack. His eyes met Lark's, and he managed to look a little sheepish.

"Are you not inclined to enjoy a spot of some scenery, Mr. Queensman?" she asked. "Or are you too accustomed to this sort of thing? Those of us who judge splendor by the size of the chandeliers in a ballroom find novelty in the great expanse of sea and sand, you know."

Mr. Queensman smiled. "I know you too well to believe your world ends at the doorway of a fine townhouse, or that you are still amazed by the prospect of chalk cliffs and beach. But, in fact, I am not so interested in the view we see, as in the fact that others may view us."

"Are you concerned for our privacy, sir?" asked Miss Hathawae.

"Or for our safety?" Lark asked, more urgently. She finally came to appreciate how vigilant he tended to be and wondered to what purpose. "I thought you said there were no enemies here."

"You are absolutely correct. I am being overly cautious."

Raeborn leaned forward. "An excellent quality in a physician, my boy. One can never be—" But his words were cut off by the sound of a fresh barrage of cannon fire. From where they sat, in the open hand of the cliff, the echoing sound was deafening.

Lark, resisting the impulse to cover her ears, looked down and noticed fine slivers of white chalk lying in her lap. Suddenly the air seemed full of them, dropping down around her like thousands of snowflakes. She turned to Mr. Queensman in wonder when a larger fragment glanced off her cheek, and she heard a rumbling sound that surely was neither thunder nor the cannons below.

He was on her in an instant, throwing her down onto the floor of the carriage with the weight of his body and shielding her from the avalanche of rock and dust. In the second before he reached her, she saw Raeborn move as well, and she thought Ben Queensman might have pulled him down with them. But she felt both arms of his embrace holding her so closely, he could not admit another person between them. He flinched once, and then again, and she wondered what this unexpected bit of heroism might cost him.

"Sir! My lady!" came a muffled sound. Lark thought she recognized the voice of the groom, and wondered if he lay buried in his seat. Then she moved her head and realized it was her hearing and not his throat that was afflicted. She reluctantly pulled her ear away from Mr. Queensman's chest.

"Are you hurt?" her protector asked, beginning to extricate himself from the tangle of limbs on the floor of the carriage.

Lark blinked and looked around her, and saw Lord Raeborn awkwardly attempting to separate himself from the squirming body of Miss Hathawae. She gave him credit for his own show of heroism and briefly wondered what chivalric instincts made him go for the older lady as Mr. Queensman went for her.

"You seem to spend too much time asking me that question, Mr. Queensman," Lark said, dusting chalk off her shoulders and seeing him for the first time. She could not help but grin, as his black hair seemed as powdered as once was fashionable, and his impeccable jacket was dusty and stained. "But it seems that once again I have you to thank for my safety."

"It is my responsibility, my lady," he said stiffly, and glanced meaningfully at his cousin. He held out his arm to support Lord Raeborn as he rose shakily to his feet. By now the groom was at the side of the carriage, helping Miss Hathawae regain her seat.

"What has happened, Benedict?" she asked.

Both gentlemen of that name looked at her, but only one spoke.

"I believe it was a—a landslide," the elder man said tentatively, and looked to his cousin for corroboration. When Mr. Queensman nodded, he went on. "The vibration of the cannons must have loosened the rock, and we just happened to be in an unfortunate place."

"Oh, dear, how foolish of us," Miss Hathawae said. "And I only wanted to enjoy the view."

"Perhaps we will do so while John cleans out the carriage for us and we shake out our clothing on the road," said Mr. Queensman, and took her hand before alighting from the vehicle. Lord Raeborn quickly followed, but Lark waited patiently, as she knew she must. Then she accepted not only Mr. Queensman's arm around her, but also his clean handkerchief.

"I might ask you what you find so amusing, my lady," he growled as he set her down.

She glanced over to the others, convinced of their distraction, before she answered. And that she did by using his own handkerchief to wipe the chalk from his nose and his cheeks in a far too familiar fashion. When he began to pull away, she stopped him with no more than a touch to his forearm and by blinking her eyelids. It was part of the familiar arsenal of flirtation, something she had never used with Mr. Queensman. And he seemed no more immune than most men.

And just now she wanted something of him.

"This is not seemly, my lady," he began.

"There is no one who cares just now. Perhaps it is my due, anyway. After all these weeks of allowing you to dictate to me, I believe it is my turn." Purposefully, seductively, she ran the linen cloth over his lower lip, snatching it away when he tried to bite down on it.

"My safety is no longer your responsibility, sir, whatever you say. You absolved yourself of it and turned me over to your lordly cousin."

"Then what will you have of me, Lark?" he asked. "For this little scene is being played out for some reason."

She hesitated, her hand in the air. He was right, of course, but the acuteness of his observation, his cynicism, was too true.

"Must I have a reason?" she asked softly.

"I fear you must," he said.

She did not speak at first, knowing he was right. It was the only way things could be between them.

"I will have you answer to responsibility of another sort," she said. "It is unjust of you to be secretive about the strange events that have taken place these past few weeks. A death, an attack on Martha Gunn at sea, this current mishap—"

"I do not believe this anything but an accident, my lady."

"Oddly enough, I do not believe you."

"If you will not believe me, I will not bother to explain at all. It will be to no avail."

"I want to know only one thing, and I desire the truth."

He looked at her, and she sensed he would be disappointed by her question.

"What is Gabriel Siddons' part in all this?"

By the expression on his face she knew herself correct. And by his answer she knew why it was so.

"You seem to take an active interest in that man," he accused.

"No more than I do other men. But that is not the point. I should like to know why you, sir, seem to take an active interest in him. What is more, why you do not trust him nor his uncle."

The words hung between them like a heavy drapery, admitting no light.

"It is no business of yours, my lady. Your business is only to prepare yourself to return to London and to leave the affairs of this community to those for whom it might matter."

"And why does it matter to you, Mr. Queensman? What is it you do that makes it so important?"

"You already know what I do."

She waved her hand dismissively, for it was the easy part. "You heal people, sir," she said.

He glanced over to the other side of the road, where Lord Raeborn and Miss Hathawae returned their gaze to the pageantry below.

"And I protect them," he added.

Chapter Thirteen

A hazy shroud draped the landscape, distorting the crisp colors of the earth and sea and weighing down the bodies of all who passed beneath it. Great clouds of dust were kicked up by the hooves of all the king's horses and settled uncharitably on dark jackets and hats. And the sun, whose intensity might be seen as a fair omen for George IV's entrance into the city he had adopted as his favorite, blinded the eyes of those who admired him most and looked up to him for inspiration.

Benedict Queensman licked his dry lips and then regretted it almost at once, for the taste of chalk remained upon them. He had not allowed Lark to tend to him, as she apparently wished to do, nor had he yet taken the time to tend to himself. It was most unfortunate should the king see him in such disarray, but he would have to plead the case of doing the crown's business.

Yet, even now, he was not sure it was the truth.

He knew they had been watched as their carriage made its way along the cliff road, for he sensed it with an intuition that was once legendary in the encampments along the Hudson River, in America. He also knew there was a reason why the small company in the carriage might be susceptible targets and why there were those who wished them ill.

But small landslides along the chalk cliffs were not at all uncommon, and might be induced by the vibrations against the rock face. Raeborn explained it thus, and it made absolute sense.

Or at least it did to Raeborn and Miss Hathawae.

Without looking down to where she sat beside him, Ben's selfsame intuition warned him that Lark was more curious about him than about the approaching entourage and that she merely awaited her chance to ask him all the questions he was not at liberty to answer. She was too damned perceptive and curious—not always the most comfortable companion. And very unusual for a woman.

Of course, if she were a man and a colleague, he would have welcomed her discernment with pleasure and respect. How rich and gratifying it would be to have someone like her as a regular companion, working at his side and continually prompting him to higher levels of endeavor. A woman might do the same, but she must be his wife to be permitted such behavior. And if she were his wife, she should not be required to work.

Of course, someone like Lark would hardly be content to sit in the drawing room, pulling thread through muslin cloth. Nor would she, for she preferred to flaunt the conventions of society and make a claim for her independence. Though true that when they had first met, she seemed no more than a very pretty miss giving herself up to a scoundrel who would only use her, it was now impossible to see her in such a passive role or to imagine her engaging in the frivolity of fashionable behavior.

She had tried it on him not minutes ago, and he saw through it as quickly as he once guessed at her more elaborate ruse. Lark, batting her lashes and cooing as she touched his face, was an entirely unfamiliar creature.

And an utterly charming one.

Of course, he reasoned, she attempted to seduce him to get something from him.

He could not allow himself to be seduced or yet give up what remained privileged information. But under the power of her spell, he might have relented and given her anything her heart desired.

Or given in to what his heart desired.

Without moving his head, seemingly intent on the scene before him, he slanted a glance down at her. It was as he thought: she looked to have no more interest in the king than in the man she would marry. Her attention was all for him.

"Do you think we ought to warn the king's men of the dangers of yonder cliff walls, Mr. Queensman?" she asked sweetly, but surely not innocently. How did she know he looked at her then, when he was at such pains to disguise it? "I believe him to be quite vain, and he should not like to be showered in chalk, I should think. Luckily, it hardly seems to bother you at all."

Ben frowned and wondered if she was once again offering to clean him off. He desperately wanted to rid himself of the chalk dust and thought about jumping into the nearby waves. Perhaps he could tempt the lady to join him there.

He sucked in his breath and resisted the impulse to sneeze.

"I am sorry, Mr. Queensman. Perhaps the chalk has settled in your ears. I asked—"

"I heard you, my lady. I hesitated because I debated which part of your address I should answer first." Still he did not look at her.

"I believe I asked only one question, sir."

"But implied another. Let me respond by saying the chalk bothers me a great deal, but I am quite capable of washing myself, thank you. And yes, I shall inform the king's men of the possible dangers ahead. And certainly warn them not to fire off any shots."

"I wonder if they would respond with the immediacy you demonstrate, Mr. Queensman. I must say, your instincts seem to be remarkably quick. I also must say how grateful I am for them."

It was impossible not to look at her now. Ben put his arm up on the rail of the carriage and one foot on the step. It was as near as he dared get to her, and she responded by edging forward on her seat.

"They have twice come to my rescue," she said.

"So they have. But I am not certain they would have been as keen if another lady's safety was the issue. Under certain circumstances they are sharper than usual."

Almost immediately, he regretted his choice of words, for Lark was too capable of thinking metaphorically. But she seemed unperturbed by his pronouncement, accepting it with the air of dead calm that had characterized so much of her behavior in recent days. Was it possible she was truly resigned to her fate, just as he was coming to believe he would not be resigned to his?

"Lady Larkspur," he began, not altogether certain where his words might lead, "there is something I would discuss with you in private."

Her beautiful eyes widened, and she parted her lips in

wonder. Surely she would not receive his words joyously, nor wish to just now, when they had an audience.

"You will tell me why you fear for the king's safety? And how you came to be his guardian?"

He looked at her, bemused by her single-mindedness, when possibly he should be wondering at his own. But it was for this information she attempted to seduce him, and she wished to have her way in this as in all else.

"That is not your affair, my lady," he said tersely.

"I am the daughter of a peer and shall soon marry another. Of course it is my business, Mr. Queensman," she said, her haughtiness effectively disguising her disappointment. She did not attempt to disguise her emphasis on the commonness of his title.

But before he could dispute her and put her in her proper place, Lord Raeborn reminded them of his presence.

"What are you two gabbing about?" he complained. "Look! He approaches!"

Miss Hathawae was already lowering herself into a curtsy undoubtedly brutal on her aged knees. Lord Raeborn held the other side of the carriage and bowed. Ben dropped his arm from the railing and did the same. He did not know or care how the lady Larkspur would manage.

Suddenly, before them, the sounds of movement ceased. Ben raised his head, hoping to use this moment to caution the guard about proceeding on the road and remembering too late how disreputable he looked.

But he need not have worried.

The king and, indeed, all his men, were looking beyond him, to the carriage. Of course, Ben realized with a sort of pain, why would they linger on a rather ordinary man coated in chalk when they could feast instead on the delicious Lady Larkspur, who knew precisely how to flirt a man into distraction. He turned towards her and was surprised to see her, in turn, looking bemusedly at Miss Hathawae.

"My dear Betsey," came the sonorous voice of the king, in the distinctive accent learned from no tutor. "I hoped to see you in Brighton."

Miss Hathawae smiled. "Am I not always here, waiting on your return, your majesty?"

Ben felt no surprise at the revelation of the relationship, only that they should be so open about it. His informers had told him years ago about some ancient affair between the two, and that a young man, currently at university on the Continent, possibly was a royal by-blow. Miss Hathawae was most certainly the mother, but the reports of the young man's florid good looks suggested something of his father.

Since the king held his other mistresses open for public scrutiny, his reticence about Miss Hathawae had seemed to disprove the relationship. Now Ben was not quite so sure.

"And who waits with you?" the king answered Miss Hathawae with a question.

"Why, several whom I believe you know, your majesty. Lord Raeborn you certainly know, as you do his young cousin, Mr. Queensman." She paused to allow Ben and Raeborn time to bow again. "And here is Lady Larkspur, Lord Leicester's daughter."

"Why do you not rise, missy?" said the king on a note of some indignation.

"If you please, your majesty. My betrothed is not well. It is why she takes the air and water at Brighton. My cousin, her physician, constrains her to her chair."

"I see. Well, Raeborn, I hope you have more luck with her than I did with an ailing wife. She looks much too pale and not plump enough; she may be a bad bargain."

Ben heard Lark's slipper scrape the bottom of the carriage and thought she would rise in protest. And so she might have, but for the arrival of a newcomer.

"And here is Mr. Siddons," Miss Hathawae added seamlessly.

Gabriel Siddons' entrance was not nearly so graceful. He walked through a hedgerow, snagging his jacket on a branch. His clothes were rumpled and damp, as if he had run a great distance, and his boots were covered in mud. Well, Ben thought ruefully, he could hardly fault the man for his appearance, for he himself looked barely presentable.

The king clearly thought the same. He looked from one to the other wordlessly, before his eyes settled on Miss Hathawae again.

"It appears the code in Brighton has become more lax

during the season of my absence, Betsey. I hope the run-abouts who dwell here can manage to make themselves presentable for a dress ball at the Pavilion in two days' time."

"A dress ball!" Miss Hathawae clapped her hands to-gether in joy. "Fear not, your majesty. I shall bring these gentlemen to heel."

The king looked vastly put upon.

"So you may, but I do not include everyone in my invita-tion. You will come, Betsey, as will Raeborn. And Mr. Queensman, if you can manage to clean yourself up in time."

Ben smiled and bowed in appreciation before he realized the serious omission.

"My lady would be grateful to be in attendance, your majesty," Raeborn said, a little nervously. "After all, we are to be married shortly."

"I would get on with it, Raeborn, for she may not last long. Not plump enough to be healthy. And I will not have the infirm at my dinner table."

Ben could sense Lark bristling beside him, knowing she would speak her mind all too plainly to anyone but the Lord of the Realm. But the king's authority was unanswer-able, and, in any case, the little manipulator got precisely what she deserved. Ironically, her own clever masquerade was the very thing to prevent her invitation to a costume ball.

"Of course not, your majesty," Raeborn said and bowed. Ben noticed the look of disgust he sent to his bright-eyed lady love. Of course, it was nothing next to what he eventu-ally would reveal when he found out how he had been duped.

Gabriel Siddons cleared his throat, reminding Ben that the man still lacked an introduction. He himself saw no reason to offer one, and Lark had been effectively stifled by her indignation. Raeborn did not know Siddons, and Miss Hathawae preferred to decline the honor.

The king studied his humble subject through puffy-lidded eyes and apparently concluded he did not care to waste his time with him. Ben felt an ungentlemanly sense of pure satisfaction.

"I shall expect to see several of you," the king repeated,

emphasizing each word, "at the Royal Pavilion in two days' time. Mr. Queensman, I hope you may call on me this very evening."

"As you wish, your majesty," Ben said, and bowed very low. He felt the eyes of all the company upon him and knew he would shortly pay for this moment of favor with the explanations they all would demand. Siddons alone understood more than the rest, but he would make Ben pay with a different sort of currency.

"I do most particularly, sir," the king said into the wind, so it became difficult to hear even his clear, decisive voice. "But now I must make haste for the Pavilion, for there are others who await me."

Ben straightened and looked directly into the eyes of the aging rake. All the world knew of his extravagant behavior with certain young and not-so-young women and his destructive relationship with the Princess Caroline. But few, Ben mused, recognized the sadness and disappointment for what it was: the desperate search for happiness. More often than not, he felt only pity for the man who would have everything.

The king turned away and assumed a regal stance. In a moment, and in a whirlwind of white dust, his carriage was gone, quickly on its way to the extravagant palace that had cost England her rich American colonies. Perhaps it would prove the most costly pleasure palace in history.

"I am surprised his majesty did not suggest you sit in his own seat, Mr. Queensman, so he might remove himself to the baggage shelf," Lark said tartly. She straightened her skirts about her, looking very prim. "That way, you would be certain to arrive at the Pavilion with alacrity."

"So I would, my lady. But then, perhaps the king thought me saddled with sufficient baggage of my own."

Lark sat quietly, and Ben, with a curious sense of disappointment, thought she did not understand his allusion. But then he saw the bright gleam in her eyes and the telltale twisting movement of her lips, usually the precursor of her barbed wit. He sat back in the cushions, steadying himself for her retort.

" 'Tis a pity you are so encumbered, Mr. Queensman," she began sweetly. "Therefore it must give you ever so much satisfaction that when you join Lord Raeborn and

Miss Hathawae at what will surely be the highlight of Brighton's social season, your baggage will be safely stowed at Knighton's. It should bother no one there."

But Lady Larkspur was very wrong. It would bother him very much indeed.

"You do not propose to leave me—you will leave me alone all this evening?" Lark asked in disbelief.

"Please do not make this more difficult than it already is, dear Lark," Janet said. "Have you not already insisted on granting me some semblance of freedom?"

"You were never my prisoner, Janet. It is horrible of you to think so."

"You willfully misunderstand me; you know you do. But I distinctly heard you say you would not stand in the way of my meetings with Matthew. And as it is he who requests my presence, surely you cannot deny me this one evening away."

"Might he come here instead?" Lark asked, a little desperately.

"You know he cannot. If Mr. Queensman is to be at the Pavilion, Matthew must be at the hospital. I consider it a very fine place to spend the evening."

"Of course it must be, if you are with the man you love. A prison cell could be heaven itself under such circumstances. And now that I think on it, I shall manage quite well. I shall spend my evening in the excellent company of Colonel Wayland, as he and I seem to be the only persons without an excuse to be anywhere else."

Janet hesitated over her ribbons and seemed confused.

"I am sorry to tell you, dear Lark, but the colonel goes with Lord Raeborn and Miss Hathawae to the king's costume ball. Did you not see him earlier? He is dressed as Napoleon."

Lark felt a flicker of anger. "How revolting! To flaunt the image of our enemy before the party."

"I do not recall hearing it said the colonel owned any taste."

"Then perhaps that is how he secured an invitation, for he and the king seem to have that in common."

Janet laughed. "I believe you regret your lack of an invitation for no better reason than that you wished to see the

Oriental chambers for yourself and then report on them to all the family."

"No," said Lark with genuine sadness. "It is not why I wished to be included. I should have liked to be at a ball again, to dance and to dress beautifully, and to stay out until the dawn."

"You would not have been able to dance," Janet dutifully reminded her.

Lark looked at her friend ruefully, fully comprehending how her excellent plan for salvation and revenge had ultimately proved reckless and futile. "But perhaps such would have been my disguise for the evening," she said. "I would have attended as a young girl in good health and spirits, imagining myself a desirable match for the most handsome of men. I would flirt and dance and move quite freely among the others. As a guise it would have been considered quite remarkable. And utterly convincing."

"Why should it not? You are a young girl in good health and spirits."

Lark shook her head, wondering if she would ever again be happy.

"But Mr. Queensman would certainly be amazed. Your instant recovery would prove quite a blow to his self-assurance."

Lark of course knew perfectly well that he would not be at all amazed, having seen through her disguise almost at once. But she very much desired to surprise him and wondered what he might do if she approached him on her own two feet and demanded a dance. She remembered the dreadful evening of Hindley Moore's defection, when she danced with Ben Queensman for the first and only time, and wondered if the sensation of his body moving alongside hers would prove potent enough to last a lifetime.

Perhaps it would fade in time and she would be utterly bereft. Might she challenge Mr. Queensman's sense of duty to renew the acquaintance? If she asked him to elope with her to the north, would he be sufficiently amazed?

"I see you smiling, Lark. I knew your bad temper would not last for very long," Janet said comfortingly. "It must be the thought of confounding Mr. Queensman that revives your humor. I believe him a man who is very rarely wrong."

"He provides a very strong contrast to me, it would seem. I believe there is nothing I have done right in some time."

Janet tied her cape about her shoulders. "You have been a very loyal and generous friend. Surely it must count for something." She leaned down and kissed Lark on the cheek.

"Perhaps not. The same might be said for the little cinder girl, and she did not go to the ball either," Lark said.

"You forget the story, my friend. She did go to the ball, after all, disguised so well her sisters did not recognize her." Janet walked to the door, and then turned, as if in afterthought. "And in the end, she married the prince."

Lark felt the breeze caused by the closing of the door. *But it is not the prince I wish to marry,* she said to herself, and had not the heart to pray for what she most desired.

The patients at Knighton's were very much in the habit of retiring early, and the servants who saw to their every need usually took advantage of the opportunity to do the same. Lark opened her door to the soundless, darkened hallway and wondered how much she might dare with so slim a prospect of an audience.

She could not sleep, nor had she the patience to read anything in her small collection. She had worked and re-worked Mr. Siddons' little maps until she knew the territory by memory and the light was not strong enough for needle-work. The night air seemed full of music, both from the distant Pavilion and from the closer, more insistent waves upon the beach, and it proved invigorating for her already restless mood.

Lark stepped out into the hallway.

No bells rang, nor did cries of alarm stop her in her tracks. The voices of the night sang on, tempting none of the residents of Knighton's but her.

The smoothly polished floor felt hard beneath her slip-pered feet, so unaccustomed was she to treading upon her toes, and once or twice she felt as if she would lose her balance. But she made her way to the great room with no mishaps and pushed open the doors onto the scene she had come to know best during her respite in this place.

The great room, with its huge plate windows open onto

the veranda and the sea beyond, was at once familiar and strange. She had never known it so dark and quiet, but yet there was the book she had abandoned earlier in the day, the morning's flowers fading on the library table, a deck of playing cards spread across a gaming table. Several of Mr. Siddons' tedious dissected maps were laid out upon a corner table, awaiting completion on the morrow.

Feeling just a bit mischievous, and remembering something of an old tale about the shoemaker's elves, Lark thought it would be fun to make some progress on the pieces and confound their owner. She positioned the table to take advantage of the gentle moonlight and considered the matter.

But she was disappointed to realize she had once worked this map, and she remembered how it seemed the least exciting of any that Mr. Siddons brought. It was of the coastline, from Winchelsea to Brighton, falling short of the extensive properties of the Seagate estate, which would have been the only features to truly hold her interest. And yet it seemed, for a while, to hold that of Mr. Queensman, who seemed perversely antagonistic about the whole subject when he questioned Mr. Siddons about his choice of map. Lark mused as she fingered one of the pieces, thinking she knew Mr. Queensman so much better now, and how his actions and words were never arbitrary. If he had bothered Mr. Siddons about his gift, he must have had a reason.

He might have, but to Lark the whole question of the relationship between the two men remained perplexing. At one time, her vanity had insisted that Mr. Queensman acted in jealousy against a man who brought her little gifts and amused her. But surely he came to realize, as did she, that Mr. Siddons withstood her charms very easily and made no untoward advances. Whatever set them off against each other had nothing to do with herself.

So much for the beautiful, wealthy daughter of Lord Leicester. Her earlier self-effacing comparison proved apt: She might as well have been the cinder girl.

And, lacking an invitation to the ball, she might as well be happy in her own lonely corner.

She looked at the map piece in her hand and saw that it

included the shoreline very near where she now stood. Surely this little fragment of the universe held no great significance, and yet it was where a dead man had only recently washed up on the beach, where Mr. Queensman's hand had been slashed and where Martha Gunn had met with her accident. Mr. Queensman and Mr. Knighton could not have imagined such misadventures when they chose their separate sites for their hospitals.

But surely the events were no more arbitrary than Mr. Queensman himself. Might such disasters have occurred on this beach precisely because of who dwelt here? And might Mr. Queensman already know the cause?

Lark again focused on the piece in her hand and noticed the fine line between the land and the water. With absolute clarity, she recalled the conversation about the king's arrival at Brighton and how Mr. Queensman allowed his rival to mistakenly believe the entrance would be via the sea. She did not believe him so petty as to merely deny the man the spectacle of the king's entourage; therefore, he must have had another reason to coax him away from the scene.

But he did not succeed. Mr. Siddons found his way to the cliff road anyway, although he looked like he had run through swamp and briars to get there. Why had it been so important?

The piece dropped to the floor, and Lark knelt to retrieve it. At first, she thought she had found another part of the map, for this piece had writing scrawled across its tiny form, but then she realized she saw its back side.

"King's Pie . . ." was distinctly legible. Surely no one doubted the monarch liked his pie, but why on earth would such a thing be written on a map? Lark held it closer to her face and thought perhaps the second word was incomplete. Piecrust? Pieman? Pied? Pier?

The King's Pier? There was such a place, where the royal barge docked when the king was in Brighton. If George had arrived by sea, as Mr. Siddons believed, he would have made landfall at the Pier.

Lark stared down at the little missive and made a curious cry. Instinct and sense finally came together as she scrambled the assorted pieces on the table and turned them all onto their reverse. Even in the dim light, she could see scrawling writing in the same hand forming words and phrases when linked together.

"Our man waits King's Pier. No opportunity for error . . ."

Fleetingly, Lark prayed she was being too melodramatic to think what suddenly seemed obvious.

". . . must be done before Friday. Palace last chance if all else fails. Way land . . ."

Perhaps an alternate plan, if the king came by way of the land. But that did not seem to make sense, and Lark squinted into the darkness.

Not "Way land"—of course, it read "Wayland." The colonel himself, the tiresome fool who spoke endlessly about his American campaigns and yet remembered none of the particulars. The man who received visits and maps regularly from his nephew and who regarded them as matters of great importance. Scarcely a gentleman, but one who somehow secured an invitation to the king's costume ball, a privilege denied even Lord Raeborn's intended.

Why did Wayland need to document the movements of the king, and why did he receive puzzling little messages on the back of dissected maps? Why did Gabriel Siddons receive these seemingly innocent gifts, delivered by men he met on the beach early in the morning?

Lark felt her knees give way, and she fell down onto a chair. Her weakness had nothing to do with any physical frailty, though she felt as if she had been hit by a powerful wave. When she returned to the surface, gasping for breath, she saw certain things with a clarity that had eluded her until this moment. And she saw, as vividly as if he stood before her, the traitorous Colonel Wayland in his Napoleon's costume.

It was then that Lady Larkspur knew that her stealthy journey through the darkened halls of Knighton's was not the most adventurous deed of this night's work.

Lark paused in the shadow of a tree, hoping the gang of young roughs passing drunkenly on the street would ignore her. They looked to be the sort of men who might easily torment an innocent youth, but if they should prove aggressive and discover the softness of her woman's body under the rough shirt and trousers she wore, the consequences would prove disastrous. She stood still, not daring to move even though the trousers scratched her flesh most annoyingly.

In the moonlight she glimpsed their faces, broad, whiskered, damp with sweat or ale. Their odor confirmed the latter.

When Lark allowed herself the luxury to breathe again, she realized this guise was her most futile one yet. Somehow, she had managed to convince at least some people she was an invalid, but she suddenly realized that not a single person would allow her to pass inspection as a boy.

But she had no choice. She could not walk the streets in woman's clothing, nor could she reveal her plan to anyone else at Knighton's. She did not know whom she might trust.

Though she had grown up in a household of women, knowing what to do with the garments she retrieved from one of the servants' closets did not cause much consternation. The shirt pulled tightly over her breasts but just managed to button closed, and the trousers were secured with a bit of twine. Her hair caused a greater problem, but she braided it tightly and stuffed it neatly under a tweed cap. She might be forced to remove it at the entrance to the Pavilion, but she had no choice but to chance the consequences.

As she ran through the dark streets of Brighton, following the lights of the Pavilion as a beacon, she tried to rehearse what she might say. She needed to talk to Mr. Queensman in a matter of much urgency. Should she mention the names of one of his patients? Or would he dismiss her errand as foolish, since he had left the very capable Matthew Warren in charge? What could she plead as important enough to get his attention?

"Halt, boy! You are nearing the palace of the king!" A brusque voice, suitably menacing, stopped her in her tracks.

Lark cleared her throat.

"If you please, sir. I am a servant sent from Knighton's with an urgent message for Mr. Benedict Queensman, who is a guest here."

The guard stepped out of the shadow of the doorway and held out a very large hand.

"Let me have it then, and away with you."

"It is impossible, sir. I have nothing in hand." Lark

cursed herself for this oversight. "It is committed to memory."

"Let me hear it, then," the guard said impatiently.

"Lady Larkspur suffers a serious relapse and may die this night. Do not upset Lord Raeborn with the news, but come at once."

"Is Lady Larkspur your mistress?"

"Mr. Queensman is my master," Lark said, thinking it might carry more weight. She hoped the guard did not see her blush. "Please, sir. It is most urgent."

"Those who approach me for favors usually offer some compensation."

Lark blinked like a fool, not at all understanding what the man demanded of her.

"I see you are untutored. I cannot understand why Mr. Queensman would want you."

Lark thought the man sadly close to the truth of the matter, though not in the way he intended.

"But I will admit you nevertheless."

"I am sure you will be amply recompensed, sir."

The guard grunted his doubtfulness on the matter and pushed open the heavily ornate door to the palace. "I will have you wait here while I send someone to find Mr. Queensman. He is with the king, you say? Do you know his costume? It is very difficult to recognize even the regulars this evening."

Lark realized she had no idea what Mr. Queensman might be wearing, though she could think of a few ensembles that would suit him very well.

"You are a simpleton, are you not? Stay here, and out of trouble, boy. And take off your hat in the palace of the king."

But even as Lark's trembling hand went up to remove the offending article, the guard turned abruptly on his heels and did not look back as he marched from the room.

She was in! Feeling a great rush of satisfaction, Lark took the opportunity to inspect her surroundings and to pass her own judgment on the building that had been the cause of so much censure by everyone who saw it. She studied the broad painted expanse of the ceiling, so cleverly done it rivaled the afternoon sky. She blushed at the statuary around her, which revealed not only all the particulars of the human form, but also a very active imagination. Several of the marble faces resembled George himself.

Lark was well on her way to getting an education of a certain sort when the sound of men's voices caused her to duck between the statues. Once there, she could not be sure which was worse, being discovered or being forced to press up closely against a man's marble bottom.

Master William Shakespeare and Sir Walter Raleigh passed by without noticing her, as did Queen Elizabeth, who followed closely at their heels.

"Are you certain you heard the boy correctly? The lady Larkspur was in no danger when last I saw her," argued a familiar voice, and Lark summoned the courage to step out from her sanctuary.

From one end of the long hallway, two men approached, one towering over his companion. Though he wore a half mask and a curiously feathered hat, his very manner, if not his voice, reassured her completely. She watched him as they neared, and felt only relief that once again he should come to her rescue.

"There he waits, sir," the guard said. "An insolent little rogue, he is. Still wearing his hat, I see. Why, I should like to—"

"Leave him be," Mr. Queensman said as he stopped the man's hand. "I have urged him to wear his cap, to prevent a chill."

"My good man! The heat is nearly insufferable! I—"

"Even so," came the evasive answer, spoken with a great deal of authority. "Is there a place I may talk with the boy?"

"Why, yes. There is a small anteroom just there. Is that adequate?"

"I daresay it is. Come, boy. And be quick about it. I am engaged for the next three dances."

Ben Queensman slapped Lark's shoulder a little too energetically as he handed the guard a coin with his other hand. Once the man retreated to his post, Mr. Queensman pushed her past the row of statues, muttering something about their inappropriateness for a young boy's eyes.

She knew he was angry, and knew he would be even more so if her journey proved ill founded. What did she know, after all, but that something was to occur this night?

Perhaps the king expected a shipment of dissected puzzles with which to entertain his guests. Perhaps Mr. Queensman already knew what was amiss, if anything.

Once inside the room, he closed the door and turned to confront her. She thought she saw his expression soften, but realized it might be nothing more than the wish of her imagination.

Suddenly he reached for her and pulled the offending little cap off her head, releasing her loosening braids. He said nothing, waiting for her response, teasing her with his fingers in her hair.

She did not speak at first, but responded by lifting her hands to his face and lifting the mask from his eyes.

"I believe I have just unmasked Robin Hood," Lark said softly. "Am I right?"

"Indeed you are, my lady. A Robin Hood unmasked is only at risk of his life. But I have just unmasked Lady Larkspur, and much more is at stake."

"What might it be?" Lark asked, melting to his touch, his words.

"Why, her reputation.'Tis a fragile situation when a lady dons trousers and passes herself off as a boy."

"It was not intended to be provocative."

"And yet it is," he said, and before she knew what he was about, he lowered his head to the neck of her shirt. She looked down, and too late realized the buttons against her breast had become undone and Ben Queensman was kissing the flesh revealed above her corset. She reached up to grasp his neck to support herself and pressed against him. Forgetting her desperation and sense of urgency, she was compelled by emotions of another sort and gave herself up to him.

Suddenly he leaned back and gazed down at her in amusement.

"I do not think you risked your reputation merely to seduce me. Nor do I imagine the furnishings of the Pavilion sufficient inducement to steal into the king's palace. What is it, then, my lady? A new masquerade? Has the other finally bored you?"

Lark blinked uncomprehendingly for a moment, and then pushed herself away.

"You knave!" she whispered. "I have come to warn you of danger, of matters of great importance."

"Concerning Lady Larkspur's health? I already received that message, and I suspect she will live through the night."

"Then she will have better luck than our king!"

The look of astonishment on his face provided nothing but the highest satisfaction.

"You had better explain yourself, my lady."

"So I shall, if you are quite finished molesting me."

"I—" he began and then apparently thought better of it. "What do you know?"

Lark saw his concern was real, and felt largely vindicated of her doubts. Ben Queensman would not take her seriously if he did not already have some secret knowledge, some suspicions.

She told him what she knew, as fragmented and speculative as it was. She mentioned Mr. Siddons by name, prompting a knowing nod, and implicated Colonel Wayland, which seemed to take him by surprise.

"I must away, Lark. There is no time to waste."

"It is as I thought. I am coming with you."

He had already turned towards the door, but she managed to stop him in his tracks.

"You will not. We are dealing with dangerous men."

"I have already proved my worth in an emergency."

"And you could have been killed. Do not think I am willing to risk it again."

"My safety is not yours to risk, sir. You would do well to remember that."

He sucked in his breath, looking angrier than she had ever seen him.

"As your physician, I order you to remain where you are, in this room."

"You have already absolved yourself of that role. It has no merit."

He suddenly reached for her, and Lark knew if it were any other man she would expect violence. But there was only desperation in the kiss he gave her, and he released her almost at once.

"There remains only one claim I might have on you, and I fear it may not have merit enough for you either."

"I cannot judge if you will not tell me."

"I would ask you, as the man who loves you more than his own life, not to do anything to risk yours. Will you accept that, true and simple?"

But he did not wait for her answer. With just the briefest gesture of running his finger across her cheek, he turned from her and ran as Robin Hood might, quickly and stealthily, from the room.

Chapter Fourteen

*L*ark rose unsteadily to her feet. She had received other declarations of love, of course. Lord Dunlop once professed great passion as they stood together in the protective embrace of an arbor. His sentiments were very fine, but he ruined the effect by having a sneezing fit. Undaunted, he continued his suit in the safety of his father's great hall.

The Duke of Kelsford once accosted her in the privacy of a little hunting lodge, to which Lark had retired after an active day of riding. She thought his words very flattering.

Two years ago, she received a pretty proposal at Almack's in a suite that might have been designed for that very purpose.

And Hindley Moore, the scoundrel, had approached her in the moonlight, surrounded by the heady scent of her mother's prized dahlias.

Great romantics all, and yet their currency proved false.

So perhaps she ought to regard in an entirely different light a pronouncement of love delivered on the run by a costumed man to a boyish young woman. Worse—a young woman already determined to be a liar and a schemer. And worse still—a young woman affianced to the man's cousin.

There must be merit in it; how could there not?

Lark put her icy hands up to her cheeks, but found little comfort there. She ought to feel the heat of passions long suppressed, but instead felt only a chill at her heart, infecting her spirit. Why would Mr. Queensman risk honor and reputation by declaring himself unless he thought it would not matter?

And why should it not matter?

Lark then knew why this profession of love felt truer and stronger than anything she had ever experienced. There was danger inherent and imminent, and the very real chance that her lover would not need to answer for himself on the morrow.

If there was danger, she must help him, for she had every

bit as much to lose as he. In any case, she knew a good deal more than she ought about this evening's events and could provide a real service of the sort genuine boys might be asked to do for their country.

Buoyed by an absurd sense of heroism, Lark glanced one last time at the walls of the room in which she had been held a voluntary prisoner. They were very stylish, very well painted, exactly the sort of thing a young lady might enjoy if she had nothing else on her mind.

Lark laughed out loud and felt the warmth returning to her body.

As she stepped into the hallway, she realized there was yet another, perhaps more important reason why Mr. Queensman's earnest plea might be received with greater trust and gratitude.

That is, of all the men who had ever romanced her with adoring sentiments, Mr. Queensman was the only one she loved with equal reckless abandonment.

Though not dressed in the livery of the king's palace, Lark thought it advisable to look as if she belonged to the household, and so she scooped up a discarded tray from a table and walked purposefully down the hallway, very much as if she were one of the serving boys. She did not bother to formulate answers to the questions she might receive if anyone saw her, nor did she wonder if she might be accused of stealing the royal silver. She only felt she would improvise as she must and make her way closer to Ben Queensman as she did so.

She rounded a corner into yet another formidable hallway and could not help but wonder if Colonel Wayland's informants had managed a dissected map of the Royal Pavilion. The place seemed a veritable labyrinth, asymmetrical and redundant, its gaudy rooms distinguishable only by colors and themes. Twice Lark entered a masterpiece in red brocade and thrice confronted her own image in the same series of mirrored panels. The situation seemed quite hopeless.

When she passed a porcelain peacock of very recent acquaintance, she stopped and laid her tray at its bright yellow feet. Perhaps her hearing might prove a more valuable instinct than her faulty sense of direction to lead her to

Ben Queensman's side. She remained very still and closed her eyes, attempting to absorb every sound in the Royal Pavilion.

"And here is a young man who might be persuaded to help us, or else pay for it," snickered a deep, hushed voice.

Lark could scarcely hear another thing but for the beating of her heart. She remained with her eyes closed as she nursed the absurd hope that the man might be speaking of another boy in the general vicinity.

But hope proved in vain, as an ungentle hand clasped her shoulder and pulled her around.

"Boy, are you deaf and—" The voice broke off and the hand fell away.

With herculean effort, Lark opened her eyes, and was as surprised to see her assailant as he must have been to recognize her.

"The lady Larkspur, I presume?" Colonel Wayland, uncommonly spry, bowed with mock deference. "I must confess I am astonished by your costume. An excellent performance, would you not agree, Siddons?"

Gabriel Siddons stood with arms akimbo, regarding Lark with a leer and making a great point of allowing his eyes to roam up and down the length of her body. He did not even bother with mock deference.

"I expect you were aware ladies owned legs, were you not, Mr. Siddons?" Lark asked nastily. "Or do you, like your uncle, find my performance astonishing?"

Mr. Siddons grinned wickedly. "It is not so much the fact you possess legs that makes your masquerade fascinating. It is much more that they are apparently useful to you."

"I cannot begin to—oh!" Lark blushed very much like a girl.

"Allow me to congratulate you on your rapid recovery, my dear. I would like to give some credit to the good Dr. Queensman, but I fear we may not see him for some time." Mr. Siddons gave a great sigh and looked up towards heaven. Lark felt ill. "No matter. Perhaps I overstate his role in this affair. He seems to have other things on his mind, and you—you may not have been as weak as you pretended to be."

"A lady is never deceitful," Lark lied.

"But you, my dear, do not seem to be much of a lady."

He held up his hand as she began to protest. "And, in truth, my tastes run to women with wicked ways."

"Is it because they are so much like yourself?"

Colonel Wayland laughed. "She has got you there, boy!"

Mr. Siddons made a great show of looking insulted. Then he started to advance upon Lark, backing her into a corner. So close to his person, and unable to turn away, she could smell the rank odor of salt water and sweat upon him.

"How much do you know, pretty boy?" Mr. Siddons asked softly. "Did you come to the Pavilion out of curiosity—for some errand for your lover?"

"Lord Raeborn?" Lark stood up to him and tried not to breathe deeply. "I saw him not three hours ago."

Mr. Siddons laughed. "You have fooled me about several things, pretty boy, but your relationship to Lord Raeborn is not one of them. The man would be a fool to marry you when he would be cuckolded ere the wedding trip was done. I once fancied you myself, before I saw how things stood between you and Queensman."

"There is nothing between us."

Siddons made a grunting noise. "Just as well, for you would be bound for disappointment. No matter; I shall make it up to you. For I have just realized I fancy you still, even dressed as a boy."

Before Lark realized what was happening, he pressed her against the wall roughly and started kissing her. She cried out against his mouth and tried to push him off her, but he was a good deal stronger than he looked.

When his hand went hurtingly to her breast, his deeds finally met with other protests.

"Come, man, there is time enough for this later. We must complete our mission before someone spreads an alarm." Colonel Wayland pulled his nephew away. Lark would have expressed her gratitude, but he would not meet her eyes.

"What, old man? Are you impatient to have her as well? There may not be enough of her to share when I am finished." Mr. Siddons straightened up, making a great show of flattening the wool fabric of his breeches. Lark, recently wise to such matters, knew exactly what he demonstrated.

"I will remind you it is a grievous offense to rape the daughter of a peer," Wayland said, with no attempt to gloss his words.

"And I will remind you we are in this for far worse," Siddons said, looking briefly at Lark. "If we accomplish our mission, who will care about Lady Larkspur? Perhaps she will be forced to marry me. Then she could play the part of the grieving widow when I pay the ultimate price at the Tower. She is very good at playacting, you remember."

"I shall not be a very convincing widow if I am forced to kill you myself," Lark shot back.

Siddons grabbed her again and pressed painfully against her.

"Come, my boy—"

"I think you should listen to your uncle, Mr. Siddons," Lark said, striving for some level of composure. It remained her only defense.

"My uncle?" Mr. Siddons laughed nastily. "Perhaps you are not as well informed as we feared, pretty boy. For, you see, we are quite capable of some subterfuge as well. Colonel Wayland is no more my uncle than you are an invalid. Nor is he a colonel."

Lark's eyes widened in sudden realization.

"Nor was he in the American campaign," she said with certainty.

"Of course not. He had better things to do for his country."

Lark, knowing she had little to lose, risked it all. "Like murdering his king? I fail to see how that will benefit England."

"Even an Englishman might dispute you on that, my lady," the man she knew as Colonel Wayland said with a grin. "But my country is not England."

She gazed at the man, in his Napoleonic finery and re-called wisps of conversation they had shared during simpler times. "You are French." It was not a question.

Colonel Wayland bowed low. "At your service, madame. Or should I say *'petit garçon'*?"

"You can say whatever you want, sir. It does not change the fact that you are a collaborator and a murderer. When Mr. Queensman—"

"I would not count on Mr. Queensman for anything just now," Mr. Siddons reminded her.

Lark closed her eyes, allowing the horrible words to wash over her. Benedict Queensman was dead. He had gambled and lost. And she, who had held him at arm's length in the stupid name of honor, already forfeited her one chance of happiness, her one hope for love. What harm could the evening's consequences bring upon her now?

"Thank you for your advice, sir," she said haughtily. "Now if you would pardon me, I believe it is time for me to quit the palace and return to Knighton's."

As she started to walk away, Mr. Siddons reached out and grabbed her.

"You are quite accustomed to having your way, are you not, missy? What would you know of sacrifice and deprivation, and commitment to a cause? I am sorry to disoblige you, but like other young boys, you shall be pressed into very immediate service."

"What have you in mind, Siddons? She is probably good for nothing," murmured Wayland, ignoring Lark's look of indignation.

"I disagree, man. She demonstrates a fair degree of versatility. She would be an excellent asset to our cause, if only we could trust her."

"You will not trust her!" Wayland said in some dismay.

"Of course not! But she will serve us just the same. Think of the scandal, the shame upon her family, when it is revealed that the lady Larkspur was part of the conspiracy to kill the king. And how her recent history of deception was no more than a ploy to set herself up in Brighton. All her family will be marked, including her pompous brother-in-law Southard. In fact, the more I think on it, the better it seems." Mr. Siddons chuckled maliciously. "You see how much your company is desired, pretty boy," he said, twisting her wrist mercilessly.

"Why should I do what you ask?" Lark argued.

"To save the life of your Mr. Queensman. At least there will be one who will remember you fondly." Mr. Siddons sighed dramatically.

Lark blinked several times, trying to make some sense of the web in which she was entangled. She shrugged off Mr. Siddons' hand.

"You have already told me he is dead. I believe you have gambled away your only chip, sir. There is nothing you can do to threaten me into a treasonous act."

Mr. Siddons' face turned bright red as he spat at her feet.

"Get moving," he said roughly. "You will do as I say."

Lark walked between them, hastened by Siddons' angry thrust. Her eyes darted from one side of the room to the other, looking for some avenue of escape, but she knew there was nothing, so framed as she was by her enemies and so unfamiliar with the palace layout. She tried to calm herself, knowing that any move would be precipitous. She must await an opportunity.

They entered a long corridor, so modest in its appearance that it did not seem to be part of the palace design. A young woman passed before them, carrying a wet cloth.

"My good woman," Colonel Wayland called out and she stopped, looking uncertainly at the three of them. Lark tried to give her some sign of her distress, but the woman's attention was all for the older gentleman. "We have been momentarily detained. Is the king's party already retired to the dining hall?"

"They are just leaving the ballroom, sir, and a few of the guests have returned to the dressing rooms. If you please, sir, would you like direction?"

Wayland smiled and pressed a coin into her palm. "We shall manage just fine. Our young cousin here was ill, but is sufficiently recovered to rejoin the guests. We shall do so immediately."

The maid passed indifferent eyes over Lark, seemingly more interested in the generous gift in her hand.

"You will find your way shortened if you pass through the courtyard to the north stairway. It is little used, but will bring you to the dining hall."

Lark sensed the look that passed between the two men, but did not know what it could mean. Perhaps it figured into their plan, and the unsuspecting maid had just given them confirmation of what they already intended.

"Excellent! We shall hasten to join the party," Colonel Wayland said graciously. "I do, however, have a favor to ask of you. Our cousin is somewhat embarrassed by her . . . his illness. Will you say nothing of it to anyone? If we meet the others shortly, they might never suspect our brief absence."

This time, undoubtedly prompted by Wayland's slip of the tongue, the maid looked at Lark more closely. Seizing on the small chance, Lark shook her head, releasing several

locks of her long red hair from under her cap. She started
to pull away, so the young woman would see how tightly
she was held prisoner, and tried to mouth the word "help."
The maid returned a blank stare.

"I will say nothing," she said softly.

Lark was drawn away, knowing the full failure of her
small attempt at freedom. The maid must be very carefully
schooled in her behavior to secure a position at the palace,
and undoubtedly had witnessed other men manipulating
young girls to their advantage. The king himself was probably guilty of such charges.

Wearily, she started up the long staircase with her two
guards, wondering what she might say or promise to per-
suade them to release her. Would they want money? Position? Weapons? What did she know of such matters?

"Sir!" A loud feminine voice rang out beneath them.
Siddons and Wayland turned in unison, surely each unaware that the other had just released Lark's wrist from his
tight grasp. Lark, unthinking, turned also and looked down
into the face of the maid. The woman's indifference to her
plight had been a ruse, for she now looked very alert as
she shouted, "Run!"

Lark did not need to be told twice. She stepped back
from between the villains and dashed up the stairs.

"Get her!" Siddons growled, and Wayland cursed
colorfully.

Lark wasted not a second to witness their dismay or to
thank her cunning savior. She ran with all the unfettered freedom of a young boy in trousers, taking two steps at a time.

She reached the balustrade, feeling the painful strain
upon her lungs. But hearing footsteps just beneath her provided the antidote to her distress, and she rushed down the
hall in the direction of light and noise.

Pausing only to fling a vase behind her, in an attempt to
slow the passage of her pursuers, she raced headlong, thinking of nothing but what must be done in the name of honor
and patriotism. Of her own risk, she thought not at all, for
anything would be preferable to remaining prisoner at the
treacherous hands of Mr. Siddons and Colonel Wayland.
And on Ben Queensman and his profession of love for her,
she could not bear to reflect. He might be dead, but so
might she be by the evening's end.

"My lady!" Wayland shouted, but she would not be tricked by the same stratagem employed by the maid. "You are too late!"

Too late for what?

She reached the end of the hallway, barely ahead of her pursuers. As she turned the door handle, she heard a little click and thought for one horrible moment it was locked. But when it yielded to her touch, she immediately improved upon her own impetuous plan and slipped through.

Throwing herself against the solid oak door from the inside, gasping for air, she quickly fingered the heavy brasswork until she touched the reassuring outline of a key, and turned it against her enemies.

Almost immediately, she felt the impact of their bodies smashing into the outside of the door, and she trembled at the thought of how close behind her they actually had been. A stream of vile language oozed through the wood, full of promises as to the injury to befall her once they caught her again.

She stepped away, and the noises ceased. But all at once she became aware of other voices, sounds of a more agreeable sort. Certainly of a nature more familiar.

Lark turned into the great dining hall of the Pavilion and realized she was above the main floor, along A balcony too narrow for musicians and too modest for the king's guests. Perhaps it was a servants' passage or—more likely—a viewing gallery for those who could not be a part of the affair but were nevertheless privileged to look upon it. In any case, she seemed to be its only occupant, though the sole privilege she owned was the respite with which she might catch her breath.

Treading carefully on her suddenly aching feet, she leaned against the balustrade and gazed upon the dizzying sight beneath her.

It was glorious, the very stuff of legend. Brilliantly costumed guests moved gaily about, their jewels sending off reflective flashes against the candlelight. Feathers tickled partners' noses, gloved hands reached for each other. An array of historical personages preened for the general delight. Laughter mingled with the charming music.

But nowhere did Lark see a tall man in green, sporting a cap upon his dark hair. She noticed Lord Raeborn, standing very closely to the diminutive Miss Hathawae. She recognized an elderly gentleman who had once or twice visited at Knighton's. And she saw several people known to her from parties in town. But none of them mattered if Ben Queensman was missing from their company.

Again, she felt the great ache of emptiness and despair, brought on by the almost certain knowledge that he was lost to her, no matter the outcome of this night. He might be suffering and alone, in pain or dying. He might be dead.

The wood behind her splintered, and she became acutely aware of her current danger. Siddons and Wayland had nothing to lose by murdering her; they had made that quite clear. And how easy it would be to push her over the balustrade to certain death below.

Her eyes scanned the upper levels of the great hall until they alighted upon a narrow staircase, neatly camouflaged against the painted molding. Steadying herself against the rail, she moved quickly around the perimeter, distancing herself from her pursuers, though she knew they would be able to spot her almost immediately once they smashed their way inside.

The staircase was rickety, unacceptable in a modest townhouse, let alone a royal palace. As Lark descended, overstepping an array of small hand tools and pots of paint, she suddenly realized the purpose of the curious structure and why it was not entirely integrated into the general grandeur of the place. It was a workmen's scaffold, still in active use but likely to be dismantled once the painting of the ballroom was completed. She wondered if Colonel Wayland and Mr. Siddons knew of its hazards.

Her foot touched the smooth surface of the dance floor in a darkened corner of the room, and she doubted if anyone noticed her arrival. If so, she surely would be dismissed as someone of no consequence, for her costume had none of the distinction of the others. Nor would anyone be looking particularly for the lady Larkspur—except for two men.

But here, among the guests of the king, sanity finally prevailed, and Lark was able to think clearly about her circumstances.

To Siddons and Wayland she was nothing more than an obstacle, a thorn in their sides. Their objective—their target—was the king himself, and anyone who stood in their path needed to be cut down. Ben Queensman was such a one, and he had undoubtedly been killed for his tenacity. Lark proved to be another, and she somehow had managed to elude them.

But they aimed for the king.

Ducking beneath the outstretched arm of a harlequin figure, Lark searched the throng for their unsuspecting host, hoping his costume did not overly obscure him. But when her eyes finally found him, it seemed exactly the opposite was true.

The king's costume obscured almost nothing, revealing a good deal of flesh and bulky form. He looked to be a cherub of some sort, though utterly lacking in physical attractiveness. If Janet were here, she would certainly share a giggle in the corner and then dutifully remind Lark that to do so was surely treasonous. Lark thought it would hardly improve on her present troubles as an uninvited guest.

Her rushed thoughts and impressions were interrupted by a crashing sound from above. She looked up quickly to see the stumbling entrance of her two pursuers through the barrier she had erected for them no more than five minutes, before and their almost immediate surveillance of the scene below. As they walked, catlike, along the scaffolding, she moved stealthily behind those guests most likely to hide her, and made her way into the royal presence.

Then, suddenly, she saw Mr. Siddons raise a pistol and take aim at varioius points around the room until it seemed to stop just ahead of her. She turned slightly, revealing herself, and knew it was just as she guessed: He targeted the king.

She cried out and started to run, and saw only the open-mouthed, startled faces of those around her. Surely they thought her a madman—which might explain why someone decided it wise to put out his cane and trip her up. The wood bar came across her shins like a knife edge, and she stumbled blindly before she fell on the person in her path.

And just as she—and he—fell to the floor, she heard a bullet whiz over her head and shatter the exquisite stained-glass window behind them.

She became immediately aware of the smell of wine, and hairy flesh, and being wrapped in some diaphanous fabric that clung to the rough wool of her trousers. All around her people were screaming and running, though they did not seem very interested in the tangle of limbs and clothing on the floor.

Lark struggled to a seated position and looked dazedly around her.

All attention was for the scene being enacted high on the balcony above the dining hall, where two men seemed to be struggling with a third. One suddenly recoiled and brought a dark blue sleeve up to a bloody nose. The other grappled with his assailant and pushed him back over the unsteady balustrade. A green cap fell like a leaf to the floor below, revealing a dark head and a familiar profile.

Lark's cries were lost with those of the others, though hers were surely more sympathetic. Ben Queensman lay over the balustrade, his attacker trying to send him after his woodland cap. She could not see Mr. Queensman's face, but she could see Mr. Siddons', and knew that desperation, frustration and anger would make this a fight to the death. A voice started screaming, "Ben, Ben!" and several minutes lapsed before Lark realized the voice was hers.

Later, in a private moment, Ben Queensman would confess that he heard her above everything else and was thus given the strength to fight back. Lark rather doubted it, but knew that was when the tide changed. His body twisted against that of his enemy, and he suddenly seemed to have power above him. She saw him pummel Siddons' face with his fists and take advantage of the man's momentary blindness to slip out of his hurtful grasp. And then he was saying something, provoking a genuine fury and a renewed attack.

Mr. Siddons rushed him, but Mr. Queensman deftly sidestepped and could not grasp him in time to save him from breaking through the delicate balustrade.

For one extraordinary moment, frozen in time, Gabriel Siddons seemed to fly high above them, his expression more triumphant than fearful. And then he was gone, drawn by gravity to a wretched end. Lark heard the thud of his body in a room that had grown eerily silent.

She heard, but she would not look. Utterly sickened by the hideous death of a man who would have yet had her dead, she turned away to gaze instead into the bloodshot eyes of the king himself. Realizing the full extent of what her heedlessness had wrought, she drew back in horror.

"Quite a little hero, are you not, my boy?" the king said, sounding a bit drunk.

"Your majesty, I am so sorry—" Lark scuttled on the floor, oddly aware that her legs did not seem to work. Knowing not what else to do, she made some effort at a bow.

"You have nothing to be sorry for, boy, for you have saved your king's life. Very few men could say such a thing, and even fewer boys. I know not your name, but I know what it shall be. You shall be known henceforth as the Earl of Brighthelmstone, in honor of the town in which you rose to glory. It is an ancient title, with lands and honor attached, and I would have them yours for what you have done on this day."

"Your majesty, I am humbled by your beneficence, but I cannot accept—"

"I will not be swayed," the king interrupted and thrust out a thick lower lip.

Suddenly Lark was aware they had an audience, and she watched as the king raised his arms so he might be lifted up by his guards. At the same time she felt herself grasped under her breast and pulled to her feet. But her injured legs would not hold her, and she fell against a hard, damp chest.

"Oh, Ben," she began as he turned her around into the shelter of his body. "I thought you were dead."

"So I might have been but for your interference. And so I might have wished myself if anything had happened to you."

And before she knew what he was about, she felt his warm lips on hers and his arms pressing her even closer.

So she would have liked to stay forever, but the sudden applause of the king's guests reminded her abruptly of their audience.

Ben Queensman recovered almost immediately and, still holding her, managed to bow before his king.

"Your majesty, it is Benedict Queensman at your service. I apologize for the closeness of the encounter."

George IV looked surprised and oddly amused. "I do not believe you need apologize, for all has ended well. I will confess to surprise, however, when I thought I knew you rather well."

Lark felt Ben Queensman's body stiffen beside her. "Your majesty?"

The king made a snorting gesture at Lark, the disguised girl he had just made an earl.

"I did not know your tastes ran to boys, sir. I will tell you I do not approve of that sort of thing. And certainly not in public."

Lark felt the very moment that the king's words hit home, and she looked up into Ben Queensman's face to see his reaction. She expected indignation, apologetic explanation or acquiescence.

She did not expect laughter.

She heard it bubble up in his throat like some great wellspring, before it showered down on all the confused guests around them.

Chapter Fifteen

$\mathcal{B}$ enedict Queensman did not think he would ever grow weary of the subtle delights of sight and sound that graced Seagate in the early-evening hours. The echo of waves rushing against the cliffs below composed their own melodies through the ancient dungeons of the original keep and rose up throughout the rooms of the large house. Fading sunlight danced off the sea and reflected images onto the walls. And the servants, left with only one significant task for the day, were perfectly content to move along at an easier pace, speaking to each other and to their master in hushed tones.

It was the time of day, Ben fancied, when a man might be rewarded with time to be alone with his wife and family and discuss the day's events. Or perhaps sit in companionable silence and not say anything at all.

In fact, Ben now shared this most rarefied moment with a member of his family, and as all had seemingly been said in the three days since the Great Event at the Pavilion, he and his elderly cousin sat quietly, each to his own thoughts.

Lord Raeborn tapped his wineglass nervously, making little pings in discordance with the music of the sea.

Ben studied him and realized he must only think kindly upon his cousin, though he would be the means of destroying Ben's fondest hopes of happiness. But Raeborn was good and just and revealed a great forbearance, as not a single word had yet been said about the scene in the king's dining hall in which the lady Larkspur had been kissed a little too passionately by the man who would soon be her cousin twice over. Indeed, the older cousin demonstrated a good deal more forbearance than the younger.

For no accusations had been brought forward.

Ben was not privileged to know if, in private conference, Lark had already explained everything to Raeborn, from her indecent but flattering garb on the night of the ball to that illicit kiss before a frankly fascinated audience. He did not know if she had explained away her miraculous recovery or her apparent collusion with the physician whom Raeborn trusted. He only knew she planned to return to London with Janet Tavish, and was likely to remain there.

He would see her at the wedding of their friends, and at her wedding to his cousin. But necessarily, they would grow farther apart.

He swirled the sherry in his glass, and understood—for the first time in his life—why some men turned to drink as a balm against misery.

"I have a large favor to ask of you, my boy, and I am searching for the words that would shed a more generous light on it than the ones I currently cast." Raeborn spoke gruffly, looking at the opposite wall. The pinging ceased.

"Indeed, my lord? You may be perfectly frank with me. I will not think more or less of you for the grammar you employ."

Raeborn seemed to laugh, but then Ben realized he hiccuped.

"It is a most delicate matter. Concerning a lady."

"Might she be a lady I am privileged to know?"

"Only too well, I believe. It is the lady Larkspur."

"I see," was all Ben said, but his expression would have betrayed the enormity of his feelings. Here it comes, he thought. I will be made to answer for my most injudicious actions and will be asked to pay for them, as I must.

"I believe you may not," Raeborn continued, apparently oblivious to his host's distress. "You undoubtedly are not aware she has been engaged to be married on several occasions, the most recent occurring—and ending—only days before I offered for her myself."

"I know something of it, my lord. By all accounts the men, with the exception of yourself, were dishonorable knaves—not at all deserving of her."

Raeborn looked distinctly uncomfortable and loosened his cravat.

"That is precisely my difficulty, my boy. I fear I am about to join their ignominious band."

"My lord?" There was just the hint of censure in Ben's words, tainted by his uncertainty of what was to follow.

"I am compelled to jilt the chit as well, for I have decided I cannot marry her."

Ben thought a tidal wave had descended on Seagate, so deafening was the rush of water in his ears. He shook it off, realizing the storm waged from within.

"Do you fear the scandal?" he asked in a voice not like his own.

"Oh, scandal be damned. I am too old to worry about such things. But I am also too old to play the fool, and I am thrice the age of the chit."

"You believe Lady Larkspur will not suit?"

"I am convinced of it. But more to the point, I believe another lady would suit me better."

Suddenly, Ben felt practical and far more worldly than his senior relative.

"Then by all means you must act in accordance with your best judgment," he began, trying not to feel traitorous. "It is your happiness, after all, and you would not wish to be saddled with a burden."

Raeborn squinted at Ben and nodded thoughtfully.

"You agree with me that Lady Larkspur would be a burden? I knew not what I was getting into when I offered for her. I only saw her beauty and thought how pleased I would be if such beauty were mine. And then she seemed ripe for the taking, having just been spurned by that wretched fellow."

"I believe you mean Hindley Moore."

"Just so, my boy. Well, he treated her badly, and I took pity on her. Her family is quite excellent, though the mother is allowed to do anything she wishes. Paints or something."

"Something, indeed. She is regarded as a talent, my lord."

"So she may be, but I should not wish for my own wife to display her work anywhere, or call base attention to herself." Raeborn resumed pinging the glass. "I was assured by her father she would be most compliant. The girl, of course, not the mother."

Ben looked down into his glass again, smiling too warmly. The sherry no longer held the slightest temptation.

"The girl has disappointed you, my lord?"

"I need not point out her faults to you, boy, as you were witness to them yourself. The whole disguise business was enough to cause pain to the most tolerant soul, and her abuse of the king is a calumny she might never live down."

Ben tried hard to control his glee. "Do you really think so, my lord? The king commends her for a hero and does not seem to mind the deception responsible for saving his life. If he did, he surely would not have offered the earldom to the man she would marry. Who, I believe, is you."

Raeborn shook his head. "It is not enough to tempt me. I have all the title I need, and I lack only Elizabeth Hathawae to make my happiness complete."

"Miss Hathawae?" Ben heard with pleasure the not unexpected news. "You wish to marry her?"

"I should have married her thirty years ago. Instead I sought a titled lady, and then watched as the true love of my life was loved by one even loftier than I. I should not speak of such things. But do you know of whom I speak?"

Ben nodded sagely.

"Betsey has waited too long to be a wife. I only hope I may spend the rest of my life proving my worth as a husband to her."

"I wish you all the best, my lord. She is a wise and witty lady." Ben was about to add "feisty" before realizing it might not be an asset that Raeborn would find admirable. "But what is it you wish of me? Surely you do not require my services as a go-between for Miss Hathawae and yourself?"

Raeborn preened in his seat, somehow managing to look twenty years younger. "I can manage that myself, thank you. But there is the other, somewhat more ticklish matter that I am reluctant to handle. I thought I might ask for your assistance there. Strictly in a professional light."

"I will do whatever service I might, my lord."

Raeborn clapped his hands together. "I should like for you to break off my engagement to Lady Larkspur."

Ben saw the delicacy of his position at once. "I am a physician, not a lawyer, my lord."

"But you are the lady's physician, and you know her in a professional way. Surely you are capable of explaining the business dispassionately to her."

"I rather doubt it," Ben said under his breath.

"What is it you said, my boy? Will you not provide this service for me?"

Ben sighed deeply and closed his eyes. The sound of the water lapping against the walls of his home calmed his agitated spirit.

"I will do as you say, my lord," he said. "But there is one matter complicating the business."

Raeborn waved his hand dismissively. "If it is the matter of the settlement, I should—"

"It is not that, my lord. It is only—I may declare for her myself."

Raeborn's eyes widened in apparent disbelief, though Ben could not guess why. After all, the gossips in Brighton had been talking of little else but how the lady was compromised in full view of local society.

"You need not do so, my boy. Is it the title you wish? I assure you, you shall be Raeborn when I have retired to my sepulchre. Dear Betsey and I surely will have no children, and her son—you are aware she has a son?—will receive some compensation from his father. You need not marry just to become the Earl of Brighthelmstone."

"Nothing was further from my thoughts. Surely you know me well enough to understand that such considerations are not compelling for me. I wish to marry the lady for her own qualities, and because I do love her. Forgive me."

"How could I not? You have given me an excellent escape from a difficult entanglement. But you love the lady, you say? Do you not think her headstrong?"

"She proved headstrong enough to save a king's life."

"Willful?"

"If she were a man, she might command an army."

"Feisty?"

Ben could not help but wonder how his uncle hit upon the very word he himself avoided.

"I confess I admire it."

"Then God give you strength, my boy. You shall need it."

In the aftermath of Lark's evening adventure at the Royal Pavilion, she and Janet quietly moved out of Knighton's and into a small hotel overlooking the beach.

Their windows did not afford as tempting an early-morning view as their previous accommodations, but there were other compensations.

Not the least of which was the fact that Lark was able to move about unencumbered, having happily relinquished the role of invalid. She promptly reported the news to all her family, who now proposed to their friends that Brighton be the place to effect a cure for any ailment, from bee sting to broken bones.

"I believe the most remarkable feature of our little adventure is that we never managed to meet the famous Dr. Knighton in all the weeks we spent here. And yet he surely will be credited with my miraculous cure. And that of Colonel Wayland, come to think on it. He seemed absolutely steady when he attacked me in the hall."

Janet looked up from a box she unpacked.

"If you believe our lack of an introduction to Dr. Knighton is the most remarkable occurrence of the past few weeks, then I believe your reputed illness has settled in your brain. Modesty is becoming, but in this case it is too false. You have been hailed as a heroine throughout the neighborhood, and the news of your deed is spreading quickly. It is not every lady who has the opportunity to serve her king." Janet paused for a moment, clearly reflecting on her words. "In a manner such as this, I mean."

Lark watched her friend turn bright red, and smiled.

"You recall, I fell against his body. There is no other way I can imagine serving him, so saving his life will have to suffice. But I believe Mr. Queensman deserves all the credit, as he surely anticipated disaster and did a great deal more than I to avert it. I am only an accidental partner in the affair."

"And yet everyone, including Mr. Queensman, seems perfectly willing to let you have all the glory. Why is that, do you suppose?" Janet asked, smiling too gleefully.

"There is the novelty of it, I imagine. A woman in man's clothing, doing a man's mission," Lark explained guilelessly. But then, more seriously, "And were we not correct in imagining Mr. Queensman something more than we were led to believe? We observed how well-known he was to the king, and paid a good deal of attention to his comings and goings. You noted it first, Janet, when you considered his interest in Mr. Siddons' tiresome maps."

"They were not tiresome to everyone. We now know Colonel Wayland used them to plot the whereabouts of the king and to formulate a plan. He and Mr. Siddons were at once closer than their relationship would imply."

"Why, I now know they were not relations at all. But poor Mr. Siddons! What a horrible end!"

Janet dropped a folded corset onto the bed. "You would pity such a one? He would have killed you as well as the king, if Mr. Queensman had not gotten to him first. And he would have certainly killed Mr. Queensman."

"He told me he did, Janet. It was partly what gave me the strength to fight him off and run away. I thought if Mr. Queensman were dead, I would not have so much to live for. I could risk—"

Lark's voice cracked, and she looked away.

"You do not have to say more, my dear. I believe I know how you feel."

Lark gazed out the window, looking at the distant shore.

"I believe you cannot, Janet," she said quietly.

In the early afternoon, a messenger arrived at their hotel, requesting the presence of the lady Larkspur for tea at the home of Mr. Benedict Queensman.

"Of course you shall come too," Lark said to Janet.

"I do not see my name on the invitation and, in any case, I intend to go out for a drive with Matthew. Perhaps Mr. Queensman has something most particular to say to you."

"If he does, should he not come to me directly? I am a lady, and I deserve some degree of deference."

"You would have it both ways, would you not? You would be a boy set off on adventure, as well as a proper lady. You would be an invalid, and yet frustrated when you are not invited to a dance."

"The argument does not stand, Janet. You know it does not. Mr. Queensman knows everything."

"Of course. His eyes never seem to miss anything of consequence. Perhaps he intends this meeting as a celebration."

"Or, more likely, a valediction," Lark said unhappily.

*   *   *

Indeed, Ben Queensman looked very solemn when Lark arrived in his cabriolet at the entrance to Seagate. He leaned against a column, looking very fine in a blue jacket, light brown breeches, and Hessians that shone in the sun. But he looked somehow uncomfortable, as if he would prove to be the bearer of bad news, and he lingered at his post a bit longer than necessary or strictly polite.

Lark, helped to the ground by the groom, stood hesitantly, gazing up at the image of the man she loved framed by his splendid home.

"Lady Larkspur, welcome to Seagate," he said quite clearly when he finally came forward. And then, when only she could hear, "I never hoped to see the day you would be able to walk up my stairs."

Lark laughed nervously as she allowed her arm to be pulled into his. He felt warm and instantly reassuring.

"And yet you practically dared me to reveal myself and demonstrate such abilities. Surely you know me well enough to believe I cannot resist a dare."

"I do now. At the time, I believe, I only knew you already quite capable of managing to walk wherever you wished. I confess, I wanted to provoke you."

"Of course. It is something you do quite well."

He led her into the entrance hall, where the smell of fresh sea air mingled with the more domestic scents of wax and lemon oil. The marble floor glistened underfoot, and shafts of sunlight filtered in through each open door.

"It is perfectly lovely, Mr. Queensman. Seagate looks to be a home designed for comfort as well as beauty, which is a good deal more than I can say for the Royal Pavilion."

"It is an excellent house, but then, I am biased because I have spent all my life here." They walked into the drawing room, with its large plate windows facing out onto the sea. "And yet I confess I am often lonely. The house lacks its mistress."

Lark felt her heart beat faster and her cheeks grow warm.

"Surely that is a situation you can remedy whenever you wish. It is an advantage men have over women: they can decide whom and when they marry."

"I think women have something to say in the matter."

"Then they are a good deal luckier than myself. For I have had no choice but to marry Lord Raeborn."

"And you do not wish to."

Lark studied Mr. Queensman thoughtfully, wondering why he trifled with her. He surely did not invite her here to determine what he already knew, or to test her loyalty yet again.

"Is there anyone who knows it better than yourself, Mr. Queensman?" she asked sarcastically. "You suspected my deception almost at once, and certainly guessed what I hoped to accomplish by it."

"It proved a daring ruse. And another physician—one less skilled, shall we say?—might never have doubted your picture of ill health."

"You have a very keen sense of yourself, sir!" Lark laughed, somewhat ruefully.

"Yes, I do," Mr. Queensman answered gravely. "Of course, one might say the same about you. For it seems your deception has accomplished exactly what you hoped."

Lark caught her breath. "You cannot mean—it will not—"

He nodded and took a step forward.

"Lord Raeborn has already pronounced his intention of marrying me, no matter what my health."

"He has deputized me to inform you he has changed his mind, my lady," Mr. Queensman said, bowing deferentially.

Lark felt a little flicker of anger, even more potent than her considerable relief. She marched over to Raeborn's messenger and clasped his shoulders. When he straightened, her hands remained where they were, and her body moved very close to his.

"What do you mean to tell me, sir? Is your cousin—"

"Jilting you? Yes, it appears he is. But he has begged me to do it under the most polite terms."

"No terms can be too polite for such a thing! I will be once again humiliated, made the object of derision by all the *ton*! There will be those who will cut me—"

Lark was interrupted yet again, but this time by Ben Queensman's lips. His hands pulled her against him and moved up the lines of her back until they nested in her hair. Soon, he released the red curls from their pins, and Lark felt the weight of her hair fall upon her shoulders. But it was impossible to protest, for he did not let her breathe.

When, finally, she did protest, it was because he stopped.

"I have, however, thought of a solution to minimize the insult to your reputation. I shall have to marry you myself."

"And not ask me first? Do you consider me so desperate?"

He smiled, in the way Lark had come to know and love so well. He looked to have a secret, the very knowledge of which gave him unbidden pleasure.

"You are not so desperate, my lady. You are the trustee of an earldom, after all, and everywhere hailed as a heroine." He paused and looked at her a bit clinically. "And as your health seems to be excellent—"

He caught her hand as she tried to slap him.

"So you will marry me for Brighthelmstone? It is a very mercenary title."

"Do you think a title would tempt me? I am already in the way of Raeborn's, and as he is to marry Miss Hathawae—"

"Miss Hathawae! How very wonderful! Why did you not tell me this at first?"

"Because, dear love, you never give me the chance to finish a sentence."

"I am sorry. What else are you holding back from me?"

His lips moved wordlessly, and then he bent to caress the wrist of the hand he still held.

"As Raeborn is to marry Miss Hathawae, I doubt if I shall have any young cousins to stand in line before me."

"So you would not marry me for Brighthelmstone. Is it for pity, then? Because no one else would have me?"

"I think you have been courted by too many fools, dearest Lark. No one would ever doubt the motives of the man who would be your husband."

"And yet you will not reveal them." She circled her arms around his waist and rested her head against his chest, where she heard the strong, regular beating of his heart. "I suppose I could be rather useful about the hospital. I might work with the herbs and see what potions I might create."

"I believe you have already discovered one of considerable potency, for it seems to have worked a spell on me."

He rested his chin on the top of her head, and she, fully contented and no longer in the mood to tease him, closed her eyes to savor what would yet come. "I believe I already gave you reason enough to wish to marry you, Lark."

"I heard a declaration from a Mr. Robin Hood several evenings ago. Of course, he dashed off almost immediately, believing himself some sort of hero and perfectly willing to sacrifice himself and leave me all bereft."

"He never thought to sacrifice himself if that meant abandoning his soul's desire. But neither did he imagine the young lady to be in any sort of danger. Of course, in the end his heroics did not matter, for the lady upstaged him and made his rescue rather superfluous."

"Do not imagine it for a minute."

"I will not. I prefer to imagine much more pleasurable things."

"Such as?" Lark asked, her lips against the taut skin at his throat.

"Such as the selfsame lady in my home, in the herb garden, bathing in the sea, and playing with my children."

"You wish a governess, then?"

"I wish only one thing. When I hear it, I shall know complete happiness."

"What might it be?"

He said nothing, and it was several moments before she realized what still remained between them, what he would not take for granted.

"That I love you, Ben? Is that what you would hear? That I love you as I have never loved anyone, as I never could imagine loving again? I think I myself did not truly understand how very much it was so until several nights ago when my recklessness—what some have called heroism—in the Royal Pavilion was motivated by a belief that I had nothing more to lose, because you were already dead. It was an act made in unhappy desperation."

"It seems to be a way you have. If it were not so, our paths might never have crossed."

"So ill-favored a meeting I cannot imagine." Lark sighed. "When I think of how much time ladies spend in their chambers to guarantee complete perfection in the picture they present to eligible gentlemen, there is much irony in this. You have seen me at my very worst."

"Beloved, be assured your very worst is infinitely better than most ladies' very best. Let us only say that, for all the cleverness of your deception, I have managed to know you in complete honesty."

"As I have known you . . ."

She paused, too modest even in this most intimate moment to confess what she witnessed each morning on the beach.

"Yes?"

She looked up into his clear eyes with the little creases caused by laughter and sunshine in the corners, and thought of the wide blue sea and how much she wanted to spend her whole life beside it and with him.

She caught her breath, almost overwhelmed by the extent of her emotion.

"As I have known you," she repeated, "as the only man meant for me to marry."

"And so you shall," he answered slowly. And for some time, there was very little else that needed to be said.

Penguin Group (USA) Inc. Online

What will you be reading tomorrow?

Tom Clancy, Patricia Cornwell, W.E.B. Griffin,
Nora Roberts, William Gibson, Robin Cook,
Brian Jacques, Catherine Coulter, Stephen King,
Dean Koontz, Ken Follett, Clive Cussler,
Eric Jerome Dickey, John Sandford,
Terry McMillan…

You'll find them all at
http://www.penguin.com

*Read excerpts and newsletters, find tour
schedules, and enter contest.*

Subscribe to Penguin Group (USA) Inc. Newsletters
and get an exclusive inside look
at exciting new titles and the authors you love
long before everyone else does.

PENGUIN GROUP (USA) INC. NEWS
http://www.penguin.com/news